Tag chaser

By kandi steiner

Published by Kandi Steiner
Edited by Betsy Kash
Cover Photography by Austyn Bynon
Formatting by Elaine York/Allusion Graphics, LLC

*I dedicate this book to the people
who inspired it most. You know who you are.*

Chapter one
The Bet

"Why do you make it sound so dirty?" I ask, my face pinching up in resentment as I apply the last touch of liner under my left eye. "It's not like I'm a prostitute or a stripper, Kenz." McKenzie is absentmindedly swinging her legs off the edge of my bed and texting God knows who as she judges me. I want to be furious, but honestly I've come to learn this is just the way she is – blunt and sassy. It's actually a relief from the group of girls I used to hang out with in college.

I gently use my finger to wipe away a small smudge just below my brow and cringe at the sight of the small wrinkles appearing at the corners of my emerald green eyes. Crows feet, my mom always called them. *Damn.* How is it that I just suddenly became twenty-seven? In my mind I stopped aging at twenty-one, but my body refused to accept that logic. I turn to face McKenzie abruptly, "Are my wrinkles as noticeable as I think they are?"

She looks up from her phone and stifles a laugh, "Paisley, you do not have wrinkles. Besides, aging is beautiful. Unless you're Heidi Montag, then you're just kind of screwed."

I roll my eyes and walk swiftly to my closet, pulling out the little black dress I reserved specifically for tonight. It has a lacy overlay and an open back with a deep v-neck in the front that accentuates all my assets that haven't failed me yet. As I slip it over my head, McKenzie continues.

"All I'm saying is, you used to be this little angel back in college and then you graduate and just decide all of a sudden you're chasing tags. I don't think it makes you a whore, but I mean I would maybe say it makes you whore-ish," she says matter-of-factly, shrugging her shoulders and turning her attention back to her phone.

"It's not like that. I'm not running around sleeping with everyone I meet, Kenz. I just happened to learn near the end of my college career that I desire a man in uniform," I shoot back, trying not to sound defensive. If anything, I hope she hears the exhaustion in my voice. We've discussed this who knows how many times over the past four years but it doesn't seem to change the fact that it's still one of her favorite topics. I could tell her the real reason I enjoyed being a tag chaser, but it wasn't something I felt comfortable talking to her about – or anyone else, for that matter. Visions of my mom's face flood my mind and I can still see the look in Dad's eyes. The guilt.

I shake the memory.

"Besides," I throw in with a laugh, "Technically I'm not even the true definition of a tag chaser. I'm not trying to marry these guys, I just like having fun. Consider it me thanking them for their service."

McKenzie laughs too, chucking a pillow across the room at me, "Seriously, Paisley?!"

I shrug and wink at her in the mirror. She goes back to her phone, so for the moment I'm safe from any more questions. After one last look over in the mirror at the dress, I run my fingers through the loose curls in my amber colored hair and grab my clutch. "So now that you're finished judging me, can we focus on the fact that we are going to have a blast tonight and pretend like we're not too old for this kind of shit?"

McKenzie hops off the bed, head still engulfed in the apparently very amusing conversation occurring on her phone and lets out a deep sigh, "Ugh, fine. But I'm just saying it might do you some good to explore other options, since apparently none of the men you've caught so far have filled whatever void you have." She finally puts her phone away in her purse and links her arm in mine. "And yes," she adds, "We are going to have a blast. And who said we were too old for anything? You act like we're 70. Calm down, Grandma."

I let out a breath of relief and return her smile as we head out the door. It's been a rough week but I'm feeling great tonight, and I can't wait to see what's waiting downtown.

McKenzie is applying one final coat of lip gloss in her compact mirror as we sit in the back of the cab. Even for a cab it smells pretty bad, like an old gym locker, so we roll the windows down and try desperately to control our hair.

I watch her as she covers her lips flawlessly, wondering how she got all the great looks. Her long, thick blonde hair is straightened and flowing down to the middle of her back and her legs look like they go on for miles in the red dress and pumps she's paired tonight. I sigh, looking back at my own reflection on my phone screen for my last touch ups. I looked great when I was standing in the mirror by myself at home, but next to her I feel like the ugly step sister.

"You ready? I need a drink in my hand stat," she says, fastening the lid back on her gloss as we pull up to where the streets are closed downtown. I shove my phone in my purse in defeat and hand the cab driver a twenty.

Downtown Orlando is buzzing as usual for a Thursday night. There are plenty of college kids running around, but there's also plenty of post-grad twenty-somethings like me and McKenzie. Some of them are with their significant others, the rest just as lonely as me. Or at least I like to think they might be. I can't be the only woman approaching thirty who's not wifed up. Can I?

It's hot and muggy and I wish I would have applied another layer of hair spray to keep my loose curls from turning into a frizzy hot mess but it's too late now. As we walk I'm clinging to my clutch and watching my heels wobble beneath my clumsy ankles. "I hate this damn cobblestone," I say, almost tripping and falling into what looks like a college frat boy.

McKenzie laughs, "You would think you might be used to it by now. You've lived here long enough." She's right, I've been in the Orlando area my entire life. You would think I would be able to walk downtown in heels by now.

I stick my tongue out at her and praise baby Jesus when we finally reach normal sidewalk. It's easy for her to laugh, she's got the posture and strut of a runway model. It's still unbelievable to me that she hasn't been scooped up yet, even though she and Derek are basically dating but don't want to put a title on it. I'm not arguing, though. I need my wing woman.

"Okay but seriously, Paisley. Talk to me for real. Let's pretend I don't fall for your bullshit, for a minute," McKenzie has stopped right outside the front of Diggs, our favorite downtown spot. She's got her hands on my shoulders and she's staring at me like I'm a child about to be put in time out. I try to laugh and shake her off, but her left brow keeps rising as she waits for me to respond and she crosses her arms with purpose. When I realize she's serious I sigh in defeat.

"Honestly, Kenz, I don't know what you want me to say. I don't think it's that big of a deal."

"Well, if it's not that big of a deal then date different guys. Try something new. Do you want to be single forever?" She asks, as if it was just a normal everyday question. *"How's work going? Isn't the weather lovely? Do you want to be single forever?"*

I turn to her and try to explain, "Listen, I promise it's not as serious as you're making it. I'm not hurting emotionally or hiding from anything," that she needs to know about, anyway. "And I'm not sleeping around or doing anything dangerous. I really don't see a problem with me casually dating some of the best men in the country. They are all really, really nice."

"Then why don't you stay with any of them? Things are good for a few weeks and then you're back to square one," she throws back.

Now I'm getting frustrated. Why do we always have to talk about this? You would think she was my mom. "I'm fine. Now can we go inside? What happened to needing a drink?"

"I bet you couldn't date a normal guy. I bet you've got some sort of fear of falling for a guy who'll actually stick around," she says, tossing her hair behind her back. As she starts for Diggs, I tug on her wrist and spin her around to look at me. Her little blue eyes are challenging me and I can't help but feel offended.

"I could, too! If I wanted to, I could date a regular Joe. But the point is that I don't want to. So, if you're done now – "

"Prove it," she adds, the words like ice off her tongue.

Shit.

Suddenly I feel overwhelmed by my competitive nature. I knew this shit would catch up to me. Back in high school and college it was fine to be competitive, great even. It meant I went hard to win and to be the best, no matter what. I would even go as far as saying it has helped me get where I am in my career. But now, I feel the slight disadvantage of needing to win everything sneaking up.

"I will!" I shout over the music from Diggs spilling out onto the street. "From this point on, I won't date another military man. Period. Now can we go – "

"Shake on it," she says, extending her perfectly manicured hand to mine. Her left eyebrow is raised in amusement, like she knows I won't really accept the challenge.

I can feel uncertainty bubbling inside. Can I really do this? Ever since college, dating military men has been my only safe way of getting the emotion I craved without giving the trust I knew didn't exist. I can feel the anxiety showing on my face and I'm biting my lip in concentration. McKenzie drops her hand.

"That's what I thought, you can't do it." She turns once more to walk into Diggs, her head held high in triumph. I almost let her walk away, but I refuse to let her win. *I can do this.* I'm ready for a change and I don't need anyone, especially not McKenzie, to tell me what I can and cannot do. I grab her hand and whip her back to face me again.

"No! I can do it. Like I said, it's really not that big of a deal. In fact, I'm stoked to prove you wrong," I lie, shaking her hand like I'm the cockiest bitch in the world.

McKenzie smiles, her eyebrow still raised at me. "Great. Now, what are the terms?"

I snort, "Terms? What terms?"

"Of the bet," she states matter-of-factly.

I roll my eyes at her and try to lead her toward Diggs where she'll hopefully drink too much to remember this conversation, but she blocks me from walking past her. "I'm serious! What are the terms? What do you want if you win?" she asks.

I sigh, frustrated that I'm not two shots in at this point. "Fine! If I win, I get those bad ass glittery pumps of yours," I say, hoping this strikes a nerve.

"My Jimmy Choos?!" I think she might faint as she clutches her dress over where her heart is. I laugh in response and urge her to finish this craziness so we can drink.

"Yes, so what about you? What do you want if you win, which you won't by the way," I add in, crossing my arms and waiting for her response.

McKenzie steps close enough to me that I can hear her without her having to scream over the music. She's stopped laughing and she leans in to look me in the eyes, "If I win, you have to tell me the *real* reason why you're a tag chaser. Not the bullshit answer you always give me before you change the subject, but the real one." She steps back from me and her eyes are softer now, the way they are when I need her to eat a gallon of Moose Tracks ice cream and watch *The Notebook* with me after a bad week. Wow, what a best friend I am.

I almost call the bet off, anything to avoid bringing up my past that really means nothing to me anymore. I don't want to think about Dad or Mom or any of it, but I want to win this – to prove her wrong. I nod in agreement, and add in one final question, "Okay, but when do we judge who's won? We obviously can't wait out my entire life because I want to wear those pumps before my age exceeds my bust size."

McKenzie laughs, tossing her blonde hair behind her again. "And I don't want to have to put in my hearing aide to learn what I should already know about my best friend," she chimes in. I feel shitty again seeing the truth in her eyes behind that statement. The only person who knows anything about the real reason behind my dating preferences is Tanner, my best guy friend from college. I think it always upset McKenzie that I was closer to Tanner than I was to her, at least until he left for grad school. I wonder if I should just make something up to tell her so she'll feel more connected, but that would probably make me even worse of a person. God, I'm such an asshole sometimes.

"Okay, so how about a month?"

"A month!? That's nothing!" McKenzie yells back, obviously not satisfied with my proposal.

"So what then?"

"A year. One full year of no tag chasing."

I grit my teeth at her response. Maybe this wasn't such a great idea, how am I going to stay away from the one type of guy I've found solitude in for the past four years? I sigh, so eager for a drink at this point that I would agree to sell my kidney, "Fine. One year. Now, Ms. I-need-a-drink-but-not-until-I-harrass-my-best-friend-about-stupid-shit, can we please go inside?"

McKenzie links arms with me and smiles like she's won a wet t-shirt contest, "Yes we can. And I'll buy your first shot to make up for the loss of time."

"There's my best friend!"

We both laugh, but inside I feel like banging my head into a wall. What did I just get myself into?

Diggs is a little bar on Church Street with loud music and decently priced drinks. Compared to all the other places downtown it's practically free. McKenzie and I found it on the night of our graduation when we were stumbling from bar to bar to see how many wristbands we could get in one night. I remember we were both wearing our grad caps and yelling in the streets, "We're the smartest bitches alive!" Needless to say, no one else was quite as amused as we were.

It's been our favorite spot ever since. I'm not sure if it's the drinks, the local art strewn all over, or the fact that most of the employees know our names but we've made it our regular spot. Thursday night is our favorite night to come because it's ladies night which means free everything. We may have day jobs, but who can say no to free? Plus, they have the best burgers in town which makes for the perfect drunk food.

"Hey ladies," Drew says as he slaps wristbands on us. "You both look stunning, as usual." McKenzie bends to give him a kiss on the cheek before practically skipping inside, "Race you to the rum!" I shake my head and laugh with Drew before following her inside.

It's definitely more crowded than usual, but at least there is room to breathe. I don't see any stools open so I follow McKenzie's lead to squeeze in at the bar for a drink. She's leaning over trying to get Sean's attention behind the bar and balancing on her tip toes when I see the scruffy looking guy beside us checking out her ass. I roll my eyes and try to ignore him, hoping Sean will notice her soon.

Finally, Sean gives McKenzie a nod and a smile before pouring us the usual starter – two shots of Captain. "Captain and Coke tonight, ladies?" he asks, adding a slice of lime to our shots.

"Like it's even a question!" McKenzie laughs as she takes her shot and hands me mine. Sean starts in on making our drinks when she turns to me, "Alright, princess. Time to finally get the night started." She lifts her shot to mine, "To you hopefully overcoming your crazy obsession with military men."

"Here, here!" I laugh and we clink our glasses together before downing the shot. I can feel it burn in my chest as it goes down and Sean is right on cue with our drinks. As I sip from the glass I notice the guy next to McKenzie again, still eying her greedily and nudging his friend to look, too. Seriously?

I grab McKenzie's arm and tug her away from Sean as she slides him a tip. I can see he's enjoying her company, but I can't stand to be near Mr. Creepster any longer, "Come on, Kenz. Let's go dance."

She's draining her glass through her straw and her eyes light up as she nods, "Yes! Let's go." She chugs the rest of her drink and slams it down on the bar and I follow suit.

When we reach the dance floor after pushing through a few people I finally start to relax. Work has been hell all week and I'm on the verge of getting a whole new list of clients, so it's not getting easier anytime soon. The last thing I want is any added stress or I'll be baking up everything in my apartment tonight. Who cares that I made a bet to not date military men? I knew one day, eventually, I would have to let it go. I'm twenty-seven, I guess that day can be today. Besides, it would be nice to not date someone just because I know they aren't permanent.

McKenzie is slowly winding her body with her eyes closed and her hands up when a waitress brings us two more drinks. We take them and cheers Sean across the room before chugging them down as well. We had a late start but getting caught up is no problem for us. As I dance, I soak in the smells of one of my favorite places – beer, smoke, and sweat. God, I'm such a class act.

I can feel the alcohol buzzing through me. The music is thumping loud and McKenzie and I are laughing as we dance when suddenly Mr. Creepster pops up behind her. He grabs her waist and pulls her into him, grinding his pelvis on her. Usually, if the guy was hot, she wouldn't mind. But when she sees him she steps toward me, declining his advance.

"What's wrong baby?" he slurs, trying for me this time. "Let's dance."

"No thank you," I spit back as I pull away, not even bothering to hide my disgust. Is it so hard for guys to *ask* a girl to dance anymore? Or is throwing their penis on our asses the only way now?

Creepy guy's eyes narrow and his dirty hair falls in his face, sticking to the sweat on his forehead, as I grab McKenzie's arm and turn to leave. Suddenly, I'm ripped back around and he's crushing me in his grip. I can smell the tequila reeking off his hot breath as I squirm. "You're not going anywhere, sweetheart," he breathes and I almost vomit from the stench. "I said I want to dance, and we're going to dance."

I feel my chest tighten and I try violently to squirm free but his grip locks tighter. McKenzie is pulling on the sleeve of my dress and I vaguely hear her muffled screaming. Everything is slow, morphed. The smell is so strong, overpowering every other sense. I try to scream but my voice is frozen in my throat.

Suddenly I feel arms wrap around my stomach and rip me from Creepster's grasp. As soon as both of my feet are back on the ground I'm immediately engulfed by McKenzie's hug and she's checking me for wounds.

"Are you alright?!" she shrieks, pulling my arms toward her and checking me like a toddler. I'm still shaken, but this is just ridiculous. I nod in half shock, half wonder and gently push her off of me. "Yeah, yeah I'm fine," I mumble, but my interest is now completely locked on the arms that were just wrapped around me.

And damn, are they big, muscular, incredibly sexy arms.

There's a space forming around us as the crowd backs away. The music is killed and I can vaguely see the bouncers making their way over, but I can't pry my eyes away from the man holding Mr. Creepster up on his toes by his shirt. He's wearing a white t-shirt that's blazing against his incredibly tan body and his jeans are hanging around his waist and accenting what I can only imagine is the tightest ass under the sun. I can only see the back of him and I'm mesmerized. I must look like a fucking idiot, standing here with my mouth all open but I can't move an inch. Luckily, no one is looking at me since he's the center of the scene, anyway. I'm sure I'm not the only one with my jaw on the floor.

"I think she made it very clear that she didn't want to dance," Dreamboat says, still holding Creepster inches from his face and clenching onto his shirt. Creepster doesn't look as intimidating, now. His eyes are wide and he looks about three feet tall as he stares up at

Dreamboat. I wish I could get a glance at his face, but there's no way I'm moving from McKenzie's side – she's got a death grip like no one I know and right now it's latched onto my arm. His dark chocolate hair is shining in the bar light and once again I'm locked in on him, biting my lip like a fool. I haven't even seen this guy's face and I want to take him home.

What is wrong with me? I was just assaulted and all I can think about is Dreamboat whisking me away. Am I having post-traumatic stress?

"Y-yes, she did. I'm s-sorry, won't happen again. Let's just d-drop this now and have another drink, eh?" Creepster pleads, his eyes still wide. I'm actually quite amused at the sight, even though McKenzie's grip is still locked tight on my arm and she's looking at the scene like she's witnessing a drive-by shooting.

Dreamboat clenches his free fist and I know he's about to throw it into this guy's jaw. That'll get him thrown out, and that can't happen.

"It's okay! I'm okay," I scream, breaking through the crowd and throwing myself between them as much as I can. "I'm fine, really it's all good," I try to sound convincing as I spout out randomness. My heart is pounding in my chest so hard I think I might fall over. I have no idea what I'm doing, but I definitely don't want to lose sight of Dreamboat. Creepster looks over at me and smiles nervously.

"See? She's cool, man. We're all cool. My mistake."

Dreamboat seems to hesitate, but he lets go of Creepster's shirt and relaxes his shoulders a bit. As soon as he releases his grip, Drew and two other bouncers are escorting Creepster out of the bar. Dreamboat melts into the crowd as the music roars to life again. Everyone around us goes back to drinking like nothing happened at all, filling the silence with laughter and ice clinking in glasses.

I inhale a large breath as McKenzie grabs my shoulders and turns me to face her, my eyes still searching for Dreamboat, "Oh my gosh! You are crazy, you know that? You should have just let that guy have at that creep!" Her eyes are still franticly searching me for bruises.

I laugh and pull my arm away. "I'm completely fine, Kenz. Really. I promise," I lie, still shaking a bit. "Let's just go get a refill on these drinks. I'm completely sober after all that."

McKenzie exhales in relief, "Okay, yeah. To the bar!" She pumps her fist into the air in declaration and I stifle a laugh.

"I'll buy," I hear a smooth, rich voice reply. I just about melt into a puddle right there on the dance floor but somehow manage to calmly turn around. Fierce, icy blue eyes gaze back at me, lighting my insides on fire.

"After all, I am the one who spilled your drink."

Hello, Dreamboat.

Chapter two
Dreamboat

I should probably speak. I should probably stop staring like a crazy person. *Look at those eyes!* Pull it together, Paisley. Act casual. Better yet, act confident.

"Yeah, I guess you do kind of owe me. Not like you already saved me tonight or anything," I smile at the last line, praying there's no hint of a blush on my pale face.

He smiles back and his eyes intensify even more. I honestly feel like he is stripping my dress off with his gaze it's so piercing. I swallow and feel the heat rush to my cheeks. There's no way I'm not blushing right now.

Dreamboat lifts his brow and smirks, a soft dimple forming at the left corner of his mouth. As he turns toward the bar, McKenzie grabs my shoulders from behind.

"Oh my God, I'm freaking out right now! This guy is so hot!" she yells in my ear over the drum of the music. I turn and mouth, "I know, right?" and then scurry to catch up to Dreamboat. As he moves between breaks in the crowd the muscles in his back flex under his shirt, pulling me in a trance. Dear God, I hope I can form a sentence when it's time to talk.

Sean is already pouring two shots and a refill on our drinks when we reach the bar. "Damn, Paisley. I told you you'd bring down the house with that dress tonight," he says, sliding the shots in front of me and McKenzie. McKenzie doesn't hesitate and downs hers before I've even grabbed mine from Sean's hand. I can't tell for sure, but I think I might see a bit of jealousy sprinkled across Dreamboat's face.

And I love it.

I wink at Sean and take my shot, the burn returning to my chest as it flows down. McKenzie is already asking for a second one when I turn to Dreamboat.

"Well, I guess since Sean already filled my drink, you'll have to think of a different way to pay me back," I smile as sexily as I can and sip from my glass, eyeing him. He grins, his dimple showing again, but I think he still might be a little pissed.

"I guess you're right – Paisley, was it?"

God, he even makes my name sound like a sex object.

"Mmm hmm, and that's something else you owe me. Shouldn't I know the name of the brave knight in shining armor who saved me tonight?"

At this, his grin turns to a full blown smile and I fumble with my drink a bit. Holy shit, he has the most gorgeous smile I've ever seen. His teeth are blazing white like his shirt against his skin and his dimple deepens, "I think I'm more of a dark knight than a knight in shining armor."

Holy. Fuck.

He smirks at what I can only imagine is my jaw flopping to the floor again. "Corbin," he finally says, extending his hand for mine. "Corbin Ray."

When he says his last name I notice the touch of twang in his voice. He's Southern, too? Dear God, help me. He takes my hand in his and squeezes lightly, sending a quick thrill through me. I focus on keeping the drool inside my mouth and squeeze in return. "Nice to meet you, Corbin."

"Likewise, doll." His eyes glow fierce again and the music in Diggs is lost to me. All I can hear is the thumping in my chest increasing. I'm suddenly extremely warm, though I'm not sure if it's him or the alcohol.

McKenzie hands me another shot and I take it slowly, my eyes still fixated on Corbin. His bold gaze is unwavering and challenging, like he wants to see how far he can push me before I give in to him. Should I just tell him he doesn't have to push very hard? The man is fucking gorgeous. His eyes are a blue fire, burning hot and consuming me. I feel naked standing in front of him, like he's taken all I have and left me to feel nothing but a driving desire.

"Hellooooo, earth to Paisley!" McKenzie waves her hand in front of my face and hands me another shot. Did I finish that other one already? I notice my drink is gone, too. Jesus, I should probably slow down. I'm not trying to be a hot mess express, but apparently McKenzie has a different plan in mind. "Derek just texted me. He wants to come pick me up," she slurs, her eyes desperately trying to focus on mine. I can still feel Corbin's hot gaze on my skin. Combined with the shot I just took I could practically be in a sauna. "What should I do?"

"What do you want to do, Kenz?" I don't even know why I ask. McKenzie and Derek have been dating for the past year, though neither of them really want to admit it. It's always the same story – they both go out, do their "own thing," but then always end up together by the end of the night. He has his toothbrush at her place, she keeps pajamas at his. I don't understand why they don't just slap a title on it and give in already. But then again, who am I to be talking? I've sworn off titles all together since college.

McKenzie bites her lip and grabs another shot from Sean. How many does that make? My thoughts are jumbled and I forget what we were even talking about until she turns back to me and nods her head, "I really want him to come." She slides back down on her stool and rests her head on my shoulder, her immaculate blonde curls tumbling down around her face. "What is wrong with me, Paisley? I can't stay away from him," she mumbles, exhaling a fluff of hair up in frustration. I pat her head and soothe her like a child.

Corbin is grinning at us, probably trying to think of an escape plan. I mouth, "Sorry," pointing down at McKenzie. He grins wider and shakes his head, signaling that he understands. God, this must be so fucking boring for him. I'm actually stoked that Derek is coming. Now I can get Corbin alone and get inside that gorgeous head of his.

Though I'm not sure that's a good idea.

"Alright, take care of her, Derek. She's got some aspirin stashed in her bathroom cabinet." I tuck McKenzie's hair behind her ear and make sure her dress is inside the car before shutting the door. We're just down the block from Diggs and the streets are clearing out now. It has to be at least three. Conscious that Corbin is still standing behind me, I slowly lean down to look at Derek through the passenger side window, resting my weight on my right hip and popping my ass out as much as I can. I've always been more top heavy, but at least this dress does a little something for my backside. Here's hoping yoga is paying off.

"You know I've got her," he says, grabbing her hand sweetly. She smiles and closes her eyes, leaning her head back against the seat. They both seem so happy, so content.

So trapped.

I nod and smile, standing up and moving from the car. Derek gives me a half wave and pulls away, leaving me alone with Corbin. Finally. Besides a few scattered bursts of laughter the streets are quiet, though the signs still buzz above the closed bars and the white lights strung across Wall Street illuminate the cobblestone with a soft glow.

Corbin moves toward me, tucking his hands in his pockets. "Well, Paisley, now that I've got you alone, can I finally pay you back for that drink I spilled?"

"And how do you suppose you do that, Mr. Ray? All the bars are closed," I reply, moving closer to him. Away from the cigarette smoke and beer stench of Diggs I can smell his cologne. It's rich and earthy, like a forest, mixed with cinnamon.

He takes my hand in his, "Food, of course. Only the best thing I can offer after a night of drinking."

I think I can find a solid argument for what the "best thing" would be right now.

"The thing is, you have to pick the place. I'm only visiting Orlando, so I'm not exactly sure where the best three o'clock in the morning restaurant is," he adds.

I laugh, motioning to all the closed stores on the street other than one small pizza diner, "Well, we have so many choices."

He laughs as I lead him across the street to Antonio's. It's either this or the hot dog stand, and I'm not that drunk. We sit down at a booth by the window facing the old railroad track and the waitress pops over long enough to flick down two menus in front of us and say she'll be right back, although she does take a second glance and perk up a bit when she sees Corbin. Who could blame her? Even in the rustic light of the pizza parlor his eyes are glowing blue. It's a good thing he didn't flash that smile of his or she'd probably have fallen to the floor.

"So, how long are you in town?" I ask, thumbing through the small menu. The aroma of the pizza dough lingers throughout the restaurant and I realize I'm hungrier than I thought.

"Just a couple weeks," he replies. I look up and notice he hasn't touched the menu, but instead he's focusing on me. Again, if his eyes had hands I swear they would be all over me. I can't help but flush and I quickly look down at my menu again. *Pull it together, Paisley.*

"Nice. Visiting family?" I return his gaze now, feigning confidence.

His smile returns and he shakes his head, "No, business."

Could this be any more perfect? Maybe dropping this tag chasing bit won't be so hard, after all. Business men. Yeah, I could get used to that. Corbin gives his order to the waitress who has returned more put together than before. As he speaks, I imagine him dressed in a suit giving a presentation. I have no idea what he does, but it's definitely a nice image.

"And for you?" The waitress is impatiently tapping her pencil on her notebook waiting for my order. Corbin tries to hide his smirk.

"I'll have one slice of cheese, please."

The waitress nods and takes our menus, grazing Corbin's hand as she takes his, and then saunters back to the kitchen. I want to be pissed at her, and frankly I kind of am, but honestly I think I would do the same thing.

"One slice?" He asks, his smirk still plastered on his face.

"Yes, it's late," I smile back and pull my straw from the wrapper, taking a quick drink of water to attempt to sober up a little more. I'm not even sure if he drank at all tonight, I definitely don't want to be more of a mess than I already am naturally. "Plus, I baked a whole batch of red velvet cookies earlier today. My yoga instructor would be pissed if she found out I ate pizza and cookies in one night."

"You bake?"

"All the time," I say, tying the wrapper into tiny knots. "I always have, since I was like seven. My mom let me help her bake my dad's birthday cake and she said I played with the frosting the entire night, trying to make it perfect. Ever since then, I've been addicted."

Why did I just tell him that? I've only known the guy a few hours and I'm getting into baking?

"Sounds like how I am with running," Corbin says as he runs his right hand through his hair. "I started when I was really young and I get hooked more and more every year. I get a sort of high from it."

He's a runner? Well, that explains his physique a little more. Although, he's way too toned to be just a runner. I notice his arm muscles even more now as he props them on the table. God, I want those arms around me again.

"I think it's okay to have little habits like that, though," he adds, shrugging. "We all need some sort of distraction from life sometimes." He smiles softly and I feel my stomach tighten. I can think of a few ways we could distract ourselves.

"Yeah, well at least your habit doesn't add five hundred calories to your diet every time you get stressed out," I add, laughing.

He gives a short chuckle and takes my hand in his again. "Trust me, whatever calories you have suit you just fine." His eyes grow dark again and he runs his thumb over mine.

And there goes my composure.

The waitress returns with our plates just in time, saving me from trying to form a sentence. His eyes never leave mine as she sets the dishes down. When she's gone again, he leans toward me. "Can I just be completely honest with you right now, Paisley?"

I nod, biting my lip and trying to contain the heat building inside me.

He pulls me closer, his mouth hovering right over my neck. "I think you're incredibly beautiful," he breathes, his breath hot as he gently nips at my skin. "I don't know why, but I am drawn to you."

My breath is hitched in my throat and my mouth has fallen open in a soft "o." I close my eyes and give in to the electricity between us. He moves his lips from my neck and speaks softly into my ear, sending a current racing down my body.

"And at the risk of being too forward, I would really like to take you back to my hotel."

Dear God, yes. YES. YES. YES.

He leans back, his hand still holding mine and his gaze intensified. I swallow and bite my lip again, trying to steady the shakiness in my voice as I say the only word I can manage.

"Okay."

The next thing I know we're tangled together in the back of a cab, our pizza left untouched on the table.

"Give me a minute?" Corbin asks, pulling his incredibly soft lips from mine. I'm pressed against the inside of his hotel door at the Sheraton, my hair still tangled in his fingers. I nod, straining to catch my breath as he pulls away. "I just need to make a quick phone call."

"A phone call?" I ask, confused. "It's almost four in the morning."

He chuckles and moves back toward me, taking my face in his hands. His hands are surprisingly rough, calloused. "I'll only be a few minutes," he says, pulling my neck to his lips and planting soft kisses in a line down to my collar bone. My toes go numb and heat explodes inside me, lighting my desire. He pulls back again and I swear if I ever wondered what blue balls felt like I was pretty damn close to finding out. "Just make yourself comfortable and I'll be right back." Corbin smiles as he backs away and finally turns and heads for the bedroom, closing the door behind him.

Holy shit. I'm in his hotel. I'm in his fucking hotel.

The suite is quiet other than the soft hum of the air conditioner. I smooth my hair down and straighten my dress the best I can before strolling over to the couch. It's a light brown, plush couch and the red accented pillows look as though they haven't been moved since Corbin checked in. I push one to the side and fall into the cushion, kicking my pumps off and sighing in relief. I love looking nice as much as the next girl, but seriously who in their right mind decided walking on the balls of our feet all night was a good idea? I could kill whoever invented high heels, right now.

I hear Corbin's voice from the bedroom, "Hey, did I wake you? No, I'm just getting in. Yeah yeah, could have been you, too, if you would have come with me." I stiffen at the last line, straining my ear to hear more. Who was supposed to come with him? His girlfriend? His wife? Wait, was he wearing a ring? I didn't even check.

What the fuck is wrong with me?

Who cares who he's talking to, I'm not looking to be serious with him, anyway, so what does it matter? It's not like I'm his girlfriend. I laugh softly to myself, shaking my head at my ridiculousness. I wonder if my mom was like this in the end, always listening, questioning. I shake my head again, forcing myself to relax, and grab the remote for the TV. I hit the power button and it clicks on to ESPN. I quickly change it to The Food Network and a rerun of Sweet Genius fills the screen as I exhale, Corbin's voice completely muted now.

As Ron Ben-Israel talks inspiration with his chefs, I glance around the suite. Corbin's black luggage set is spread out all over the living area, most of the cases open with random clothing and toiletry items hanging out, and the kitchen is bare except for the solo Five Guys to-go cup sitting on the bar. Checking back over my shoulder to make sure Corbin is still preoccupied, I stand and walk over to his luggage, my curiosity piqued.

His smallest bag is a briefcase and is wide open, revealing his phone charger, tablet and case, a light blue folder labeled "Inspiration," and a few pens. My fingers find the edge of the folder and flip it open slowly, a few papers sliding out. It looks like mostly notes, but there are a few photographs, too. One is of Corbin at what looks like a high school football game. He has his arm around another guy and they're smiling ear to ear. God, his dimples were killer back then, too. Am I getting turned on by a high schooler right now? I shake my head and put the photo back, sifting through the rest. There's one of a running path, a waterfall, a scruffy looking white dog with his tongue hanging lopsidedly out of his mouth, and the last is another one of Corbin, this time with a young woman. She has bright blonde hair even lighter than McKenzie's and it's cut short in layers around her face. Corbin has his arm around her and they're both covered in dirt standing next to a sign labeled "Tough Mudder 2012." Corbin's muscles are practically exploding through his wet shirt and Pixie Cut Princess has her arms wrapped around him, her head leaning back in laughter. I have to admit she's pretty gorgeous, but she looks so young. Too young. Like 18 young. Could this be the woman who's supposed to be here with him?

I shuffle the photos back in the folder and move to the next bag, the largest one, which is slightly open with clothing sticking out on each side. I tug on one of the sleeves and pull out half of what looks like a workout shirt. It's bright green with thick black stripes on each side. Without even opening it further I can smell his cologne, the same scent from earlier only without the touch of himself that was so earthy and organic. I flip the top of the suitcase open and my heart stops dead in my chest. The sound from the TV blurs and everything is intensified around me as I stare in disbelief.

Laying folded right on top of the shirt in my hand is a pair of Army ACU's with "RAY" stitched on the Velcro tag.

I pull back my hand and the top falls back down, pushing a little puff of air through my hair. *Shit. Shit, shit, shit.* I quickly turn back to the bedroom and tip toe to the door, praying Corbin isn't off the phone yet. I hear his muffled laughter and exhale, panic threatening to seize me. *Calm down, Paisley. Chill out.* I thought he said he was here for business? There are no Army bases in Orlando, what business could he possibly be here for?

My heartbeat races in my chest, thumping so hard it threatens to knock me over as I sneak back to the couch to retrieve my pumps. Why did I have to make that fucking bet tonight? He's so gorgeous, so heartbreakingly gorgeous. Grabbing my shoes by the heels and cursing under my breath, I turn and head for the door. Every step feels like a mile and I swear I'm breathing like a fucking rhino. I trip over the corner of another suitcase and tumble toward the door.

Sprawled out on the floor in what I can only imagine is the most unattractive position in the entire world I raise my head just in time to see Corbin emerge from the bedroom, his face turning concerned as soon as he sees me.

"Oh my God, Paisley, are you okay?" He rushes toward me, extending his arms to help me up. I awkwardly shuffle to my feet, grabbing my heels once more and backing toward the door.

"I'm fine! I'm fine. I, uh, I have to go," I blurt out, turning for the door again.

"Wait, where are you going? What's wrong?" Corbin asks behind me. *Don't turn around, Paisley. Get out the door and do not turn around.*

"It's uh, my, uh, boss. She just called. Emergency at the office. Sorry, um, but I had fun!" I say over my shoulder, reaching for the door knob. I pull twice with no luck before Corbin reaches over me, his hard body pressing against me as he unlocks a top lock I hadn't even noticed. I pull the door open and glance back at him, immediately regretting it. His icy eyes are soft now and I swear it's like he's a lost puppy begging me to take him home with me.

"It's four in the morning, Paisley. At least let me get you a cab," he says softly, brushing a strand of my hair behind my ears. I feel myself leaning toward him and almost give in, but there's no way I'm ready to lose this bet to McKenzie. No way that I'm ready to tell her what she wants to know.

I pull back and shake my head, "No. Um, no I'm okay. It's not too far from here, I'll be fine."

Corbin's eyes don't leave mine as he leans in to kiss me. I allow myself that one last pleasure, breathing in his scent and tugging at his bottom lip with my teeth. He pulls me closer to him and I feel his excitement pressed against my stomach. I push my hands against his chest, breaking our kiss, and duck out the door. *Just focus on getting to the elevator, Paisley. Don't look back.*

When I finally get there and step inside I turn one last time to face him, trying my best to contain the heat still building inside me. He stands solid, his eyes not wavering from mine as the doors slowly close.

As the elevator descends, I close my eyes and lean my head back against the wall, exhaling and sinking down to the floor in defeat.

Fuck.

Chapter three
New Client

My head is pounding as I walk in the doors of Intrigue Advertising. In one hand, I'm balancing the red velvet cookies from the night before along with the three dozen cupcakes I baked when I got home at four thirty and in the other, my grande white mocha from Starbucks. I didn't sleep, couldn't sleep. I didn't even try to sleep. I just walked straight into my kitchen when I got home, chucking my heels in my room, and found peace in baking strawberry cupcakes with beach themed frosting. I even took the time to add the perfect coloring to the fondant for a realistic beach and ocean texture. I may be tired, but at least my mind was occupied for a few hours.

"Was" being the key word there. On the drive in I found myself thinking about Corbin. I couldn't shake his incredibly blue eyes and the sadness they held when I ditched him. I almost drove to his hotel to apologize, explain the whole bet thing to him and at least part as friends, but I knew if I saw him again I would lose my control and give in. There's no way I'm letting McKenzie win that easily.

I tried calling Tanner last night when I got home and then again this morning, but he didn't answer. I didn't even bother leaving a voicemail because I didn't want him to worry. He always worried about me, always looked out for me. I miss having him here, especially at times like this.

The office is already alive and buzzing even though it's just barely past eight. The door to my boss's office is closed and I can vaguely see shadows moving inside. She must already have a few of the new clients. Even though I already have seven major projects, one of those new clients will be mine, too. Oh joy, overtime.

Shannon pops out of her seat at the reception desk and follows me back to the kitchen and I know the questions are coming. "Don't even ask, Shannon," I say, setting the cupcakes in the fridge and taking the cookies to the center table.

"Oh, Paisley. What's wrong? I haven't seen you bake cupcakes like this since we lost the Orange Country Club account last May." Shannon grabs a cookie as I place them down and rests her hand on her hip waiting for me to answer. Her long brown hair is tied in a neat bun and she's paired a simple black pencil skirt and white button up that makes her breasts look even larger than they already are. I've always thought myself to be well endowed, but Shannon could put a whole house of strippers to shame. She is a little thick, but she owns it. We've been friends since she started a few years ago, and she quickly caught on to my baking charades. I should probably do some baking when I'm happy like I used to back in college, but for some reason it only happens when I'm stressed, sad, or pissed off anymore.

"Nothing happened, Shannon," I try to lie, but Shannon just grabs another cookie and sits down, waiting for a better answer. I sigh and fall into the chair beside her, resting my head in my hands. "Oh shit, Shannon. I met a guy."

"You met a guy?!" Shannon asks with her mouth still full of cookie. Her eyes are wide and she's bouncing up and down like a school girl in her seat.

"Calm down. You know I don't mean like that. I mean like I was going to hang out with him for a while, he was the perfect distraction."

Shannon's face falls a little, "Oh, well then what's the problem? Why all the baking?"

"He's in the Army."

Shannon wipes the corners of her mouth with a napkin, "And? Isn't that like the only kind of guy you date, anyway?"

"It was. Until I made this stupid bet with Kenz."

"Bet?" Shannon leans over excitedly, "What bet?"

"That I won't date military men anymore," I let out with another sigh.

Shannon lets out an exaggerated gasp and clutches her napkin, "Paisley Bronson? Giving up the tag chasing days? Why, say it isn't so!" She starts fanning herself and pretends to faint back in her chair.

I smack her arm playfully, "Oh ha ha, Shannon. You little –"

"Ladies, if I'm not interrupting anything too important, could you please return to your desks and perhaps get a little work done this morning?" Our boss, Mrs. Lydia Holmes, is standing at the doorway of the kitchen with her arms crossed in a rigid fashion. And by rigid, I mean rigid bitch. Her dainty lips are pursed in dissatisfaction and her pale skin is reddening by the moment. It'll match her bright fire red hair soon if she doesn't calm down.

"Yes, ma'am," Shannon responds, hurrying off to her desk and turning around to make a "blah blah blah" hand motion once she passes Lydia.

I stifle a laugh and start toward my desk, but Lydia stops me short. "Don't forget I have that new client for you this morning. I'm expecting him in about twenty minutes, so I expect you to report to my office in fifteen," she spits, turning on her heels for her office.

Bitch.

I have been at Intrigue for a little over four years now and I still can't figure out what's always up her ass. The rest of the office is so fun – everyone is friends, we all laugh and joke around – but she just won't let loose. If one deadline is missed by a fraction of a second, she's pissed. If you don't create the exact shade of purple she's expecting for a client, she's pissed. If you have a strand of hair out of place during a pitch, she's pissed. In the entire time I've been here, I've seen her smile a total of four times. Twice when she fired someone and the other two times when her husband showed up surprising her. She must be an entirely different woman around him, otherwise he'd be crazy to give her a ring.

I barely have time to check my emails before it's time to head to Lydia's office to meet my new client. I'm excited for the commission and for a new challenge, and I honestly love creating new campaigns, but I'm already so overwhelmed with my other clients I'm barely treading water. I'm just about to head that way when my phone rings. Shannon.

"What, skank?"

"Oh, be nice. Just wanted to give you a heads up that your new client just showed up. He is H.O.T. hot!"

"Shit! She wanted me in there before he got here. Shit shit shit," I respond before slamming the phone down and scrambling for my papers. It immediately rings again but I ignore it and race towards Lydia's office, grabbing a pen off Shannon's desk as I whisk by.

She rolls her eyes and laughs, "You're welcome!" I turn back and mouth a "thank you" before slipping into Lydia's office, straightening my skirt as I do.

She has her back to me, shaking the hand of our new client, but of course she hears me enter. Ears like a fucking cat. "Ah, and that must be Ms. Bronson joining us. Paisley, I'd like you to meet your new client," she says, stepping aside to reveal Mr. Hot.

When she does, I fumble my pen to the floor and stare in shock.

"Mr. Corbin Ray."

Holy shit.

Corbin is staring at me with just as much disbelief on his face, although he seems a little more amused than embarrassed. He's dressed in a gray pin striped suit with a white shirt and gray tie to match and his dark hair is slicked over, every little strand in its perfect place. His pants are hanging just right off his hips and I can't help but glance just under his belt, imagining him pressed against me like just a few short hours ago. Good Lord, help me.

I bend quickly to retrieve my pen and reach my hand out to Corbin's. He has a half smirk fixed to his face as he takes my hand and shakes it softly, sending a spike of electricity through me. "Pleasure to meet you, Ms. Bronson," he says, his voice like a fucking symphony.

This cannot be happening.

How is this even possible? I saw his ACU's with his name on them, and now he's showing up as a client at my agency? This doesn't make any sense.

"Yes, thank you for coming in, Mr. Ray."

I know I'm at least seven shades of red right now. Lydia is eyeing me questioningly as she speaks, "Ms. Bronson is our Senior Account Executive and one of the best on our team. I have faith she will do nothing but excite and amaze you with her unique style and creativity."

Corbin's smile widens, his glorious teeth bared and his dimple showing in full, "I have no doubt you are correct, Mrs. Holmes."

Fuck.

The heat rushes to my cheeks and I look down at my folder to escape the burning in his eyes. I'm in trouble, here. Where is the S.O.S. smoke signal when you need one?

"Well then, I will let you two get started. Paisley, I've reserved the back conference room for you and Mr. Ray. Please brief me when you've finished," Lydia says, handing me Corbin's profile. I nod and smile, trying to appear collected, and lead Corbin from her office.

We don't say a word as we walk, and when I finally get him to the back conference room I shut the door and set my folders on the table. "So, Mr. Ray, tell me a little about your company," I say casually, taking a seat and motioning for him to have the one across from me. *Please just sit down. Please pretend like last night didn't happen.*

"Absolutely," he says, sitting down and leaning back in his chair. "But first, I have to know that the 'emergency' at the office was handled this morning. After all, it did interrupt my very pleasant evening."

Damn it. I should have known he wouldn't just let it go. I fidget with my pen and bite the inside of my cheek, trying to think of an explanation. "I'm sorry, Corbin," I sigh, "I just had to go. I just... I realized something, and I couldn't be there any more. I can't really explain."

"So don't," he says, cutting me off. The tone of his voice has shifted and his eyes are dark. *Shit, he's mad. Great job, Paisley.* "But," he continues, leaning over the table toward me. "I think this does mean that it's now *you* that owes *me*." He smiles and leans back again, his hotness just radiating everywhere as he unbuttons his jacket and lets it fall open.

"Wait a second, how do I owe you?" I play back, tapping my pen on my fingertips. "If I do recall, I never got the drink *or* the food promised to me."

With this, Corbin's face falls a little, and he sits upright. "Well, I guess you are correct, Ms. Bronson. I'll have to make up for both of those. How about tonight?"

Oh, great. Why don't you just shove your head in an oven while you're at it, Paisley?

"I don't think that's a good idea," I say, opening my folder to his profile details.

"What's wrong," he asks, a challenging tone lingering in his voice. "Did you find something incriminating when you were looking through my bags last night?"

I drop my pen again and laugh awkwardly. "What? I wasn't going through your bags," I lie, desperately hoping my nervous mouth twitch isn't giving me away.

Corbin's brow rises and he puts his fingertips together, waiting for me to confess. "Really? So my running shirt was just laying out for no reason and you "just realized" something completely unrelated before you ditched me last night?"

I swallow and grimace, running my hands through my hair. "Listen, Corbin. You are a great guy, I'm sure. But you're just not a good guy for me."

"So let me be the bad guy," he says softly, just above a whisper. I look up into his eyes, dancing in the fluorescent lights. I'm going to faint. I'm literally going to faint.

"Okay, fine," he adds, throwing his hands up. "We'll eat somewhere very public and you can leave whenever you feel the urge. But at least let me take you to dinner tonight. I owe you, and I always pay my debts."

Everything inside me is screaming "YES!" but I know this is bad news. I try to think of some excuse, some way to get out of it, but I fail and finally give in, "Okay, but just dinner. Then we're done, Mr. Ray."

"If you insist, Ms. Bronson."

My heart beat descends a little as I exhale, thumbing through his profile. Dinner. Yeah, I can do just dinner. Just a few short hours and then I can move on and he never has to know why I ran last night.

Right?

I shake my head and try to focus on actually doing my job. "Alright, so now can you tell me a little more about your business? It says here you're looking to open a gym next year in the Orlando area," I say calmly, snapping into my professional persona.

"That's right. It's going to be a competitive gym for athletes who didn't make it pro. Basically a place for them to train, join teams, and compete," Corbin replies. He's leaning forward again, but this time with pure excitement lighting his face. "I've been saving for a while now, and I'm ready to finally start making concrete plans."

"That's great," I say, relaxing a bit. "Why are you waiting another year? Are you waiting for property?"

"No, I have the property lined up," he says, his face falling a little again. "I have to wait a year because I won't be in the area until then. I'll be deployed."

I bite my cheek again and search for something to say. That explains the ACU's, I guess. Corbin has fallen quiet again and he seems lost in his thoughts. "Well, that just gives us plenty of time to work in the perfect campaign. When will you be back to put all this into action?"

He lights up again, "I should be back in about ten months, but nothing is really ever certain with the Army. That's why I want to have as much of this hammered out before I leave next week, so that when I do come back everything is ready to roll."

I can't help but smile. Corbin is like a child as he rattles off the details of his gym. He wants to call it "B String," and he has an idea for the logo to have some sort of strong animal tied in, like a lion or a snake. The more he talks, the more I daze – getting lost in his smooth voice and dazzling eyes. Why did I have to make that bet with McKenzie? Why last night, of all nights? For the first time since my senior year, I feel myself starting to care for this guy.

Stop it, Paisley. I can't get caught up in this. I made a bet, a promise, not only to McKenzie but to myself. And there's no way this guy is as perfect as he seems. Every guy has some sort of douchey quality, no exceptions to that rule.

I always thought my dad was a perfect guy. He treated my mom like a queen, was father of the year to me, and had everything else in his life completely figured out. He was successful, healthy, and I always thought he could do no wrong.

But no guy is perfect.

I shake my head and close Corbin's profile after jotting down my last few notes. "This all sounds great, Corbin," I say as professionally as I can manage. "I think we're done for today. I'll have Shannon set up our next meeting on your way out."

Corbin nods and stands, extending his card to me. "And can Ms. Shannon also set up our dinner tonight? Or should you provide me with your phone number before you throw me out of your office?"

I smile, "I think we should save Shannon the stress of planning our date, Mr. Ray."

Shit. Why did I just call it a date?

"I couldn't agree more," Corbin replies, his eyes dancing with intensity. Could he be any sexier? I hand him my card with my cell phone number on it and walk him to the front, where Shannon is more than eager to take over. She perks up in her chair and brushes her hair out of her face, batting her lashes.

"Shannon, please set up another meeting for Mr. Ray and I. He's only in town for a short while, so make it for Tuesday. You can move around my other appointments as needed." I turn back to Corbin and hold out my hand, "It was a pleasure meeting with you, Corbin."

"The pleasure was all mine, Ms. Bronson," he says, taking my hand softly. "I look forward to seeing you again."

I flush and nod, turning for my desk and shooting Shannon a warning glare as she stares at me open-mouthed. When I reach my desk, an email is already waiting with the time of my next meeting with Corbin. A second one pops up with the subject line, *"WHAT WAS THAT? COME CHAT!"* from Shannon. *Shit.*

I fall into my chair and bury my face in my hands, trying to reassure myself. *He said one dinner – one dinner, then he will leave me alone.*

My phone buzzes on my desk and a text pops up from a 405 area code.

- Meet at my hotel tonight, 7:30. –

My heart races as I read, visions of last night flooding my mind. I should be running. I should not answer and not show up. He'll be gone in two weeks and I can just pretend like it didn't happen.

But he did say he would leave me alone if I just had this one dinner. It can't be that hard to resist him for one dinner, can it? Eating, talking - I can handle that. And truthfully, he says he'll go away, but is that really what I want?

My phone vibrates again.

- P.S. I can't wait to pay you back. –

I'm screwed.

Chapter four

Dinner for Two

"You sure you don't want to come with us? It's going to be a lot of fun!" McKenzie's voice echoes through my room from my phone's speaker.

"I know, but I'm still feeling pretty rough from last night," I lie, spraying my favorite perfume, Chanel Coco Noir, on my wrist. "I think I better just take it easy tonight."

I turn sideways and check my figure in the mirror. The new cherry red dress I picked up last minute hugs my skin and shows off my legs. Paired with this push up bra I feel like a double for Julia Roberts in *Pretty Woman*, only with darker hair and paler skin. I have to admit, it's pretty hot.

"Alright, if you say so. I'll see you at yoga tomorrow?"

"Yeah, see you then. Have fun!" I press END before McKenzie can say anything else and throw my phone in my clutch, heading for the door. I glance at the sticky note on my fridge as I pass by, "Call Mom." She called three days ago and I still haven't called her back. I know I need to, but right now all I really want is a distraction. Even if I can't fully have it.

My hand is shaking as I reach for the door knob, hesitating. *Can I really do this?* I shake my head, "Get a grip, Paisley." I feign confidence as I shut the door behind me, knowing the trouble I'm heading for.

It takes me three times of walking back to the elevator, changing my mind again, and walking back to Corbin's hotel door before I finally knock. I exhale slowly, trying to gather myself. When the door finally opens, my breath hitches in my throat.

Damn.

Corbin is wearing dark jeans and a simple gray T-shirt, the sleeves just tight enough around his arms to accent his glorious bicep muscles. He's got a lop sided grin that makes my stomach tighten it's so sexy and he's wearing a clean white apron.

"Wow," he says, letting his eyes devour my entire body. "You look amazing, Paisley."

I blush, "Thank you. Although, I feel like I might be a little overdressed for the occasion." I eye his jeans questioningly. He laughs and moves aside to let me in, and then I realize why he's not dressed.

The table that was empty except for a few folders last night is now covered with a deep red table cloth and is set for dinner for two, complete with a fondue pot in the middle and a bottle of wine chilling in a small bucket of ice. So much for a "very public place."

There's some sort of herby aroma blanketing the entire suite and I inhale deeply, realizing how hungry I am. Probably because I haven't touched food all day. How could I? My stomach has been a tangled mess since Corbin left the office earlier.

"I thought we could have dinner here," Corbin says behind me, taking my purse from my hand and tucking it in the closet behind the door. "That is, if you think you can stand my cooking skills."

I giggle softly and turn to face him, "I think I can manage. Just be warned, I have Pizza Hut on speed dial just in case."

He laughs, baring his gorgeous teeth, and motions for me to have a seat. "Since the cooking appliances are limited," he points to the small, two-burner stove and microwave. "I figured fondue would be perfect."

I smile and sit down at the chair where I can watch him work in the kitchen, "Fondue sounds amazing." It falls silent and Corbin's eyes take me in once more. I can't help but do the same with him. Even in just jeans and a t-shirt he is absolutely breathtaking. His skin looks so smooth and I'm a little jealous of the apron tied around him. What I wouldn't give to wrap my legs around him, instead.

"Ah, I almost forgot," he says, walking toward the TV. He reaches for his phone and plugs it in to a cord connected to the TV. A soft and slow country song fills the room, making me smile again.

"Who is this?" I ask, admitting my absolute lack of music knowledge. I love just about every type of music there is, but I have no idea about who sings what. I usually never follow up or download songs, I just hear whatever is on the radio. In fact, McKenzie gives me shit about it every time she tries to thumb through my phone for a playlist to get ready to and comes up empty handed.

"Brad Paisley," Corbin says, joining me at the table long enough to pour me a small glass of the chilled Moscato. "He's one of my favorites. I hope country music is okay? I can always put on Pandora instead."

"No, country is fine. I just don't know much about it," I reply, taking a sip of the wine. It's fresh and sweet and I devour almost the entire glass. *Take it slow, Paisley. You're already walking a thin line.*

"Well I can teach you anything you want to know about country music," he says from the kitchen. He's leaning into the fridge, retrieving who cares what, and I can't take my eyes off the muscles moving on his lower back as he bends and reaches around. His jeans are hanging just right and I find myself thinking about his incredible ass again. This is going to be so much harder than I thought.

"How do you know so much about it? You a southern boy?" I ask, trying to focus on conversation instead of the images playing out in my head.

"Midwest, actually. Oklahoma born and raised."

"Oklahoma?" I laugh, filling my glass a little more. "What brings you to the sunshine state, then? I know there aren't any Army bases around here."

"Really? How do you know that?"

Shit. Way to go, Paisley. Might as well tell him you're a tag chaser, too, while you're at it. "I've just lived here all my life, in Central Florida that is. So I know the area," I lie. The truth is I know because I have only dated one Army guy, and the only reason I even met him was because I took a vacation up north and met him in New York City one evening. We "dated," if you can even call it that, for the week and half I was up there and then when he wanted to try the long distance thing I took that opportunity to call things off. A little fun, a little romance, and none of the hurt that goes along with it. It was perfect. But I knew there were no active Army guys in Florida unless they were just visiting. It's all about the Air Force, Navy, and Coast Guard here.

"Oh, well I'm not exactly sure what attracted me to Florida honestly," he says, bringing a couple of bowls over to the table. One is filled with shredded cheese and the other with little pieces of bread. "I've just always had this dream of opening this gym. Well, ever since my best friend in high school came up with the idea, anyway. And I knew I didn't want to do it in Oklahoma." He goes back to the kitchen and returns with a few more bowls; carrots, broccoli, and apples. "One day I just saw this ad on TV about Orlando and I figured it was just as good a place as any. Besides, I think I could get used to the sunshine… and the heat," he says the last line as he leans close to me setting down the last bowl, his eyes gazing into mine. I can definitely feel the heat.

"Well, it really is a great area. I can't seem to leave," I say, grabbing the napkin on the table and adjusting it on my lap as an excuse to break our eye contact. He smiles and stands up straight again. He knows what he's doing to me, I just wonder if he knows how much I like it.

Damn it, Paisley, stop! How am I supposed to do this dinner with him and then never think of him again when my mind keeps thinking things like that? It's like it's out of control and I'm just along for the ride. I don't have a say in anything.

"Do you mind if I dim the lights?" he asks. I shake my head nonchalantly and try to gain my cool. He lights the two small candles on the table and a few more on the bar before shutting the kitchen and main light off. In the new glow, his frosty blue eyes are darker and they dance with the flames. I try to look away, but they're so beautiful I'm entranced without a prayer to save me.

He walks back to the table and begins melting the cheese in the fondue pot, adding a can of beer and a few other ingredients and stirring the cheese in slowly. I watch him in a daze, wanting so bad to reach out and touch him. To just feel his skin on mine. I shake my head and go back to the conversation, "So, where's your best friend?"

He stops stirring and looks at me, the warmth in his eyes vanishing. "What?"

"Your best friend? You said the gym was his idea..." I trail off, unsure of the sudden shift in his mood. He stares at me for a moment and his eyes seem hollow, vacant. He goes back to stirring in the cheese and I find myself wanting to reach out to him again, this time to comfort him and bring back the shine in his eyes.

"I don't really want to talk about it right now, if that's okay," he says, setting the spoon he's been stirring with on a plate next to the pot. He grabs two sets of fondue forks, one white and one red, and hands me the white ones.

"Yeah, of course. It's no problem. I shouldn't have even asked, it's none of my business," I reply, taking my forks. He sits down across from me and exhales one large breath before looking at me again, the light coming back into his eyes. And the heat back into my stomach.

"It's all good. I just don't want to think about work right now, not in the company of such a beautiful woman." Corbin takes one small piece of bread and dips it in the cheese slowly before popping it into his mouth. I let out a soft moan under my breath when he licks his bottom lip. *Good Lord, this is impossible. Why does he have to be in the Army? Why?*

"Sounds good to me, work is the last thing I want to talk about, anyway," I say, trying to change the subject. I try a carrot in the cheese and once again realize how hungry I am. It's smooth and tangy, and so delicious paired with the sweet Moscato.

"Oh?" Corbin eyes me questioningly as he pours himself a new glass of wine. "Seemed like you were practically running the place when I was there. What could be so bad?"

I shake my head and roll my eyes, sticking a piece of bread with my fork. "Not even close. I mean, I'm good at what I do, but I'm just not sure I'm… I don't know the words,"

"Happy?" Corbin asks, his eyes watching me closely. I feel the word weigh down on me and my shoulders deflate a little. Am I happy? I don't really think of myself as unhappy, but am I really *happy*?

I shrug, "I'm not sure, really. I don't really think about it. I just get up and do what I have to do, and I'm good at it, so people respect me for that."

He laughs and runs his hand through his hair before taking a long drink from his glass. I watch as his arm muscles shift under his t-shirt, tightening and loosening. I'm completely mesmerized.

"Well, if you could do anything in the world, if money wasn't a factor and it didn't matter what experience you had, what would you do?" Corbin lets me finish off the last of the cheese before removing the pot and heading back into the kitchen. I guess we were both hungrier than we thought.

"Bake," I say, a small fleeting dream of owning my own bakery flooding my mind. There's nothing that makes more sense to me in my life than baking. It's measurable and simple, yet there's so much room to create and make changes. Baking has been there for me no matter what – when I'm incredibly happy, when I'm heartbreakingly sad, and everything in-between. It's dependable.

"Ah, I thought that was just a stress reliever?" He questions, stirring a pot on the mini stove top. It smells like earthy herbs and delicious spices. I pour myself another glass of wine and frown a little when I realize it's the last of the bottle.

"It is, among other things. Baking is kind of my release for every emotion, not just stress." As I set the empty bottle down, Corbin walks over right on cue to replace the ice in the bucket and fill it with a brand new bottle of wine.

"Are you trying to get me drunk, Mr. Ray?" I tease, motioning to the new bottle.

Corbin's gorgeous smile comes alive in the candle light, "Maybe just a little, but I'm not the one pouring your glasses anymore." He winks at me and returns to the kitchen, retrieving a plate of raw steak and chicken seasoned with garnishes. He brings the plate along with the new pot to the table and sets it on the burner. I watch as he meticulously adds a bit of red wine, four small potatoes, two mushroom heads, and a few more spices before taking his seat again.

"Two minutes for the chicken, one and a half for the steak. If you like it tender, that is," he's pointing to each of the meats on the plate, but his eyes are locked in on mine, gauging my reaction. "If you like it a little tougher, two to two and a half minutes."

I swallow and nod, picking up my fondue fork and sticking a small, thick cut of steak. I slide it into the boiling mix and let it begin cooking, starting a piece of chicken on my other fork. For a moment it's silent other than the clinking of our forks on our plates and in the pot and the occasional sip of wine. When I take out my steak, Corbin laughs a little, his eyes still fixed on me.

"What is so funny over there, Mr. Ray? Care to share with the class?"

He takes another sip from his wine, chuckling, "Just taking note, is all." I raise my eyebrow, intrigued. He laughs softly again and eyes the steak on my plate. "A little over two minutes."

I look down at my steak, "Yeah, I guess I do like it tough."

Corbin's eyes sparkle once more and he smiles, "Good thing I like a challenge."

My eyes shoot back to his. They're darker now, and the heat from the pot suddenly feels too close for comfort.

I'm completely helpless.

Corbin is finishing up the dishes in the kitchen as I relax on the couch where I sat the night before, right before I fled like an idiot. Or was I smarter then? Am I the idiot now, thinking I can resist him? I'm lost in my thoughts and startle a little when Corbin sits down next to me, handing me a new glass of wine. My head is already a little fuzzy, but I immediately take a gulp.

"So, Ms. Bronson, are you ever going to tell me what that emergency was at work this morning that made you have to leave so quickly?"

I flush and take another, longer sip from my glass. I look up at him, my guiltiness written all over my face, I'm sure. He laughs a little and shakes his head, "Relax, you don't need to explain anything to me if you really don't want to. I'm curious, but I'm just glad you met me for dinner tonight."

"I am, too." I blurt out. *Shit, Paisley, you're supposed to not be interested.* "It was delicious."

Corbin's eyes are searching mine and I feel him leaning in closer to me. Shit, shit, shit. "But, uh, I have yoga really early tomorrow. So I should probably get going," I fumble, setting my glass of wine down on the coffee table. I go to stand but Corbin's hand reaches out for mine, stopping me in my tracks.

"Wait, what about dessert?"

I turn to face him again and melt to the floor when I see the look in his eyes. They're dark, daring. He's daring me to stay. Daring me to take a chance.

He slides his other hand around my waist, leaning closer with every word, "You've got three options." I know I should leave, should stand up right now and walk toward the door, but I'm frozen in place and captured by his eyes. " I could whip up some delicious chocolate fondue with fresh cut strawberries," he breathes, tickling my back a little with his fingertips. My breath is hitched in my throat and I can hear my heart beating in my ears, the rate rapidly increasing with every syllable that escapes his mouth. "We could make a trip to the store and pick up the perfect ingredients for you to show off your baking skills," he pulls me a little closer and I have to turn away, the intensity in his eyes too much for me to handle. My legs start shaking a little and I try to steady them and focus on breathing. His body is so close to mine now, I can feel his chest against mine. "Or," he pulls his hand from mine and touches the side of my face, running his fingers up through my hair, and begins planting soft kisses on my neck. "We could stay right here, and I could make you dessert, instead."

Holy. Fuck.

I turn to him, breathless, and crush my lips onto his.

Every thought leaves my mind and all I can focus on, all I breathe, is Corbin. He pulls me up toward him and runs his hand down my body as his mouth explores mine. His tongue moves with mine between short, quick breaths, both of us losing control. He bites my lip and a moan escapes my mouth. Corbin lets out a growl and his eyes roll back, "Fuck, Paisley. That is the sexiest sound I've ever heard." Hearing his words makes me moan again and he moves his mouth to my throat and bites and sucks as he moves between my legs, forcing my dress up to my hips and thrusting hard against me. I can feel him grow harder as I let out another moan, my control completely gone.

I run my fingers down his back and reach for the bottom of his t-shirt, pulling it up and over his head as he lifts to help. His muscles are swollen, alive with movement. He stares down at me, his eyes hungrier than I've ever seen them before as he falls back down on me. He thrusts again between my hips and a current of heat runs through me. I'm gasping for air, for a long breath, but I can't catch one. I'm completely engulfed in his touch.

I run my hands down his chest and pull at the hem of his jeans, sliding my finger tips just beneath his boxer line. He lets out a breathy, "Fuck," and slides his hand up my thigh, gripping my ass and pulling me into him. I push my hand under his jeans and feel him through his boxers, sending a throaty growl through him.

Fuck. He is so big.

I run my hand up and down him, feeling every inch. His breath is choppy in my ear as he kisses my neck, thrusting into me. This moment is electrifying, everything feels alive. I start to reach under his boxers when suddenly Corbin's ringtone fills the suite. He stops kissing me and I pull my hand from beneath his shorts, searching his eyes. He hesitates, then lets out a frustrated, "Shit," and lifts himself off of me, rushing to retrieve his phone from the bar counter.

I sit up and pull my dress down, smoothing my hair and wiping the corners of my mouth where I'm sure my red lipstick has stained. I watch Corbin carefully as he answers the phone. Who is calling? Who's so important that he stopped what was happening? Maybe he really is married… I try to shake the thought from my mind, or the fact that I even care, but I can't. I just sit fixated on his expression as he answers the phone.

"Hello? Hey, now's not really a good time – what? Ugh, hang on a second," Corbin puts his hand over the phone and mouths an, "I'm sorry, give me a minute," before tucking into the bedroom and shutting the door.

What the hell are you doing, Paisley? So much for just dinner! I shake my head and reach for Corbin's glass of wine on the table, downing the entire thing. I can't do this. I made a bet, and I'm not going to lose it. I'm not ready to talk to McKenzie about Dad and how fucked up I am in the head, am I? No. I need to leave.

I glance back at the bedroom, Corbin's muffled voice creeping through the crack in the door. I think I'm clear. I slide into my heels and retrieve my purse from the closet behind the front door. My legs shake as I take one last look at the couch where his hands were just all over me, where I felt him. *Every inch of him.* I shake my head, turn on my heels, and rush out of the suite.

I'm practically running down the hall. When I reach the elevator and step inside, I frantically press the "FLOOR" button, my heart pounding in my throat as I imagine Corbin coming out of the room looking for me. When the doors finally slide together, I lean my head back and let out a long, shaky breath.

I'm out, I'm okay. I didn't break the bet… not all the way, anyway.

But when the elevator touches down and I head for my car, I can't help but think of the real reason I wanted to leave. Is it really still about the bet, or is it because I know that for the first time since college, I feel something for someone. I care about someone, and the fact that he is on the phone with someone I don't know bothers me. The fact that I can't have him bothers me.

Shit. I fucking like him.

Chapter five

Running

"You cannot bail on me again. Not only did you not come out last night, but you didn't show at yoga this morning, either. Do I have to come over there and pull your lazy ass out of bed?" McKenzie is talking so loud I have to hold my phone a few inches from my ear to not add to my splitting headache. I knew I had a lot of wine last night, but I forgot how bad the hangover is.

"I just don't want to go out tonight, Kenz. Can't we do a movie night instead?"

"Why? So you can bake and feel sorry for yourself and we can cry watching some stupid romance movie we've seen a million times?" It doesn't sound like that bad of an idea to me, but apparently McKenzie isn't satisfied. "No. Absolutely not. Get your ass in the shower. Right now. I'm on my way over." I can hear her mumbling a few curse words before the line goes dead and my "But Kenz," goes unnoticed.

I sigh and let my phone drop into my lap. I wanted to throw it in a river after last night. Corbin called three times not too long after I left. He didn't leave a voicemail, didn't call me a crazy amount of times, but the three times he did call it took everything in me to not answer. I just wanted to explain, to tell him everything so that I could spare us both the misery. But the problem is, it's not just the bet anymore. He had to go and talk about himself, and ask about me. He had to go and do the cutest fucking dinner ever.

As if he can hear my thoughts, my phone buzzes with a text from him.

- You don't have to talk to me, but please let me know you're okay.
I'm going crazy over here. –

I let my head fall back against the couch and close my eyes. *Fuck me.* Now he's being all concerned and shit. I lift my head and stare at the text, debating a response. I don't want the guy worrying about me, but if I text him there's a chance he'll ask more. Or what if he calls?

Ugh.

- I'm okay. –

I immediately regret sending the text as soon as I see it go through. I should have just ignored it, but I still have to work with him and the last thing I need is him showing up to his appointment on Tuesday thinking I'm dead or a complete asshole.

Though I'm not sure I'm safe from the asshole part just yet.

I wait for a few minutes, but no other text comes through. Maybe he really did just want to make sure I was okay. I let my mind wonder what he might be doing right now. Is he staring at my text trying to find the words to text me back? Or maybe he is out running, frustrated that I bailed… again. Maybe he doesn't give two shits about me.

But I want him to.

I shake my head and get up from the couch, heading for the shower. My phone buzzes in my hand and my heart leaps in my throat. When I check the screen, I immediately deflate. It's Mom. I sigh, knowing I can't put off talking to her any longer. At least I can't talk long, this might be the best time to answer.

"Hey Mom," I answer, grabbing a towel from the linen closet.

"Hey sweetie! How are you?" Mom's voice sounds a little happier than usual which makes me smile. She hasn't sounded completely happy in a long time, I'm not sure she ever will again.

"I'm good, Mom. Sorry I haven't called, it's been a very… busy week." I laugh to myself at that description. "Busy" would be an understatement.

"Oh that's okay, honey. I know how busy you are. I just wanted to check in on you. You know your Dad's birthday is next week," Mom's voice trails off a bit and I feel a pain in my heart. I toss the towel on the bathroom counter and turn on the shower, shutting the curtains with more force than I mean to in frustration.

"So?"

Mom sighs and I know she wants to give me a lecture, but she doesn't. "So I just wanted to remind you, is all. You're an adult, you can decide what to do with it from there."

"Yes, I am an adult. And because I'm an adult I know that what he did to you is still fucked up and I know that I still don't give a shit about his birthday."

"Paisley! That's enough with all the cursing. You're too pretty for that," Mom is trying to be stern, but I can hear her giggling a little. I relax and pull my hair out of the messy bun it's been in all day, letting it flow over my shoulders.

"Yeah yeah, we all know my filter is broken," I laugh back. Mom seems to lighten up a little as she tells me about work. She never worked when I was growing up, but when her and Dad split up she had to figure out some sort of income. So she started working part time at the Publix supermarket near our old house and has been there ever since. I send her money when I can, and by that I mean when she doesn't refuse it and send it back, but for the most part Mom insists she doesn't need much. She likes her simple pleasures, bowling with her league and the occasional six pack. As long as she has that, she doesn't complain.

When I tell her I have to get ready to go out, she sounds disappointed but lets me go and asks me to call her later this week. I agree and this time actually set a reminder in my phone so I can't bail out. I love my mom with all my heart, it's just hard sometimes hearing her voice on the line. I wish I could make everything better for her, make her happy again.

When I end the call, I see a missed text from Tanner.

- Hey, beautiful. Sorry I missed your call yesterday. Can I call you tonight? –

I want to talk to him, but right now I don't even know where to start. I toss my phone on the counter and decide to text him later. Right now I need to clear my mind, so I throw on my Guns N' Roses Pandora station and turn up my phone as loud as it goes before jumping in the shower. I may not know much about music, but I love it. I love every single kind. There are only a few songs that I can actually say I don't like, and most of those I have to hear when I go out and they end up growing on me, anyway. The best thing about music is that I can turn on the radio or throw in an old CD and the songs can either bring out the emotions I'm keeping inside, or it can help me forget whatever I'm thinking. When *Night Train* comes on, it does the latter and I forget about everything and for a while it's just me and my air guitar. But when I turn off the shower and the song ends, I'm alone again with every thought focused on one thing.

Corbin.

Every time the bass gets loud in the music I think it's my phone and I jump to check it, but there's never anything new. An email came through at one point and that just pissed me off more. I want Corbin to call, even though I don't want him to call. Hell, I don't know what I want. All I do know is that I *don't* want to be sitting in Diggs watching McKenzie and Shannon giggle through Power Hour. I'm trying to keep up the fake smile and drink as much as I can stomach so they won't suspect anything, but honestly I'm failing miserably.

McKenzie leans over the bar and calls Jordan, the busty bartender behind the bar, over to put in another order. Jordan is funny as shit and always entertaining, but I tend to prefer Sean or Mike. It's much easier to get cheap or free drinks when a guy is on the other end of the bar.

"I need three more Blue Moons, please. And a shot of Jack for this girl so maybe she'll stop bringing down the mood," she eyes me as the corners of her mouth creep up into a sly smile.

"Damnit, Kenz, I haven't even finished this one yet. Take it easy on me here."

"Hell no! You're lucky I've let you slide by with the pitiful excuse for drinking you've been doing so far. When are you going to get tipsy enough to tell us what's wrong?" McKenzie isn't smiling anymore and Shannon's now leaning over the bar a little so she can see my face, too. I look back and forth at them and finally bury my face in my hands, grumbling under the music where they can't hear.

"Come on, what's going on? Is this about that client of yours?" My head pops up and I give Shannon a stare of death to warn her. Her eyes get a little wide as she remembers the bet between me and McKenzie and she takes a big drink of the fresh beer Jordan has just placed in front of her.

"Well, there's no shitty client that a shot of Jack Daniels can't fix," Jordan chimes in, sliding the shot down to my hand now practically gripping the bar. Without hesitation, I throw it back and let it burn, not even reaching for my beer to chase it with.

McKenzie rejoices and lifts her beer in the air to cheers Shannon, "That's more like it, let's get this shit started!" As their glasses clink together and they take a big gulp, I throw on the best fake smile I can manage and raise mine, too. I'm going to have to do this, for a few hours I'm just going to have to push Corbin out of my mind and put on an act.

McKenzie gives me a concerned look again and I know it's game time. I nudge her and point to a few guys on the other end of the bar, "Come on, let's get another round of shots and then get those guys to buy the rest."

A shit eating grin spreads across her face and she slams her fist down on the bar, "That's what I'm talking about! She's back, ladies and gents. Put your party panties on and let's do this!" She motions for Jordan and orders a round of cherry bombs and Shannon calls the guys over to take them with us. I laugh and start talking to one of them as they walk up, channeling my inner actress the best I can, but when he puts his hand on the small of my back I can't help but think about the other set of hands that were all over me the night before.

I'm drunk. Like, really drunk. McKenzie is finishing up her goodbyes with the guy who's been buying her drinks all night, much to his dismay. I can already see she's got Derek on her mind. She's been glued to her phone texting away like a mad woman for the past thirty minutes, which means he's probably on his way now to pick us up. I wonder when they will just give in to each other.

My head is foggy as we walk, McKenzie holding my hand as we stumble along behind Shannon. Shannon lives in a small apartment above a wine shop a few blocks from Diggs, so we head that way since there's really no where else to go. It has to be at least four in the morning, but I stopped checking the clock what feels like hours ago so I can't be sure.

As McKenzie goes on about Derek to Shannon, I let my mind drift to Corbin again. I did a decent job of blocking him out for most of the night. The more shots the guys bought and the more I tried to put on an act, the easier it eventually got. But now, walking down the cobblestone streets where we walked together not even 48 hours ago, I let him fill my mind like paint fills a canvas. I let the image of his beautiful eyes dancing in the candlelight wash over me, blurring my mind even more than the alcohol.

I don't know what it is about this guy, and I know it's only been two days, but whatever it is makes me want to let down my walls. Or at least peek over them. Maybe hop up on top of them and swing my legs over, just to see what it's like. There's something about his genuine care for me and the way he says my name. I go crazy thinking about his insane body, and he's incredibly driven and passionate about this new gym. But these are just baseline things, there's something more there that I can't really put my finger on. Something dazzling.

In my daze, I collide into what feels like a brick wall and bounce backward, stumbling and falling to the ground. My hands stop me from falling all the way back and hitting my head, but my ass is aching as I look around trying to figure out what the hell happened. My head still a little fuzzy, I look up and see a bright neon green blur. I shake my head a little and squint, and suddenly I'm sober as a fucking judge. The neon green blur is clear now, and I see that it's the shirt I held in my hands two nights ago. Only this time, it's not lying in a suitcase.

It's filled out fucking flawlessly by Corbin's body.

I sit up and grab my head that now feels like it's pounding as I try to regain composure. My phone is shattered beside me and I curse out loud, Lydia will be so pissed. Shannon and McKenzie are stumbling back toward me shouting, "Oh my God, are you okay?" and "What the hell happened?" I nod and hold my hand up toward them signaling for them to calm down. It's not embarrassing enough to be on the ground in front of possibly the hottest guy in the entire world but now they have to scream it so everyone else drunkenly cruising by will notice, too.

Corbin reaches down to help me get back on my feet and I wrap my arms around his hot, sweaty shoulders as he lifts me. When I finally find my balance, I look up into his eyes and feel my breathing grow shallow. His ear buds are still in tact, though I'm not sure if he's listening to music anymore. He searches my eyes with his, but the fire that glowed so fiercely in them the night before has been doused and replaced by a cold, heartbreaking sadness. He pulls his arm from around me and steps back, making me want to pull him back in or just hide until he leaves. I try to find something to say, but no words come. I just stare at him in his running gear, wondering what is going through is mind.

McKenzie jumps in between us and checks me over for injuries as Shannon gathers the broken shards of my phone. Right now I wish she would just jab one of those shards into my heart so I could be spared this achingly awkward situation. I can hear her and McKenzie asking me questions and feel them touching me but it's a numb awareness, like I'm about to go under anesthesia at the doctor's office and they're cooing me farewell. My eyes are still locked on Corbin's, and his on mine, and we just stare. He opens his mouth slightly like he wants to say something and moves forward, but then he pauses and his mouth clenches shut again. Suddenly, he turns and runs the other way, freezing me in place as I watch him disappear around the corner.

"Hello? Paisley? Oh my God, Shannon, I think she's gone into shock. What do we do?!" McKenzie is frantically shaking me and yelling at Shannon.

"I don't know! Shit, let's get her in a cab and take her to the hospital," Shannon moves to the edge of the street and starts searching for a cab. I shake my head and come back down to earth, pushing Corbin's cold eyes from my mind.

"No, no don't do that. I'm fine," I speak softly, just above a whisper. "Just still drunk." Shannon and McKenzie laugh and I pretend like I'm telling the truth. In reality, my head is spinning – but it's not from the drinks. Why didn't he say anything? And why did he look so… sad?

"Was that the guy from Thursday night, Paisley?" McKenzie is looking behind her now as if Corbin is still standing there. I wish that he was.

"Yeah, yeah it was."

"Oh, your new client?!" Shannon blurts out. I try to give her the "really, you whore?" look, but I'm too late and McKenzie is already freaking out.

"New client?! What the hell, Paisley, you didn't tell me this!"

I grab my head with both hands this time and try to imagine this isn't all really happening. "Can we please just go? I can't deal with any of this right now."

"Paisley, what's going on? You can tell us," McKenzie's eyes are softer now and she's holding onto my elbows and dipping her head down to my level, trying to get me to look at her directly. I drop my hands from my head and let out a heavy sigh, my shoulders slumping.

56

"I want to, Kenz, I do. I just don't know what to say right now. Can we please go?"

McKenzie seems a little hurt, but she nods and puts her arm around me as we start walking toward Shannon's again. My head is reeling with the images of what just happened. I feel my stomach slowly curl into a tight knot and I want to throw up. I want to tell McKenzie everything, I want to scream at the top of my lungs, I want to cry, I want to call my mom, I want to call my dad and then hang up on him, but most of all – what I want more than anything – is to run to Corbin.

And after what happened, I know that I'm the only one who wants that. He doesn't want me anymore, couldn't even talk to me. And I care.

I care.

Chapter six
Waterfall

I want to die. I want to curl into a tiny ball in the corner of my room and die.

I'm not sure what hurts more – the hammer beating down on my head from last night's festivities or the hole being punched in my heart when I think about Corbin's face. Either way, I seriously want to die.

I push my hand out from under the blanket pulled over my head and blindly reach for the ancient flip phone my phone company gave me until my replacement ships in. There was no use trying to salvage the tiny pieces that were left of my phone after my fall last night, so I had to make a trip first thing this morning to get a replacement. To add pain to embarrassment, a huge bruise formed on my upper backside overnight and it hurts like hell to sit down on anything other than a pillow.

Finally, I feel the phone and jerk it inside the covers with me, refusing to let any light under my covers of protection. I don't know why I keep checking my messages, like he's going to text me. Like he would even want to still be my client after the way I saw him look at me last night. Those eyes that once made me feel naked and aching for his touch were replaced with ones that made me feel like a palm tree trying to survive in the icy tundra.

Maybe he hasn't texted me because he knows my phone is broken. Maybe he's thinking about me, too.

Oh get real, Paisley! He literally ran away from you last night. I drop the phone on my chest and pull the covers tighter around my head, sighing in frustration. Although it's the last thing I want to do, I know the only way to stop at least half of my misery is to distract myself, so I throw the covers off and retrieve my laptop from my desk. Maybe if I can just dive into work for a little bit I can forget about the ultimate bad luck I've been having.

As if Lydia can read my mind, my phone lights up with her name. I guess in most cases, people would be surprised if their boss called them on a Sunday. I, however, am completely used to this. I swear she thinks of Sunday as the first part of Monday. I seriously wonder how she has a life outside of those office walls.

"Hello?"

"Paisley, are you busy?" I jerk my head away from the phone as her voice echoes, sending throbs of pain shooting behind my eyeballs.

I grit my teeth and turn down the volume as much as I can before responding, "Not at the moment, Lydia. What can I help you with?"

"Good. What you can help me with is understanding how you expect our creative team to do anything for your client without a budget listed? And in one day, none the less."

Shit. I forgot to ask for his budget? How fucking stupid can I be?

"I'm so sorry about that, Lydia. We were caught up in the creative details," yeah, that's one way to put it, "and it must have slipped my mind. I will contact him first thing in the morning to hammer out the budget."

"No, call him today. I see his cell number is written in his file, let him know it's urgent. We're behind and I want this all in order for the team to take on tomorrow," her voice is short and stern, like I'm her five year old child begging to stay the night at a friend's house.

"I completely understand, Lydia, but it's Sunday and I can get to this first thing in the morning," I try to rationalize.

"No, you can do it today. If he doesn't answer in the morning or takes half the day getting back to you then we will be even more behind. Call him today and tell him it's urgent so that he responds quickly."

"But –"

"That's all, Paisley. See you tomorrow."

The line goes dead before I have the chance to utter another plea. The pounding in my head is now replaced by the anger vibrating through my entire body. I throw my phone across the room and slam my head back down into my pillow, pulling the covers up once more.

"Bitch!"

It's fucking Sunday. You would think I missed a deadline the way she was jumping down my throat. I sigh and throw the covers off again, sitting up and popping another aspirin that I left out on my dresser after taking my first dose this morning. As I swallow the pill, it feels course and dry and I can't help but compare it to Lydia's frigid bitchiness and controlling habits that choke me every day.

I have to call him. I can't fucking believe this. After what was probably the most embarrassing moment of my life, mixed with one of the worst feelings in my stomach, and on top of this awful hangover – I have to call him. As I retrieve my phone from the other side of the room, I try to plan out what I'll say in my head. Honestly, where do I even start? Do I just pretend like he's a client now and nothing more?

Is he anything more?

Before I have time to over think it or come up with an excuse to put it off, I find his business card in my work binder and dial his number. They couldn't recover my contacts from my broken ass phone, but thankfully I kept his card just in case. As the line rings, I fidget with last night's curls in my hair and pace my bedroom, checking my reflection every time I walk past my dresser mirror. I look like complete and total shit. Thank God we're not Skyping.

Just when I think I might be the luckiest son of a bitch ever and get voicemail, I hear Corbin's voice, "Hello?"

My words freeze in my throat as I let his voice spill over me. I walk in a daze to the edge of my bed and sit down slowly, trying to find the words to say.

"Hello?"

"Hi, Mr. Ray? It's Paisley Bronson from Intrigue Advertising," I say professionally. *Shit, that was so fucking stupid.*

"I know who this is, Paisley." His tone is dry. Not mean, just dry – like he's unsure how to feel about me calling him. I'm surprised he hasn't hung up on me yet.

"Shit, yeah… I know. I, uh, shit. I'm sorry, Corbin. I need to know what your budget is for B String, I forgot to get it when you were in the office on Friday," I say quickly, pacing the room again. I wait for him to curse, or yell, or ask me what the fuck is wrong with me but instead he just laughs.

Not like a sarcastic, "You're such an asshole" laugh, but a genuine, cute as hell laugh.

I can't help but smile, "What's so funny?"

"You," he says, still chuckling. "You sound like you're confessing a crime or something."

"I just don't want to bother you is all," I struggle to explain myself. He knows as well as I do that I left him, completely turned on… again. He knows he literally ran into me last night. He knows why this is awkward… right?

"It's no bother, Ms. Bronson. I was actually just about to pay a visit to the property to check on a few things, that would probably help me give you a better idea for budget depending on what needs to be done there. Can we meet and check it out together, say one o'clock?"

What the hell? Is he asking to see me again? My smile grows larger now and my stomach starts doing flips. I want to see him. So bad.

This is a bad idea, Paisley. You know you can't resist him.

"Do you need me to go with you, Mr. Ray? You can always call me after you check on the property," I offer, trying to resist the teenage girl inside my head throwing a tantrum at my reluctance.

"Oh, I definitely need you, Ms. Bronson," his voice blazes a trail of fire inside me and I have to sit down again. *Holy shit.*

"Okay," I reply, giving in to my burning desire. I know I shouldn't see him, but the reasons why I shouldn't are slowly being devoured by the reasons why I should.

"Perfect. Text me your address and I'll pick you up on my way over. Looking forward to seeing you, Paisley." The line goes dead and I'm left in my bedroom with my mind racing once more. Isn't he pissed at me? Why didn't he tell me to fuck off?

Jumping up from the bed, I decide to ignore the questions in my head and focus on getting presentable. I've got less than an hour to fix last night's mess and I'll be damned if I'm going to look anything less than mouthwatering when he picks me up.

Corbin pulls in and parks his black Chevy Silverado in the empty parking lot of a large building. He looks so hot driving it, and with the country music he's been playing the entire way I just want to make him drive me out in the middle of nowhere and do all the things these guys are singing about. Who knew country music was so hot?

The outside of the building seems to be in good shape and the parking lot is expansive, leaving room to build on to the original building if needed. It smells like a fire burning somewhere, maybe a cook out at a nearby house. I inhale the smokey smell drifting on the hot wind and let it fill my lungs. It reminds me of camping trips with my dad when I was younger. He would always let me help build the campfire and he made sure we had plenty of hot dogs to cook and marshmallows to roast. Sometimes we would stay an entire weekend camping, just the two of us.

Corbin opens my door and wakes me from my memory. As I step out of the truck, I can't help but stare at him. He's dressed in faded blue jeans and a white t-shirt that looks like he's been working in it all day. His hair is roughed up and I feel my fingers itching to run through it, or grab it and pull him into me. The slight stubble on his face only adds to his sexy look and his eyes are covered by a sleek pair of sunglasses similar to James Dean's. He's absolutely beautiful.

"Why are you looking at me like that?" He asks, flashing his perfect smile and dimple. I feel like melting into the concrete we're standing on. He makes me such a fucking mess.

"I'm sorry, it's just… well, you look perfect right now." I can't believe I let the words fall out and I have to fight the urge for my hand to fly up to my mouth to keep it shut. Corbin smiles again, stepping even closer to me. His cologne and earthy smell practically consume me and all my senses are alive.

"Trust me, I'm far from perfect. And I could say the same about you in those shorts," he says, letting his eyes trail down my body to my legs. I swallow hard. *Fuck, he's sexy.* It's good to know the outfit I picked out is having the right effect. I wanted to look casual, like I didn't have to change before he picked me up, so I threw on a pair of jean shorts and a loose, off the shoulder faded light green top to bring out my eyes. I piled my messy curls into a loose bun on my head and pinned them in place, letting a few fall here and there. Judging by the way Corbin is staring at me now, I don't think he's complaining.

"So this is it?" I say, turning toward the building and changing the subject. I want to be here with him, want to give in to him, but I know that nothing has changed. It's like I'm teasing myself just so I can feel good for a while, like I'm on a diet and allow myself to have just one bite of chocolate but leave the rest of the bar in front of me all day.

"Yeah, this is it. I know it doesn't look like much, but it's still in great shape and really hasn't had any damage done. The people who owned it before me built it originally to use as an events venue but plans changed and they ended up moving to New York. I have some changes to make, but overall I couldn't have been any luckier choosing the place to build my dream." Corbin's smile falls a little at his last sentence and it makes me want to reach out and hold him. I want to know more about his dream, more about him.

"What about your best friend? When is he coming down?" I know I've struck a cord with Corbin because his face completely deflates. He turns to me and takes off his sunglasses to wipe them with his shirt. His eyes are sad, hurt.

"He won't be coming down. He died when we were 17."

The hot air collapses around us and I feel the weight of his words crush down. I reach out my hand to touch his arm, and when he doesn't pull away I slide down to grab his hand.

"Corbin, I'm so sorry," I hope he hears how truly sorry I am. I hate seeing him hurt like this. I just want to pull him in and wrap my arms around him, kiss the worried look off his face. I want to bring back his smile. It hits me that his best friend must have been the other kid in the picture of him on the football field in his inspiration folder and my heart hurts a little more.

He looks back at the building, takes a deep breath, and puts his sunglasses back on. "He was the best friend I ever had, and now I'll get to keep one of his dreams alive," he squeezes my hand tighter and pulls me forward. "Come on, I want you to see inside."

As we walk hand in hand toward the building, I can't help feeling like this is how it's supposed to be. Him and me, me and him. Like this. How important is this stupid bet, anyway? It's not the same situation as before… or at least, I don't think it is. He's not like the other guys. There's something more there, something that I can't resist. Something I crave. Could I just call off the bet and tell McKenzie what she wants to hear?

Just as memories of my dad start to creep in, Corbin lets go of my hand and brings me back to earth. He unlocks the double glass doors and swings one open, signaling me inside. When I step in, I see what Corbin meant by getting lucky.

The place is beautiful. It's large with plenty of space and no definitive objects set up that he would have to get rid of. Whatever their idea was before, they didn't get too far before it was called off. It's practically a large, empty building with high ceilings and beautiful tiled floors. The back wall has three windows that stretch all the way to the ceiling and are at least six feet wide. They extend out past the wall and give a breathtaking view of a small pond with a waterfall and garden behind the building. They must have had a vision for weddings back in that space.

I feel Corbin watching me and turn to find his eyes studying mine. "Do you like it?" he asks, and I can tell that it matters if I do or not.

"Are you kidding me? It's perfect. There's so much room, and that back area with the waterfall is beautiful."

He smiles and takes my hand again, leading me around and explaining his vision. He tells me where the courts will go, the weight area, the cardio area, how he wants to build the field for football and soccer out back behind the waterfall. It looks like that will be what costs him the most money, because the rest is just a little refurbishing and buying the equipment. I'm lost in his dream with him, watching how his eyes light up the more he shows me. I want to be a part of his dream, too.

I stop walking and he turns, questioning me. We're completely alone in the building, nothing but an old desk and chair in the corner of the room that looks like it was used as a makeshift office space while the building was being worked on.

"What's wrong?" He asks, his voice echoing off the walls. I can barely breathe, barely think. I pull him toward me and look up into his eyes. Our bodies are pulled together tight and I feel the tension in his muscles as I reach my hands up into his hair and slowly pull his mouth to mine.

His lips are soft and gentle as we kiss. I nip at his bottom lip and he groans softly in his throat, pulling me closer as he massages my tongue with his. My brain is in overdrive trying to stop me, but I can't hear it. I'm completely dazed by him and I can't shake it. I don't want to. I just want to live in this moment, right here, right now.

My fingers play at the bottom of his t-shirt, softly grazing the lower part of his incredible abs. He smiles against my lips and lets me go long enough to lift it over his head and toss it behind him. My body trembles when I feel him press against me, his leg between mine and his arm muscles tense. I move from his lips and bite down his neck, his collarbone, his shoulders, and up to his ear. I must have hit a sweet spot, as I nibble on his ear and breathe heavily I hear him groan and clutch me a little tighter.

He's taking it much slower this time, both of us are. I feel his hands exploring every inch of me. Our kisses are long, gentle. Corbin keeps biting on my lower lip and tugging it toward him, igniting the fire inside me. I run my fingertips down his chest, smiling as he explodes with goose bumps. When I reach the hem of his jeans, I unhook the top button and pull back from our kiss to look in his eyes as I slowly unzip them and pull down just enough to get them past his hips and let them fall to the floor. Then, I step back a bit further and lift my shirt over my head, watching his chest rise and fall with every heavy breath as his eyes eat me alive.

Corbin steps close again and undoes the top button of my shorts and unzips them, but then he steps back, eyeing me as the corners of his mouth creep into a sexy smile. Oh, he wants a show? *Fuck, this is so hot.* I shimmy slowly out of my shorts, winding my hips and biting my lip before letting them fall to the floor. He stands there watching and shaking his head like he can't believe what he's seeing, then his hungry eyes meet mine again and before I can react he sweeps me up and I wrap my legs around him as he carries me, crushing my lips to his once more.

His arm is wrapped tight around me while he runs his other hand through my hair, pulling me closer as we kiss. He's carrying me through the building but I have no idea where. Corbin nuzzles my chin to the side and peppers my neck with kisses, softly biting and letting out hot breath against my skin. Suddenly, I hear a ripping sound as he grabs the side of my lacy thong and rips it off of me. Literally, *rips it off of me* and tosses it to the ground. *Shit.* He smiles against my neck and I can't help but let out a little giggle. He pulls back, his eyes devouring mine. Looking at them closer in the light I can see flecks of gold freckling the icy blue. "You have the sexiest laugh," he says breathlessly.

I smile and pull his lips back to mine before he presses my back against the smooth, warm glass of one of the tall windows. I can hear the soft sound of the water running from the waterfall and feel the sun shining in on us, bathing Corbin in a warm orange glow. He presses his forehead to mine and pulls his lips away, staring into my eyes, practically staring into my being. Our breathing is heavy and synched, our chests rising and falling in a rhythmic fashion.

"Don't run," he breathes, his eyes searching mine. I can barely stand the way he looks when he says it. I know I've hurt him, but I don't want to run this time. I don't care about the bet, I don't care about who he was talking to on the phone. All I know right now is that the one thing I do care about is him.

"Don't let me," I breathe back. He pulls me back in, his eyes closing as he kisses me deeply. I feel him strip off his boxer briefs and he presses against me, stopping my breathing. He wants me and I want him. Now.

"Please, Corbin," I beg, soft moans escaping my lips.

The sun moves out from behind a cloud, engulfing us in its rays as he pushes inside me. Everything else is gone, nothing else exists. Nothing but our fire blazing in the hot sun.

Chapter seven
Complications

"What was his name?" My head is resting on Corbin's chest while he runs his hand through my hair. Our clothes are spread on the floor around us, the sun setting outside the windows and covering us with its warmth.

"Hmm?" Corbin asks, still sedated.

"Your best friend," I giggle, lifting my head and turning to face him. "What was his name?"

Corbin smiles this time, a much different reaction from when I mentioned his best friend earlier. I wonder if he ever talks about his best friend, other than to tell people that he's no longer alive. It makes me sad to think that could be the only way people learn about him.

"His name was Jack," he says. "But I used to call him J-Dash, because all the girls used to say he was so classically charming and 'dashing.' So I gave him a hard time about it, even though I was secretly jealous that he had that reputation." Corbin laughs at the last part and shakes his head.

"Trust me, you have nothing to be jealous of. You're absolutely flawless," I chime in, planting small kisses on his bare chest. He smiles and pulls me in to kiss him – a soft, deep kiss that almost makes me forget what we're talking about.

"I want to know more about him," I say, pulling away far enough so Corbin can see my sincerity. "Will you tell me about him? About you guys?"

Corbin seems hesitant and his eyes get lost in the window behind me, though his hand is still absentmindedly running through my hair.

"Please," I plead, pulling his attention back. "I really want to know. Plus, I make the best apple pie this side of Tennessee and I happen to have all the ingredients to make it at my place. You can tell me in between mouthwatering bites." I stand up and smile, offering to help him up.

Corbin's eyes have definitely changed, but not the way I expected. They seem hungry, dark. He's eyeing me up and down and I realize I'm standing completely bare ass naked in front of him. I don't move, letting him look and hoping the pinkish orange light beaming in from the setting sun is flattering in all the right places.

"You look like an angel," he says, grabbing my hand and pulling me back down with him instead of standing up. He pulls me on top of him and presses his forehead to mine, staring deep into my eyes. Slowly, he runs his hands through my hair and pulls me closer, inch by inch, until our lips are touching again. I swear his kisses could kill me, could take all of my life and I would still want them.

"I'm no angel, just like you're no knight in shining armor," I say, thinking back to Thursday night when we first met.

"Hmm, that may be. But I still think we could make a pretty good story together," he smiles, kissing down my neck to my collarbone.

"Oh, you think so?" I laugh, letting his kisses blaze a fire down my body.

"It's worth a shot, right? Who knows, it could be a fairy tale," he says as he stands up, pulling me with him.

"Or a train wreck," I laugh and Corbin smiles. I say it jokingly, but inside I'm really wondering how I'm going to explain this to McKenzie. Wondering if I'm even ready for it, myself.

"Alright, you convinced me," he says.

"I convinced you?"

"I'll tell you more about Jack, but only because I'm starving and that pie sounds too good to pass up," he adds, tossing me my shirt. I laugh and pull it over my head and he follows suit until we're completely dressed again.

"Corbin?" I say just before we reach the door. He turns back to me with his eyebrow raised, waiting. "I just want you to know I think this place is perfect." I pull him in for one last kiss before we leave, knowing by the look in his eyes that those words mean more to him than he'll ever admit to me.

As we kiss, his hands explore my body, trailing my spine down to my ass. He cups it gently and pulls me toward him, sending a chill through me. I kiss him more intensely and grip his hair in my hands, desperate to get him closer.

"Alright," he laughs, pulling away. "Let's get out of here before I forget all about that pie and devour that delicious body of yours again instead."

I blush, wondering if I really care about the pie anymore myself.

I'm freaking out a little the entire ride home. Corbin is blasting the music and driving with all the windows down, making my hair whip around into what I'm sure is the hottest mess ever and making him look even sexier, if that's even possible. I can't believe what just happened. Did that really just happen? Did I just have sex with the hottest guy ever in quite possibly the hottest place ever?

I want to calm down, but I can't believe I have to tell McKenzie about this, about everything. I lost the bet, and now I'm going to have to tell her about all the shit in my head, which is way more than I care to tell anyone. Checking my phone, I see two missed calls from Tanner and a text.

- Hey, call me! I have something to tell you. :) -

I set a reminder in my phone to call him tomorrow and go back to thinking about the discussion I have to have with McKenzie. I groan and lean my head back against the seat. Corbin stops singing and looks over at me, turning the music down.

"You okay?"

I sigh, "Yeah, I'm fine. I just... realized something, is all." I definitely can't tell Corbin about the bet, not yet at least. What kind of girl does that make me look like that I had to make a bet to stay away from military men? *Fuck, this is not good.*

"Uh oh, you 'realized' something? Last time that happened you ran out on me in the middle of the night," Corbin laughs and grabs my leg with his right hand, giving it a gentle squeeze. It feels so right there, like I was meant to ride beside him and he was meant to always touch me.

Stop it, Paisley. What the hell is wrong with you? You just lost a bet over a guy who's leaving next week. On top of that, he's your client! I shake my head and sigh again. Corbin is still scrutinizing me and looks like he's about to say something else when his phone vibrates. He moves his hand from my leg to answer it.

"Shit," he says as we pull up to my apartment.

"What is it?"

Corbin seems frustrated as he texts back on his phone, tossing it in the console when he finishes. "I'm sorry, Paisley. I have to go."

Seriously? Who is it this time? Or is it the same person it's been the whole time I've known him? Suddenly it hits me – this is his way out. He got what he wanted and now he can just leave and go back to his girlfriend or wife or whoever and forget about me.

"Don't worry about it," I say, the words more like a hiss off my tongue than a sentence. I throw my door open and don't bother trying not to slam it as I get out. I can't fucking believe this. How stupid can I be? Am I really going to be as naive as Mom? I'm practically shaking when I reach my door, cursing myself for not realizing that there's obviously another girl. The phone calls in the middle of the night, how he always had to answer them, and now a text that mysteriously makes him have to leave. The signs couldn't be more obvious if they were lit up in neon.

As I fumble for my key, a hand reaches out and grabs mine and I feel Corbin wrap his arms around me from behind. I try to shake loose, but he tightens his hug and pulls me in closer, grabbing my keys from my hands. I try to fight, try to get inside before my emotions get the best of me but it's no use. I break down and feel the tears start to soak my face. Corbin turns me toward him and pulls me into him, crushing me in his arms. He kisses my head as I cry, overwhelmed by the last four days, by the last four years.

"Look at me," he says, pulling my chin up so our eyes meet. He pulls me close and searches my eyes with his, waiting until I focus on him. I'm still shaking, wishing he would let me go so I could run inside and hide under my sheets.

"Paisley, I don't know who hurt you in the past, I don't know what happened. But I'm not going to hurt you. I'm not like them," he says, his eyes still locked on mine. "I promise, I'm not them."

The way he's looking at me makes me want to believe him, makes me want to dive in head first and forget everything that's holding me back. But I know it'd be like diving into an empty pool, nothing but cement waiting to catch me.

I start crying again and bury my face in his chest. I wish it was that simple, wish I was just getting over a broken heart, but the truth is the guy who hurt me wasn't an ex-boyfriend. The guy who hurt me is the only guy in the world who could hurt me as bad as he did. My dad.

"I'm sorry," I whisper, controlling my tears and taking deep breaths.

"Don't be. I'm the one who should be sorry. I wish I could stay, and I promise I'll explain later, but I need to know you're okay before I leave," Corbin says, grabbing my face in his hands and staring at me with his beautiful eyes.

I nod softly and try to smile, even though I'm still convinced there's something he's not telling me. "I'm fine, I promise. Ugh, I'm such a girl right now," I laugh, wiping the tears from my face. He laughs too and pulls me into his chest again.

"Well I, for one, am really glad you're a girl."

I laugh and pull back, snagging my keys from his hands. "Yeah, I guess that does make things less complicated, huh?"

Corbin smiles and plants one last kiss on my lips, "Something tells me we're nothing if not complicated. I'll call you later, okay?"

"Okay," I nod, desperately wishing he would stay and kiss me for the rest of the night.

"Goodnight, Ms. Bronson," he says, tipping an imaginary hat on his head as he walks backwards toward his truck, his icy blue eyes blazing again.

"Goodnight, Mr. Ray," I laugh, curtseying in return. I turn and let myself in my apartment, locking the door behind me and sliding down to the floor.

I immediately grab my temp phone and dial McKenzie's number.

"Hey drunkie, I was just about to call you," she answers.

"Come over."

"Are you okay? Have you been crying? What happened?" McKenzie starts rambling off questions but I cut her off.

"Please just come over. I need to talk to you."

"Okay, I'll be right over. Give me like twenty," she says, and I know she can tell I'm hurting. I end the call and sigh, letting my head fall back against the door. Tears threaten to fall again so I shake my head and stand up.

I walk in the kitchen and start getting out all the ingredients for my apple pie. I definitely need a distraction. Just as I'm reaching in my spice cabinet for some cinnamon, there's a knock at the front door. I smile, I guess Corbin changed his plans after all. I fix my hair the best I can as I walk toward the door, hoping he'll mess it up again.

But when I open the door, it's not Corbin waiting for me. It's not McKenzie, either. Standing there in a deep purple NYU t-shirt and faded jeans and leaning up against my door frame is the last person I would have guessed.

Tanner.

And I am so fucking excited to see him.

"Oh my God, Tanner?!"

"Hey, beautiful," he says, his voice like fucking melted chocolate as he leans in to hug me. "Cancel all your plans tonight, you've got a date."

Chapter eight
Familiar Feelings

I'm sitting shot gun in Tanner's 1957 Chevy Bel Air. He's got the windows down and we're cruising through town with the hot night air pouring in, heading to our favorite spot. His car is beautiful and I can still remember when his dad first handed it down to him the night before his graduation. I'd never seen Tanner so happy, except for maybe right now in this moment. His shaggy caramel colored hair is blowing all around him and his famous sexy grin is plastered on his face. He's got one hand on the steering wheel and the other holding mine, a familiar position that he used to take all the time back in college. It feels comfortable and right.

"I still can't believe you're here," I say, the smile on my face growing. I haven't been able to stop smiling since I opened my front door and saw him standing there.

"Well, believe it baby. Sometimes dreams do come true," he sticks his tongue out and raises both of his eyebrows, glancing at me sideways.

I smack him playfully, "Smartass." He chuckles and turns up the music. I can't tell who it is, but that really doesn't surprise me. I'm pretty helpless when it comes to known music, let alone when it's Tanner's underground rock. He loves to follow the bands that no one knows about. He always told me how their songs were so much more authentic because the record labels couldn't screw them up. I have to admit, some of the few songs I did download were suggestions he had made.

I pull my hand from his and reach into my pocket, texting McKenzie again.

- Are you sure you're okay with me bailing tonight? I'm so sorry,
I had no idea he was coming. –

I feel so bad for ditching McKenzie, but when I saw Tanner I knew he was exactly what I needed right now. I told McKenzie how he surprised me and asked if we could reschedule for tomorrow, but if I know anything about her I'm sure she was probably pulling into my complex right when I called. She would never tell me though, wouldn't want to make me feel bad. Which is just one of the thousand ways she's a way better person than I am.

- Of course! Girl, I'm so excited that Tanner's here.
Can't wait to hear all about it tomorrow. XOXO –

I smile, I swear she's too fucking understanding sometimes. I text her back a smiley face and a heart and then put my phone back in my pocket just as Tanner pulls off onto a very familiar dirt road. He turns down the music and leans forward in his seat, his grin growing into a full blown dazzling smile.

"I'm so fucking stoked right now. When was the last time we came down here?"

I laugh and close my eyes, trying to remember. "Damn, I think it was that night after your last fraternity social. Remember? The theme was "Anything But Clothes" and you didn't have on anything but a stack of three pizza boxes covering your... um... unmentionables," I laugh, blushing at the memory. We were always like best friends, but I have to admit it was hard to think of him as just a friend that night. I can still remember him telling me to turn around so he could pull them off and change into the basketball shorts I brought him from my dorm. I was definitely tempted to peek.

"Ha, yeah I think you're right. God, that was an epic night. And don't hate on my pizza boxes, you know you enjoyed the view," he chimes back, giving me his signature wink that pairs so perfectly with all his conceited lines.

I roll my eyes, "Oh yes, just what I wanted to see. You drunkenly trying to maneuver your junk out of a cardboard box."

"Sounds like a pretty entertaining sight to me!" He laughs and I can't help but laugh with him. He has the most contagious laugh in the world. It's a deep, care free laugh and it fits him. His laugh would seem so odd on anyone else, but with him it's perfect.

He pulls his car under a tree off the side of the road, the same tree he parked under the first time we accidentally found our lake. I can't even remember how we stumbled on it. He was upset over something with his roommate and I saw him storming out to his car. When I tried to ask what was wrong, he told me to get in and we just drove and drove until we somehow ended up here. Ever since that day, we've claimed this lake as ours. We even named it, "Lake Whinealot," which was really just a very un-clever way for us to name it our place to bitch about everything. I swear no one else knows about it because we've never ran into anyone. It's just a small, quiet lake that's home to a few jumping fish and lazily singing crickets. It's not much, but it's ours.

"What's in the bag?" I ask, glancing at the green reusable bag swinging from Tanner's arm as we trek down to the water.

"You'll see. Did you bring the goods?"

"You make it sound like I'm a drug dealer," I laugh, pulling a medium sized bottle of Jack Daniels from my purse. "Yes, I brought 'the goods,' nerd. Now will you tell me what's in your bag?"

He laughs, unfolding a large UCF blanket and spreading it out on the sandy area just before the edge of the water, "You're just how I remember, so patient and sweet."

I shrug and smile as I sit down next to him on the blanket, taking a swig from the Jack Daniels bottle before passing it to him. "My patience is like your humility, non-existent," I pipe back, reaching for the bag over his lap.

"Wait!" he says, grabbing my wrists before I can pull the bag over him. "Can you just sit still for a second? Close your eyes."

I let out an exaggerated sigh and close my eyes, folding my arms like a five year old. I hear him moving beside me, but my senses are mostly taken over by the lake. The sound of the water gently washing up on the sand, the buzz of insects around us, the smell of the earth and water, the sticky heat of the Florida night air. I inhale deeply, but my senses are disrupted by something different. Something that smells rich and delicious. Something really familiar.

My eyes pop open and I literally shriek like a stupid fan girl, "Oh my God, Tanner! Is this what I think it is?!" I tear off the plain light blue wrapping paper that reads *Margie's Bakery* and sure as shit, it's an Oreo cream pie. Not just any Oreo cream pie, but THE BEST Oreo cream pie ever. Margie's is a small bakery in Winter Park and their pies are the only pies I've ever not been able to duplicate. I've tried to get their recipes several times, but Margie and her family refuse to share. With pies this delicious, I don't blame them.

"Wait, how did you get this? They stopped making these two years ago," I'm still freaking out and I practically rip the plastic fork from Tanner's hand when he hands it to me.

"Slow down, killer," he laughs. "I know they stopped making them, but I called in a favor. This one was made just for you."

I stop just shy of shoving a large bite in my mouth and turn to Tanner, "You really are my best friend. The fact that you even remembered how much I love these damn things is so sweet." He's grinning shyly and his soft hazel eyes are shining in the starlight. I never really noticed before how beautiful his eyes are.

"Almost as sweet as you," he replies, winking again. I laugh at his cheesy comment and take the first bite, which is complete and total bliss.

Half the bottle of Jack Daniels is gone and I just finished the last bite of the Oreo cream pie from Margie's. Tanner is telling me about his classes at NYU and I'm completely relaxed laying on the blanket beside him looking up into the night sky. I could stay here forever. No stress from work, no mom and dad drama, no bet with McKenzie, and no insanity from trying to figure out what I feel with Corbin.

Although at this point, I think it's pretty obvious what I feel.

"So, who's the lady in your life now a days?" I ask, leaning up on the blanket and turning to face Tanner.

He smiles, "You said, 'lady,' like there's only one."

"Don't be such a dick," I laugh, knowing very well that he's probably not joking. Tanner has always been a heartbreaker, it wouldn't surprise me if he's got half the female student body singing love songs about him by now.

He shrugs and leans up, resting his weight on his arms behind him. "Honestly, I really haven't been with anyone. I've been really busy with classes and residency, it's almost impossible to try to date," he says, staring out at the water.

Tanner's studying to be a pediatrician, which I think is absolutely perfect for him. Besides the fact that he's really intelligent, he's also hilarious, which is the best quality to have when working with kids in my opinion. I remember seeing him play with his nephew when his family visited for graduation and knowing he would be the best pediatrician ever. I swear that kids eyes lit up when "Uncle Tanner" was around.

"Besides," he throws in, turning on his side to face me. "We all know I'm marrying you, as soon as you get over your thing with dog tags and realize a stethoscope is way sexier, anyway."

I laugh and punch his right arm, making him tumble down on his side. "Oh smooth one, you use that on all the girls?"

He's only a few inches from me now and I can see his eyes clearly in the soft blue light of the night. I never noticed before, but there's a little ring of gold around his pupils. It's almost like they glow a little now, with the darkness all around us.

Tanner stops laughing and a sexy grin spreads wide on his face as he tucks a stray strand of hair behind my ear, "Nope, just ones I'm trying to seduce under the stars."

I don't know why, but I'm breathing a little heavier at his last words. Tanner's eyes keep flickering back and forth between my eyes and my lips like he's about to kiss me. I know he's just doing it to be an ass, he knows I used to have a crush on him back when we first met, but I can't help but be affected by him. Even though we've been in a clearly defined friend zone for several years now, I still think he's gorgeous.

Nothing wrong with looking, right?

My phone buzzes in my back pocket so I lift my hips into the air to retrieve it. My stomach does a little flip when I see it's a text from Corbin.

- Just wanted to say goodnight. I've been thinking about you. -

I smile and bite my lip, curious of what he's thinking about.

- Me too. Can't wait to see you again. Night, Mr. Ray. ;) -

Just this morning, I would have been hesitant sending him that text. But after today, after him opening up to me and taking me to such a special spot, after our afternoon exploring each other, after him not letting me storm away from him and put up my damn walls – it just feels natural.

"What are you smiling at over there? There's not a guy I should be jealous of, is there?" Tanner raises his brow at me mockingly.

I look up from my phone and try to not look guilty, but this stupid smile is plastered to my face. Tanner's smile falls a little and he leans away, "Wait, is there really a guy?"

"Maybe… sort of… I guess, yeah. It's a long story," I say, tucking my phone back in my pocket. Tanner and I have always talked to each other about our relationship issues and I've honestly counted him as my best source of advice. After all, who knows more about guys than an actual guy?

For some reason, Tanner doesn't joke with me like he used to when I told him about a new guy. He used to always say they were probably nerds, make fun of their majors, ask to see a picture and then laugh about the way they dressed – never anything mean, just little comments to make me laugh. This time, he seems more serious. I guess it's just us getting older.

"Oh, well, let's hear it. Tell me about your new private or sergeant or whatever," he says, sighing and taking another swig of the whiskey.

I tell him all about Corbin – about the bet with McKenzie, the club, running into him at work, worrying about breaking the bet and mostly about letting him too close – pretty much all I leave out is the steamy stuff, just because it feels awkward to talk about that with Tanner. The entire time I talk, Tanner is laying back on the blanket looking up at the sky. He only leans up for the occasional shot of whiskey but then lays back down, his eyes fixed on the stars as he listens intently. When I finish, he leans up and hands me what's left of the bottle.

"So he takes you to this building he's turning into a gym and all of a sudden you want to call off this bet with McKenzie?"

I frown, wondering why he doesn't see it the same way I do. "No, it's not just that. I mean the bet aside, I like the way he makes me feel. He took me somewhere that is really special for him and told me about his best friend, I think it's only fair of me to show a little trust in him, too."

"Maybe," Tanner says, shrugging his shoulders. "But do you really think you're ready to talk to McKenzie about your dad? I mean, other than me does anyone really know how much that shit affected you?"

I fall back against the blanket and let out a deep sigh. "I don't know. I mean, I called her before you showed up tonight and asked her to come over. I was going to bake and tell her everything. I mean, she's my best friend, shouldn't she already know?"

Tanner smiles and lays down next to me, pulling my head to rest on his chest. He starts running his fingers through my hair. Combined with the alcohol, it's like he's cooing me to sleep.

"Yeah, I suppose you're right. Listen, if you want me to be there when you tell her, I will," Tanner says softly. I nuzzle into his chest and wrap him in a hug, realizing how happy I am to have him here tonight.

"I've really missed you, Tanner."

"I've missed you, too, Paisley."

For a few minutes, we both lie there silently letting the insects sing to us. Finally, I pull my phone out again and check the time. Holy shit, it's almost three in the morning.

"Tanner, I'm way too drunk to drive and I know you are, too. Should we call a cab?"

He shakes his head, his eyes closed. I think he may already be drifting off. "Can you just stay here with me tonight? I'll drive you to your place early enough to get ready for work, I promise."

I smile and lay back down, setting an alarm on my phone. "Sure, get some sleep and I'll wake you up when it's time to go."

Tanner nods and just seconds later I hear him softly snoring. I finish setting the alarm on my phone and notice a missed text from Corbin.

- I can't wait, either. Though waiting is half the fun. –

I want to text back, but my eye lids are fighting me now and I feel the alcohol drowning my will to stay awake. I lay my phone down beside me and curl up into Tanner, that same stupid smile still plaguing me even in my dreams.

Chapter nine
Forgiveness

Work has been hell all morning, but surprisingly not due to my lack of sleep or insane hangover. Lydia has been on my ass the entire day about three different clients, even though I'm exactly where I'm supposed to be with them. Two people in our creative department called out sick this morning so now the projects I was on time with are likely to fall behind, including Corbin's. My high heel broke on the way to a meeting with two account managers on my team, so I had to run across the street to pick up a new pair. Normally, I wouldn't complain about getting new shoes, but given the circumstances I wasn't exactly thrilled. To top it all off, it started raining on my way back from getting the shoes and, of course, I didn't have my umbrella with me. So now, I'm sitting in my chair with a client profile pulled up on my screen, completely drenched, with a splitting headache and blisters rubbing from these damn new shoes.

Happy Monday.

I can't stop thinking about what a crazy weekend I had. Shannon already made me promise to have a long lunch with her to talk about Saturday night, she's going to flip when I tell her about yesterday. I haven't been able to get Corbin off my mind, and having Tanner surprise me was just a bonus. I'm seriously the happiest girl ever right now.

But something in my gut tells me I should be careful with Corbin. I still don't know who all these phone calls are from, but I guess I don't really need to know. Do I? I feel like after yesterday, I deserve to know a little more about him and his personal life. But then again, I haven't done the dating thing in so long, I usually don't care what they have going on when they're not with me.

Are we even dating?

Jesus, Paisley, calm down. Just have fun and let things fall into place. I shake my head, laughing at my inner turmoil. I'm just about to log off my computer and grab Shannon for lunch when I feel a pair of hands cover my eyes from behind.

"Guess who," Corbin's rich, melty voice breathes in my ear. I practically orgasm right there, he's even sexy when I can't see him.

"Hmm, could it be my knight in shining armor? Or is it just another client in a clever disguise?" I wheel around and smile up at Corbin, but before I can say anything else his lips are on mine. He slips his tongue in my mouth and massages mine gently, his hands on either side of my face. It's a little steamy for the office, but I'm a little past caring at this point.

"Well, hello to you, too," I say breathlessly as he pulls away.

"You're wet," he says.

"Mm hmm," I reply, still breathless from our kiss.

He smiles, shaking his head. "I mean you're actually wet, like soaked. You get caught in the rain?"

I sigh, "Long story, but it's definitely been an interesting morning to say the least."

"Well, hopefully I can make it a little better. I can't stay long, but I wanted to see if I could steal you this evening. I want to take you on a date, a real one, you know, the kind where you don't run away from me," he smiles, making light of the situation that we both know holds more weight than we care to discuss.

"Well, I suppose I could take off my sneakers for a night and cancel all my get away trains," I tease back. Corbin pulls me up from my chair and into another steamy, panty-melting kiss.

"Could we make it a little later, though? I promised Kenz I would come over tonight for dinner," I breathe into his lips, desperately trying to calm myself down. I'm about two seconds away from throwing everything off my desk and having my way with Corbin on top of it.

"Sure, how about I pick you up at eight?"

"Eight is perfect," I reply, kissing his bottom lip softly. "Now get out of here before I skip lunch with Shannon and opt for tasting you, instead."

A throaty growl escapes Corbin's lips and he pulls me in closer, crushing his lips on mine. His hands slide down from my hair to my collar bone to the V in my blouse. He runs his fingers along the hem, causing my skin to erupt with goose bumps. Just when I think I can't take anymore, he pulls back and steps just far enough away that our bodies aren't touching at all.

"Go eat your lunch, there will be plenty of time for dessert later." He winks and plants one last, sweet kiss on my hand before turning and walking out of my office. I'm still standing there panting when Shannon whips around the corner.

"What the fuck?! Get your purse and let's get the hell out of here, you have GOT to tell me what that was about!"

I nod and that same big, goofy grin that I had when I fell asleep last night is right back on my face. I don't stand a chance, I'm complete putty in his hands. He could mold me into whatever he wants, whoever he wants. He could play with me, hold me, love me.

Or he could completely destroy me.

I grab my purse, shaking Corbin's spell, and head out the door with Shannon. She's practically bouncing as we walk she's so excited. I'm not exactly looking forward to talking about all this, but I know I don't really have a choice anymore. Hell, it'll be good practice. I have to tell McKenzie about Corbin tonight, about everything. It's time I stop being such a pansy and finally let my best friend in.

And maybe finally let love in, too.

McKenzie and I are wrapping up dinner at a little café downtown, Green Eatz. They have the best salads in town, and after all the crap I've been eating and drinking the past few days, it's just what I needed. McKenzie is smiling the biggest smile I've seen since the first night she hung out with Derek. I just finished telling her about Corbin and everything that's happened between us since we met Thursday night. The easy part is over, but I know the hardest part is still coming.

"Paisley, this is so freaking exciting! I can't believe you didn't tell me all this sooner. I have to meet him again, you know, sober," she laughs, taking a sip of her sweet tea.

"You will definitely meet him again, I promise," I say, kind of hoping she'll be so excited about me possibly letting a guy in that she'll forget about the terms of our bet. "He's so dreamy, and he makes me want to open up to him. I can't explain it, but I think about him all the time. It's like I'm in high school again."

McKenzie lets out a girly squeal and grabs my hand from across the table, "I'm seriously dying over here! Fucking finally!"

We both laugh and cheers our drinks. I'm so happy they don't have alcohol in them, my stomach is still rough after last night's bottle of whiskey.

"So, I hate to say 'I told you so,' but I knew you wouldn't last long," McKenzie teases, pursing her lips at me in satisfaction. "And you know what that means. Time to spill, girl."

I take a deep breath, the weight of what I have to tell her weighing down on me. My chest tightens and I suddenly feel hot and uncomfortable.

McKenzie frowns, "Do you seriously dread telling me that badly? I don't understand, I thought I was your best friend."

"You are! You *are* my best friend, Kenz. It's just," I pause, trying to find the right words. "It's just really fucking hard for me. I hate talking about it, I hate that I even think about it or feel about it. I just want it all to go away."

She sighs and grabs my hand again, "Paisley, I love you like you're my own sister. I know this has something to do with your parents, and I know that whatever it is, it's really fucked you up. But I also know that I am here for you and I can help you so much more if I know everything that's going on in that head of yours. I want to be the best friend you can come to with *anything*, and I can't be that if you don't let me in."

I inhale deeply and fight back the tears stinging the corners of my eyes and threatening to fall. I want to tell her, I want to open up, but I don't even know where to start.

I don't know if I'm ready.

"Paisley," McKenzie says, pulling her chair around the table so that she's on my side. "Just start talking. It doesn't have to make sense, just talk."

I nod and bite my lip, wondering why this is so difficult. It seemed to be so easy to tell Tanner, but this is different. I hate admitting this to McKenzie, someone who's always seen me as so strong and driven.

"Kenz, I lied to you about why my parents got divorced."

McKenzie tilts her head, confused. "What do you mean? You said they had fought most of your life and you were actually glad to see them part, what else is there to tell?"

"That's not what happened, they never fought. Like, ever. They were practically fucking perfect. My whole life, I wanted exactly what my parents had. Or at least, what I thought they had," I pull my arms to my chest and cross them tightly. "My mom was so happy, and all her friends told her how lucky she was to have a guy like my dad. He treated her like a fucking princess, like she was all he ever needed in life. Like she was the air in his lungs."

"I don't get it," McKenzie says, leaning back a little. "Why did they get divorced? Why wouldn't you just tell me the real reason?"

I bury my face in my hands as the hot tears finally start to slide down. Each one feels like a burning razor blade cutting deep into my heart. "Shit, Kenz. He cheated on her. My fucking dad cheated on my beautiful, innocent, loving mom. She had no idea, didn't see it coming. She fucking loved him and he betrayed her."

I feel sobs rack through my body and I suddenly feel very awkward and aware of our setting. Dinner was probably not the best time to have this conversation. I breathe in deeply and use my hands to wipe away the tears from my cheek, looking back up at McKenzie. She's got her hands over her mouth and her eyes are glossy, probably from seeing me cry.

"Paisley, I am so sorry. I had no idea, I can't imagine how you feel," McKenzie says, reaching out to touch my hand again. She gives it a soft squeeze and tears threaten to fall again.

"Can we leave? Like, go somewhere else to talk?" I sniffle, glancing at a table behind McKenzie where an older couple sits silently staring at us. McKenzie nods her head and leaves cash on the table to cover our bills as we get up from the table. As we walk to her car, neither of us say a word.

"So," McKenzie says as we climb inside. "Is that it? Is that why you haven't dated anyone seriously since high school? Why the military men were so attractive to you?"

I nod, wiping the last bit of wetness from my face. We both sit in the car with the windows down, the warm breeze still sticky from the rain flowing through and drying my tears. "I know it sounds so stupid, I don't even fully understand it. But I just can't trust anyone, I mean my dad was the best guy in the world and even he cheated. I just don't think it's worth it, I don't want to go through what my mom did," I choke at the last comment about my mom and let my head fall back against the headrest. My poor mom, she was always so loving and caring and all she got from life was a cheating husband and a bratty daughter.

"Paisley, I completely understand why you're hurt over this, and I'm sure it will take a long time to forgive your father, but not every man is like that."

"I will never forgive him," I spit, feeling sick just thinking about talking to him again.

McKenzie's eyes soften and she places her hand on my shoulder, "Yes you will, Paisley. I know you. You're a loving person, just like your mom, and deep down you know you still care about your dad. You're mad at him, and that's completely understandable, but he loves you and regardless of what happened between him and your mom, he's still your dad."

I shake my head as McKenzie speaks, denying that I will ever forgive him, but something inside me wants to. I want to love my dad again, to not want to cry every time I think of him. I just can't do it right now, any thought containing him just fills me with hatred.

"I don't know, Kenz. I'm not sure I'll ever get over this, I don't know if I'll ever heal."

"Does Corbin make you feel safe?" McKenzie asks, tilting her head a little. I contemplate her question, thinking of all the wonderful feelings I've had around Corbin in the past few days. I know he makes me happy, I know he makes me want to be around him, I know he makes me smile, but I also know that there's still someone on the other end of those phone calls and I don't know who that person is.

"I'm not sure, yet. I mean, he makes me feel absolutely wonderful, but I'm still wary. I just feel like every great guy could be a real big dick in just the blink of an eye."

McKenzie laughs, "Yeah, you're right. Most guys can be assholes, but that doesn't mean they all are, and it definitely doesn't mean you should swear off love for your entire life. I've seen you with these military guys. You pull them in, get tangled up for a week or two, and then just let them go. It's like you love the thrill of the chase, enjoy the little pleasures, and then you just walk away before things have the chance to get difficult."

"I don't want things to get difficult," I murmur, kicking my heels off and putting my feet on the dash.

"Things have to get difficult," McKenzie continues. "It can't always be this perfect, bright eyed, fire blazing love. Things will be rough sometimes. Sometimes you'll fight, sometimes you'll cry, and sometimes you'll want to punch them in their face."

We both laugh at that, and I feel McKenzie relax beside me.

"But the most important thing is that we keep loving. We have to believe that at the end of the day, the love we have is worth all the bad stuff, because all the good stuff is what makes it so amazing."

I think about Corbin and our afternoon at the gym, the way he opened up to me, the way he touched me. I know I care about him, but is it worth letting my guard down? Is the pain I know will come worth the pleasure I get from him?

I want to tell myself it's not, but right now in this moment, I'm certain that it is.

"Thanks, Kenz. I really needed this, I'm sorry I didn't tell you sooner. I guess I just feel stupid for the way I feel, and it hurts to talk about it. I just wish it never happened."

McKenzie smiles softly as she turns on her car, "Trust me, I completely understand. I'm sorry I pushed so hard for you to tell me. I guess I was just jealous that you could talk to Tanner about stuff you couldn't tell me. I know he's one of your best friends, but I am too, and I want to be there for you. Through thick and thin."

I smile, "Yeah, I want that, too. And Kenz?"

"Yeah?"

"Does this mean I can still borrow those Jimmy Choo's?"

We both laugh and the rest of the ride to my place is smooth and comfortable, back to jokes and gossip. I feel like I've been wearing one of those backpacks I've seen my past military guys carry when they leave for deployment and I've finally been able to toss it to the ground. The weight has been lifted off of me, and now all I can think about is seeing Corbin tonight. I'm ready to try, to let my walls down and dive deep into what might be the most painful thing I'll ever experience.

But what could also be the best love I'll ever know.

Chapter ten

Put on a Show

"Where are we?" I giggle as Corbin helps me out of his truck. He's had me blindfolded since he picked me up and my heart is flipping in my chest, I'm dying to see where he's taken me.

"You'll see in just a minute. Do you trust me?"

I falter a bit at his question, but realize he just means to guide me. *Jeeze, Paisley, calm down. He's not asking for a wedding.* I nod and smile, so excited to take off this damn blindfold.

As he takes my hand and guides me, he stops suddenly and I collide into his back. "Oops, I'm sorry!" I say, taking a step back, but Corbin just laughs softly and pulls me into a deep kiss. As his tongue slips inside my mouth and swirls around mine, my head fuzzes and I feel weak. He pulls back and guides me a while longer before stopping to kiss me again, this time sucking softly on my earlobe. *Good Lord, if he continues like this I'm going to hope there's a bed wherever he's leading me.*

"Are you trying to distract me, Mr. Ray?"

"Who me? Not at all, simply taking advantage of the current situation," he laughs, his hands roaming my body in my tight, white and nude striped dress. "That's all."

"Uh huh, well I would like to take this blindfold off sometime soon so can you please try to focus?" I laugh into his kisses and he groans, pulling away and dragging me further.

Finally, he places his hands on my shoulders and begins positioning me just right. "Okay, stand right… there. Perfect. Now," I feel him fidgeting with the blindfold. "Open your eyes."

My eyes flutter open, and a tiny gasp escapes my throat.

I'm standing in the middle of a large, beautiful kitchen. The lighting is dim and there are white Christmas lights strung along the counter and above where the pots and utensils are hanging. On the island directly in front of me is a string of baking supplies, from flour and sugar to chocolate chips and vanilla extract. A woman's southern voice is floating out from the speakers above, creating a heavenly melody over the scene. As I turn around to face Corbin, I see a small video camera staged on a tripod behind him.

"This is beautiful," I say breathlessly. "Where are we?"

Corbin smiles and kisses me softly, "We're in a kitchen, silly."

"Well I know that," I laugh, returning his kisses. "But whose kitchen? Where? And what are we doing?"

"You, miss inquisitive, are in the back kitchen of Amelia's. And we are putting on a show."

I stare blankly back at Corbin, "Wait, Amelia's as in the super cute and romantic beach restaurant in Daytona? As in the one that takes like a year to get a reservation? Shut up!"

Corbin flashes his beautiful grin and shrugs, "That's the one."

"What? How?" I start questioning, but Corbin shakes his head and puts his finger to my lips.

"Stop worrying about the details, Paisley. I know a guy, he owed me a favor, and now we're here. And what matters most right now is that you've got a show to host." He raises his brow and gestures to the camera.

"And who exactly is this show for, Mr. Ray?" I tease, grabbing a nearby apron and tying it around my waist.

"Hmm, let's just call him a man with a really bad sweet tooth," Corbin jokes back.

I lean into him and kiss him deeply, running my fingers through his hair and pulling him into me. He groans into my mouth and I feel a jolt run through me. Corbin pulls back, rubbing my cheek with the pad of his thumb as he catches his breath.

"So, are you ready, Chef Bronson?"

I smile, pulling on one of the goofy chef hats Corbin has laid out. There's one for him and one for me, "That's Pâtissier Bronson to you, sir. Now turn around so I can prep you appropriately." I wink, holding up the apron laid out for him.

He throws his hands in the air in surrender and turns around. I slowly slip the top over his head and pull the sides around to tie behind him, taking my time and making sure I get a little closer than necessary to pull it around.

"You're awfully hands on with your assistant, Ms. Bronson," Corbin teases, raising his eyebrow playfully as he turns to face me. I shrug innocently and skip over to the island to examine my tools.

"I laid out everything I figured you would need to make chocolate chip cookies," Corbin says as I eyeball the ingredients. "I figured that would be pretty easy for you."

I fold my arms in resentment, "Easy? I'm supposed to host a baking show and you want me to make something easy?" I shake my head and smile, "Tsk tsk, Corbin. I thought you had better taste than that."

"Goodness, you're right! What was I thinking?" Corbin mocks, hanging his head. "I guess it's a good thing I got the all clear for you to use whatever you'd like, as long as it's in this kitchen."

"Whatever I want?"

"Anything," he says, daring me with his eyes. I feel the heat rising in me again, but I fight it down and focus on my project. Quickly, I scan the cabinets and refrigerator for everything I'll need – graham crackers, butter, brown sugar, cinnamon, cream cheese, eggs, marshmallow fluff. I put them with the chocolate chips and vanilla extract on the counter and continue searching for the rest of the ingredients.

"You're a southern guy, right Mr. Ray?" I ask, checking the labels on a few bottles of vodka. There's no marshmallow flavor, but whipped cream flavor should work.

"Yes, ma'am. Although, I consider myself more mid-west." Corbin is entertaining my antics and watching me as I flutter around the kitchen. I keep glancing at him out of the corner of my eye, wondering what's going through that gorgeous head of his.

"Well, I assume you're a seasoned camper then?"

"Of course, you can't not be in Oklahoma. I spent every summer of my life camping, especially down on Lake Eufaula. Some of the best memories of my life were made camping," Corbin smiles, and I see him light up as he speaks about his home. It makes my heart ache knowing he's surely thinking about Jack, too.

"Great, that's what I was hoping. That just means you're going to love this dessert even more," I say through gritted teeth as I stand on my tip toes trying to reach the bag of mini marshmallows on the top shelf of a cabinet. I feel Corbin sneak up behind and reach over me to grab them, his mouth hovering close to my neck. Every breath he takes is warm on my skin and sends chills down my body, all the way to my toes. It's like the air he exhales lights me on fire and shields me with ice at the same time.

"Thank you, dear assistant," I grin, batting my eyes playfully as I take the bag from Corbin. I toss it on the counter along with the remaining ingredients I managed to find and double check that I have everything.

"So, what's on the menu?" Corbin asks as he turns on the camera and adjusts it to focus on me. The small red light blinking makes me nervous for some reason, although I'm pretty sure it's Corbin who's having that effect and not the camera.

"We're making "Sex in a Tent," also known as s'mores cheesecake."

"We?" Corbin grins and tilts his head a little.

"Of course. How could I make anything without my handy assistant?" I wink at Corbin as I grab his hand and pull him behind the counter with me. He smiles and pulls me in close to him, making my heart stop. His eyes are studying mine, searching for something, before he leans in and softly kisses me. It's not needy or urgent the way we kissed in the gym, but it makes me hotter than I've ever been in my entire life.

"I didn't know we were making that kind of show," I giggle into his lips.

He laughs and pulls his hands back, "My apologies! I'll be sure to keep my hands off the chef."

We talk and laugh as we make the cheesecake together. I instruct Corbin what to do and he makes sure to mess up so I have to come close to him to make corrections. I entertain the camera and make sure to give verbal instructions and measurements for every move. We even take time for commercial breaks and make up our own ads about makeup and online dating. When we finish and the cheesecake is in the oven, Corbin pops open a nearby bottle of Ruby Port wine and pours us two glasses.

"I want to tell you about Jack," he says, handing me my glass and taking the top part of his apron off. It falls in front and hangs on his hips as he leans back against the counter.

"I want to know all about him," I reply, taking a sip of the sweet wine. "I want to know all about you, too." I hate that I'm so honest with him, that I say things like that. I immediately wish I could suck it back into my mouth and remind myself not to be so vulnerable, but there's something about Corbin that makes me not care.

Corbin smiles, circling his glass to release the flavors in the wine. "Well, if you give me the chance, I promise I will bore you with anything you want to know."

I smile, "Deal."

Corbin takes a drink before he starts talking and I notice his hands shaking a little. I wonder if he ever talks about Jack.

"Jack and I met in the third grade. I can still remember everything from that day. I was having the worst day ever, which at that time meant that my mom didn't pack anything good for lunch and the kids at school were being mean," he shakes his head and we both laugh a little.

"I find it hard to believe anyone would have been mean to you in school," I joke, but honestly I really don't see how it's possible. He's practically flawless.

"Oh, trust me, I wasn't always this sexy," He says, winking at me and taking another sip of his wine. I smack him playfully and he continues, "Seriously though, I wasn't all that cool back then. There was one kid in particular who used to love to pick on me. His name was Andrew and he was the biggest kid in our class."

"Well, I guess I was his main target that day because he just wouldn't leave me alone. At lunch, he made some snarky comment about my mom. Even though I was mad at my mom for packing a lame lunch, it still wasn't okay for him to say something about her, so I called him the first thing I could think of."

"And that was?"

"Meanie head."

I laugh so hard I almost spit out my wine all over Corbin. I'm still bent over in laughter when Corbin starts to tickle my side, "Hey, it's not funny! I didn't know any bad words back then, okay?"

I try to stifle my laughter, but I can't help the huge smile on my face, "Okay, okay, so what happened then?"

"Well," he continues, leaning back against the counter again. "That's when Jack showed up. I don't know why he stuck up for me, but he just walked right over to us and punched Andrew square in the nose. I knew right then that he would be my best friend."

Corbin's eyes shine as he smiles, remembering his best friend. I think about McKenzie and what I would do if she wasn't here with me. I shudder at the thought and take a sip of my wine, focusing back on Corbin.

"Anyway, that's how it all started. We were inseparable after that. I would either be at his place or he'd be at mine. Our parents became close, he was there for every big moment in my life and I was there for his. When we won the Regional Championship in high school we threw the biggest party Chickasha had ever seen."

"Chickasha?"

"Yeah, that's where we grew up. It was just a small town, but definitely not the smallest in Oklahoma. Anyway, Jack was there for every break up I had and I was there for every fight he had. We just worked together, and everyone in school knew us as 'Jack and Corbin.' We didn't stand alone, we were like one single person together."

Corbin's face falls a little and I can tell it isn't easy for him. I refill our glasses and wait for him to continue, knowing he will talk when he's ready. After a few sips, he sets his glass down and I notice his hands are still shaking.

"Corbin, you don't have to tell me everything tonight."

"No, damnit, I want to," he chokes out, and I hear the strain in his voice as he tries not to cry. Seeing him like this makes tears sting at the corners of my eyes. I hate seeing men cry, it just tears me up inside for some reason.

I set my glass down, too, and move from my place across from him to slide up beside him instead. I take his hand in mine and lay my head on his shoulder, thinking maybe it will be easier if I'm not looking at him. I rub his hand with the pad of my thumb and wait.

"He died three weeks before graduation. Three weeks," Corbin's voice cuts off and I feel him tremble a little. "It was my fault."

"No it wasn't, Corbin," I try to soothe him but he pulls back and walks away from me, running his fingers through his hair in frustration.

"No, you don't get it. It *was* my fault," he says, his voice a little louder. "Jack died driving my truck because I was too drunk to drive it myself. It was an old truck and there were so many tricks to keep it running, I never should have let him drive it. I never would have let him drive it if I were sober. But I just wanted to go home and I was going through a stupid break up. The girl I had been dating showed up at the party we were at and I just got hammered and then wanted to leave. I was so stupid, such a fucking idiot."

Corbin is looking down at the ground and his arms are folded over his chest. For a moment, the only sound is the distant hum of the refrigerator. Finally, Corbin shakes his head and continues.

"I loved that old truck, even with all its problems. But that night, the brakes gave out at the wrong time and that damn truck killed my best friend. We were going down hill, he tried to control it but we ended up rolling. After that moment, I hated that truck. I've never hated anything more in my entire life, except for maybe myself for letting it happen at all."

"Corbin, it wasn't your fault," I move toward him again slowly, making sure it's okay. "He was looking out for you and wanted to make sure you got home safely. The brakes could have gone out on anyone, including you."

"I would have known what to do," Corbin tries to rebuttal, but I cut him off.

"You would have known how to stop a truck without brakes?" Corbin shakes his head and crosses his arms again, tears pooling in his eyes. "Corbin, you can't blame yourself for this. For whatever reason, everything that happened that night was meant to happen. Jack wouldn't want you to feel this way, he wouldn't want you to feel responsible like this."

I slowly step a little closer and wrap Corbin in my arms. He stiffens and tries to remain upright, but eventually folds into me. I hold him for a short moment, running my fingers through his hair. I had no idea how broken he was, just like me. I want to fix him, I want to make everything okay in his world. I wish I could just take all the pain away.

"He would be so proud of you if he saw everything you've done to make this gym happen. I know he would be."

Corbin slowly lifts his head and his eyes bore into me, stripping me of words. I've seen his hungry gaze before, but not like this. It's like I touched a place in him he forgot existed. Suddenly, he swoops me into his arms and carries me across the kitchen until I'm pinned against the refrigerator, his mouth crushing down on mine. His breathing is shallow and heated, consuming me with flames.

"Corbin," I breathe into his mouth, moaning as he thrusts his pelvis into me. The metal of the fridge is cool against my back and sends chills down my legs that are quickly erased by the heat from Corbin's hands.

"God, it is so fucking sexy when you say my name," Corbin rips my apron off and throws it to the floor. "Say it again."

I moan his name a little louder and gasp when he growls and bites down on my neck. I drag my nails down his back and move to untie his apron, but then I change my mind. I move further down and unbutton his pants, letting them fall next to my apron. I then pull back and eye Corbin, biting my lip, as I strip his shirt over his head. Finally, I push down his boxers and take him in. Corbin Ray is completely naked except for a little white apron.

And it's the sexiest thing I've ever seen.

Corbin gives me a half smile, "Like what you see, Ms. Bronson?"

I can barely even nod. He laughs a little and pins me again, this time taking both of my wrists in his hand above my head. His hips keep grinding into me and the friction is driving me wild. I want to touch him so bad, but he keeps a firm grip on my wrists, biting and sucking on my neck and collarbone. I let out a soft moan and he growls again, slipping his tongue inside my mouth to take full advantage. I'm positive that out of every kiss I've ever had in my entire life, nothing has ever come close to this. Nothing ever will again.

I am completely his.

Corbin uses his free hand to push my dress up further, exposing my black lacy thong. I go to unwrap my legs from around his waist so he can remove them, but he stops me. "No need for that," he says into my neck. I feel him smile against my skin as his hand moves slowly up the inside of my thigh. He runs his fingers along the edge of my panties, then suddenly, he rips them off me.

Rips. Them. Off. Me.

Again.

Shit, I should just skip wearing the underwear.

"Fuck," I cry out, my body screaming for him. Before I have the chance to beg, he moves his apron to the side and pushes inside me. I cry out again and bite his neck, my legs aching with pleasure as I clench around him. Each time he moves I feel every sense come to life. I feel the smoothness of his lips on my breasts, hear him groaning my name in pleasure. My eyes dance over his body as his muscles move to the rhythm of our passion.

Corbin finally releases my hands and lets me explore him as he pushes in and out of me. He slides his hand down and stops to circle my nipple, teasing it. I arch toward him and moan in ecstasy, completely surrendering to his touch. He thrusts harder in response and I feel like I can't breathe, I'm so full. Full with him and full with an unspeakable pleasure. He slides his hand down further and applies pressure in just the right spot, making me whimper into his mouth as he bites down on my bottom lip.

The heat inside me is too much to handle. Corbin pulls my hair with his free hand, still circling, and I can't wait any longer. I lose it, shaking around him and biting his shoulder to muffle my moans as I explode into the best orgasm of my life. I scream out his name one last time and feel him release inside me.

"Fuck, Paisley," he breathes, switching places with me. He grabs me completely in his arms and slides down the fridge onto the floor next to our clothes. I straddle him and our breathing steadies out as we sit forehead to forehead, completely wrapped up in each other. I plant small kisses on his chest, still shaking around him.

"That was…" I try to find the words to describe the feeling inside me, but nothing comes.

Corbin nods and smiles, "Yeah, it was. You know what else?"

"Hmm?" I ask, sedated.

"The camera is still on." Corbin gestures to the blinking red light on the camera and I flush what I'm sure is every color of red under the sun.

"Corbin!" I start to protest, but he pushes his hands through my hair and pulls me in to a long, deep kiss. When he pulls back, his icy eyes capture me and I completely forget what I was thinking about. We just sit there with our eyes locked for what seems like hours.

"Can I say something without completely freaking you out?" His eyes are darting back and forth between mine.

I swallow, afraid of what he's about to say. "Yes," I breathe.

Corbin seems like he's fighting with the words. He runs his hand through his hair and shakes his head, "I know I probably sound like an idiot, but I'm seriously crazy about you, Paisley. It's like you have this hold on me, like you're my gravity. You pull me to the earth and send me out of this world at the same time. You absolutely paralyze me in the sweetest sense."

My heart feels like it weighs a hundred pounds as it thumps in my chest. This is how it always starts. They fall hard and I pull away. They get in deep and I leave them there to drown.

I stand up and stumble a little, dizzy from his words. As I straighten out my dress, Corbin jumps to his feet and pulls on his boxers. He rushes to me and pulls me in his arms again.

"Please don't run," he pleads, pulling me to him.

"I wasn't –"

"Yes you were. I saw it all over your face. I still see it, the same look you had in my hotel room that night," he pulls back and captures me with his eyes. "Paisley, don't run from me. I'll take this as slow as you want, I'll wait every day of my life if I have to for you to tell me who fucked you over so badly that you can't stand to stay with me. But I promise you one thing I won't do. I won't give up on this, on you. I'm not going anywhere, and I'm not letting you run away from me unless you tell me that's what you want."

One single tear slides down the left side of my face and Corbin wipes it away with his thumb. "I've never felt the things I feel when I'm with you," I say softly. "It scares the shit out of me."

"Don't be scared," he pulls me in again, engulfing me in his sweet and earthy scent. "Open your heart to me."

I can't help it, I sink my head into his chest and sob. I cry because I'm scared, I cry because I don't want to hurt him, I cry because I believe every word he tells me, but mostly I cry because I want to open my heart to him more than he could possibly ever know.

I just don't know if I can.

Chapter eleven

Popcorn

I think the past few nights have finally caught up with me, I'm officially exhausted. I can't stop yawning the entire ride home in Corbin's truck. He keeps smiling at me and brushing my hair from my face. He's told me several times to just get some sleep, but the cold reality that he will be gone soon has sunk in. Usually, deployment is a good thing for me – it means an easy get away from a guy. But this time is different. This time, I actually don't want him to go. And I'm definitely not wasting my time with him by snoring in his passenger seat.

Corbin pulls into the Shell right by my apartment. I glance at the clock on the dash, 11:42. Jesus, it's not even midnight and I'm tired. I'm like a grandma.

"I just need to fill up real quick and grab an energy drink, I've still got some paperwork to work through tonight. Do you want anything?"

I smile a ridiculously goofy smile and he probably thinks I'm crazy, but the fact that he just asked me if I wanted anything makes me feel special for some reason. It's such a loving gesture, something my dad would have done for my mom when I was younger. I shake my head no and he gives me a kiss before shutting the door and heading inside.

I lay my head back against the seat and close my eyes, surrendering to my fatigue for just a few moments. I'm just about to nod off completely when the console starts vibrating. I open my eyes slowly, reaching around for my phone. The vibrating continues and when I finally pull my phone from my purse, I see it isn't me that's vibrating.

It finally stops and then is shortly followed by two short buzzes. I look back toward the store and see Corbin chatting with the cashier. *Leave it alone, Paisley.* I try to distract myself, but curiosity gets the best of me. *Fuck it.* I lift the console and pull out his phone, one missed call and one text message notification lighting up the screen.

Both from "Rachel."

My hands shake as I slide my thumb across the screen to unlock his phone. The text message fills the screen.

- I'm falling asleep, long day. No need to call tonight. Sweet dreams. :) –

I glance back and see Corbin heading back to pump gas. I lock his phone once more and toss it back in the console, trying to control my breathing.

Why am I freaking out right now? The text didn't even really say anything bad. So it's from a girl, and so what she's telling him to have sweet dreams. So what he was supposed to call her. It could be his mom or something, right?

Are you fucking stupid? Of course it's not his mom! I shake my head, trying to gain control of my heart pounding in my chest. *No, he just opened up to me, there's no way this is anything to be worried about. He said things to me no one ever has before, and he asked me to trust him.*

So, for the first time in a long time, I'm going to do just that.

I'm going to trust him.

Corbin gets back in the car and hands me a Hershey's chocolate bar with almonds, one of my favorites. "Since you neglected to tell me we would have to wait eight hours to eat the delicious cheesecake you made tonight, I figured this might hold off your sweet tooth." He smiles and kisses me again on the neck, lingering there for just a little longer than necessary.

I rip open the wrapper and pop a little piece in my mouth, "Hey, wasn't it you that said waiting is half the fun?" I wink and Corbin shakes his head, laughing.

"That is right, I guess I did. Karma is a real bitch sometimes."

We both laugh and as we pull away, he grabs my hand and plants a small kiss on my fingers that are laced with his. I stare at him in wonder as we drive, feeling myself melt into him, but I can't ignore the voice in my head. Even though my heart is trying so hard to get me to forget about the text, my head is too stubborn. No matter how hard I try, one thing is clear.

Trusting him is easier said than done.

"Can we pleeeeease watch something girly? We always watch your manly, action-packed, macho-man movies," I whine to Tanner, pouring us two glasses of Jim Beam Honey and Coke. Tanner is pouring a bag of freshly popped popcorn into the same big silver bowl we've used since the first time we had a movie night together. I steal a few puffs and shove them in my mouth before putting on my best pouty face.

"Don't give me that look," Tanner laughs, pegging me in the forehead with a popcorn kernel. I pout my lip out further and bat my lashes. "Okay, okay. We can watch one of your girly movies."

I squeal and grab our glasses, following behind him as he heads to my couch. I love how Tanner can make me feel so happy, regardless of all the shit that's always piling up in my life. Work was hell today, and Corbin asked me to go out with him again but I turned him down and told him I was hanging out with a friend, which was a lie until about thirty minutes ago when Tanner showed up. I was just so overwhelmed at work and the thought of being with Corbin sounded nice at first, but then I remembered the text from last night. I tried to force it out of my mind, or should I say I've been trying to all day, but it's no use. There's something he's not telling me, and as much as I want to say "fuck it" and fall into him, my brain won't let me.

To top it all off, today is my dad's birthday. My mom made a point of texting me this morning to remind me. I'm sure she wasn't surprised when I didn't answer.

I had planned on just drowning my sorrows in a bottle of wine and turning on whatever Pandora station came up under the "I'm fucked up" search, but Tanner came over just as I was about to open the bottle. He came bearing hard liquor and a night to waste, which sounded a lot better, so I put my self-pity party on hold. For now, at least.

"How about this one? It's not too girly, and I know you love Katherine Heigl," I hold up *The Ugly Truth* and wave it behind me as I continue searching for a back up in case he says no.

"I do have a thing for a sexy blonde with long legs," he teases, knowing it will piss me off. He used to always hit on McKenzie in front of me, and knowing she's about five thousand times prettier than me just made me want to punch him every time he did.

I find the nearest DVD case and toss it at him, "Screw you, ass hole."

He laughs as he dodges the DVD and casually tosses a handful of popcorn in his mouth, "Just kidding, babe. You know you're the only one for me."

"Yeah, yeah," I shake my head as I slide the DVD in and take my seat next to him, both of us propping our feet up on my homemade coffee table at the same time. McKenzie and I made it last year as a Pinterest project. We failed miserably if you look at what we were trying to accomplish, but on its own it doesn't look half bad.

Just as the opening credits start, I get a text from Corbin. I say a little prayer to Jesus that my new phone came in and I don't have to text on that tiny ass flip phone.

- I just want you to know I'm completely envious of your friend right now. I miss you. -

I can't help it, the goofiest smile spreads across my face. He misses me? Fuck, my emotions are like a yo-yo with this guy. One minute I'm up, the next I'm down, half the time I'm just a tangled fucking mess.

- I miss you, too. Save me a piece of that cheesecake? -
- Yeah right, that thing was devoured before lunch. How about you save tomorrow night for me and I'll give you something even better. -

My face goes hot and I feel my muscles clench between my legs. I'm really hoping that means he's going to give me a repeat of last night. I'm stuck on what to say, but luckily he texts back a few seconds later.

- I would love to see the look on your face after that last text. -

I smile again, knowing he'd like to see a lot more than just the look on my face.

- Stop making me blush in front of my friend. G2G, see you tomorrow. -
- Now I'm even more jealous, I love that blush. Maybe I'll just have to watch the tape from last night so I can see it, too. ;) Goodnight, beautiful. -
- You're so bad! ;) Night, Corbin. -

I inhale deeply, breathing in his words, and toss my phone on the floor beside the couch so I won't be tempted to text him again. I'm still smiling, but it's slowly fading as I remember how much I still don't know about Corbin. Everything he says to me makes him seem so perfect, but I know there's no such thing. That text from "Rachel" last night didn't say anything bad in it, but I can't ignore the pit in my stomach that tells me there's something more to her, something bad. Something that will probably break my heart.

Tanner reaches for the remote and pauses the movie just as Katherine Heigl is yelling into her phone at Gerard Butler. "Okay," he says, leaning back on the couch and facing me. "Spill." He drapes his arm over the back of the couch and leans on his other elbow, looking confident as he always does. I can't help but notice how he fills out the black t-shirt he's wearing, his arm muscles threatening to burst out at any time.

"Spill what?"

"Seriously, Paisley? I just witnessed a roller coaster ride on this couch and all I had to do was watch your face as you texted your secret man for the past five minutes."

I blush, crossing my arms and pulling my feet up under me, "He's not my secret man."

"So then spill, what the hell is going on? Every guy you've dated since college I've barely even noticed because your interest level was at, like, maybe a two with them. This guy I noticed Sunday night and again tonight. If he's pulling you away from Tanner Time, we're going to have a problem," he teases, tickling my side to get me to relax.

I laugh and swat his hand away, "Stop! It's nothing, okay?"

He folds his bulgy arms across his chest and gives me the "yeah right, bullshitter" look.

"Ugh, FINE. I maybe like him. Okay, I for sure like him. And it pisses me off." Tanner looks confused, and I know there's no letting this go, so I tell him everything I left out on Sunday night. I tell him about the strange phone calls and cryptic text, about how he wants me to trust him but I just don't think I can. I tell him about how Corbin opened up to me and trusted me, but I still feel so unsure. I tell him about how, for once, I'm dreading deployment – and that scares the shit out of me because that means I care. When I finish, I take a deep breath and realize I've probably been talking for a good twenty minutes straight. Tanner just nodded and listened to each word, probably analyzing what a psycho I am.

"Well, as much as I want to punch him in the face already for ever putting any phone calls before you and for interrupting Tanner Time, he sounds like a decent guy. And you sound like you're letting your dad hold you back."

I look down at the floor and tug at the shaggy carpet with my toes, avoiding Tanner's eyes.

"Look, I don't want to bring this up, especially not today, but this is something you've got to let go, babe." Tanner brushes my hair out of my face and pulls my chin up, forcing me to look at him. "Your dad fucked up, but not every guy is like that."

I nod, but I'm still not so sure. "Wait, what did you mean about not bringing it up today?"

Tanner shifts his weight and shrugs, "Well, I just mean on his birthday. I'm sure you've been thinking about this shit all day and I came over to make it better, not worse."

My heart almost explodes as I look at my best friend, the one guy who has actually had the chance to fuck me over and hasn't. "Tanner, you remembered that today was my dad's birthday?"

He moves closer to me, making my stomach flutter. I don't know why, but I feel a little nervous right now, like I used to when I first met Tanner. "Of course I remembered. Paisley, you're my best friend and one of the best girls I know in this fucked up world. The last thing I want is to see you sad over a douche move your dad pulled. I just wanted to take your mind off things for a while."

An overwhelming want to kiss Tanner is coursing through my veins. I know it's fucked up, and I know it's probably just because he just said one of the sweetest things I've ever heard, but whatever the case may be I definitely want to kiss him.

"You have popcorn in your hair," he laughs, reaching up and pulling a small piece out of my hair. I blush and tuck my hair behind my ear. *Why are you being such a weirdo? It's just Tanner.*

"You know, I always think about you when I eat popcorn. I guess it's the smell or something, but it always makes me think about our movie nights and stuff. Whenever I make it in my dorm at NYU or when my family makes it or even at a movie theatre, I always think of us and our popcorn fights. Or how you always seem to get pieces in your hair," he teases, grabbing another stray piece from my hair. This time, he lets his hand hover there a bit before he lets it trail down the side of my face.

His golden brown eyes are searching mine, and he slowly leans in closer. Shit, does he want to kiss me too? My heart starts thumping wildly in my chest, beating like a fucking warrior drum. He's only a few inches from my face when my phone rings, breaking the tension between us.

It takes me a minute to move and I realize I probably look so fucking stupid. I shake my head as I fumble for my phone on the ground. How could I possibly think Tanner would want to kiss me? He's my best friend, I've known that for years. I groan out loud when I see my mom's name filling the screen, knowing she'll want to know if I talked to Dad.

I sigh and show the screen to Tanner, "Look who it is. Give me a sec?" He nods and I answer the call as I duck into the hall and head for my bedroom.

"Hey Mom," I sigh into the phone as I close my bedroom door behind me. My breathing is still shallow and I can't wrap my brain around what just happened. I'm falling for Corbin, and he's all I can ever think about.

But then why did I just almost kiss Tanner?

"Hey, sweetie. I'm so happy you answered. How's my baby girl tonight?"

"I'm good, Mom. I'm actually watching a movie with Tanner so I can't talk long, would it be okay if I called you tomorrow?" I lean over my dresser and adjust my make up in the mirror, realizing what a mess I am right now. My white running shorts and dark purple NYU tank top that Tanner brought me are not exactly working wonders for my figure right now. I turn and check my ass in the mirror. Well, at least these shorts flatter in that area.

"Of course, honey. I'm sorry, I don't want to take away from time with Tanner. I just wanted to see if you had spoken to your dad at all today. I'm not sure if you remembered, but today is his –"

"Yes, Mom. I know it's his birthday," I sigh again and flop down on my bed. "Listen, I love you with all my heart, but you have got to let me deal with dad on my own time. I don't care about his birthday right now, and you can't change that. I'm trying to work through all the shit in my head but right now I just can't, so he's going to have to just wait. And so are you."

It's silent on the other end for a moment before my mom finally answers, "Okay, I guess that's better than nothing. I'm sorry I keep bothering you with this, I just want us to be a family again. As much as we can be, anyway."

My heart breaks a little at those words and I inhale deeply to stop myself from crying. "It'll be fine, Mom. Regardless of what happens with me and Dad, you're the best mom ever and we're a great family just the two of us."

"I love you, sweetheart."

I smile and we both sit silently. I'm sure she wants to say more, but she knows there's no budging me tonight. I think if anyone knows how broken I am over what my dad did, it's Mom. She knows when she can talk to me about it and she knows when it's useless to even try.

"Well then, I guess I should let you get back to Tanner. When is he going to move back and marry you, anyway?" she teases.

"Mom," I groan, dragging it out for emphasis on how embarrassing she is sometimes.

"I know, I know. Just friends, I get it. Well, have fun, sweetie. I'll talk to you soon."

"Goodnight, Mom."

I drop the phone on the bed beside me and cover my face with my pillow. What the fuck is happening to me? Just a few days ago I was completely single and not interested in anyone but myself and my career, and the occasional cute military man, of course. But now, I'm falling for one of the most romantic men I've ever known, the same man who opened up to me more than he probably has with anyone, and I almost fucked it all up by kissing my best friend, which in turn would have fucked up our friendship, too.

Jesus, I should have my own Lifetime movie.

I throw the pillow off my face, grab my phone, and head back down the hallway to my living room where Tanner is still sprawled out on my couch.

Looking sexy as fuck.

Stop it, Paisley! I try to control my thoughts and take my seat next to him, propping my feet up on the coffee table once more.

"Everything okay?" He asks, pulling me into him. It's such a casual gesture, one he's done so many times before, but I can't help but feel there's something more to it this time.

I pull away and reach for the remote, "Yeah, everything's okay. Let's go back to your original plan of just making me forget about all this shit, okay?"

I'm about to push play when Tanner leans up and stops me, placing his hand over mine. "Before you start the movie again, I just want you to know that I'm here for you. If you want to talk about Mr. Military Man, your dad, or anything else – just know you've got me."

I smile and lean in to hug him, "Thanks, Tanner."

When we pull back, he grabs the bowl of popcorn and throws a few puffs into his mouth. "Besides," he adds, "If this guy fucks you over, I'll beat his ass and ride off into the sunset with you on the back of my white horse. We'll see who the knight in shining armor is then." He gives me a cocky look and moves his eyebrows up and down.

"Oh shut up, ass." I laugh and smack him on the arm, glad to have the tension between us gone and feel a little more normal. I push play and fall back on the couch, letting the exhaustion from my recent emotional adventures take me over. Before I have the chance to reach for another hand of popcorn, my fatigue wins out and I fall asleep, my head on Tanner's shoulder.

Chapter twelve
Yoga Pants

Breathing in deeply, I try to relax in my pigeon pose. I push all the thoughts that have been clouding my mind out of my head and focus only on my breathing and the soft sounds coming from my instructor's stereo. There are birds singing over the rush of a distant waterfall and a soft drum beats along with it, steadying my nerves.

For about thirty-five seconds, at least.

But then it's right back to the tug of war battle raging on inside my head. Last night was the first real night of sleep I've had since last Thursday, yet I feel more exhausted today than I have my entire life.

As I transition into full pigeon, I let my mind wander back to what happened with Tanner last night. How the hell did I almost kiss him? This is Tanner, my best friend. I've always thought he was sexy as hell, but I've never let it get that far before. We've been in the friend zone ever since I can remember, and we've both made that very clear. So then what on earth was that last night? Did I imagine the tension between us, or did he feel it, too?

I move into a lotus pose, breathing in deeply again to calm my thoughts. I can feel my heart threatening to beat uncontrollably out of my chest. *Focus, Paisley. Just relax. Last night was a little weird, but everything is just like it was and you were just having a bad night.* It was my dad's birthday, maybe I was just delusional. I sigh, inhaling another deep breath as the waterfall sounds rush over me. The more important thought to dwell on right now is Corbin.

Sweet, sexy, panty-melting Corbin.

As I turn and lift my legs into the boat pose, my core tightens and I remember the delicious feeling that always sits in my stomach when Corbin touches me. My heart races as I trace the lines of his strong jaw in my mind, letting my tongue reminisce on the way he tasted when he took me in the kitchen.

I'm still convinced I will never have a kiss that will ever beat that one. His lips do something to me, something no one else's ever have or ever could. He paralyzes me and sends me spinning at the same time. It's like it almost hurts it's so fucking good.

And there's more than that. Corbin makes me want to be a better person. When I hear him talk about Jack and I think of all he's doing to make this gym happen, it makes me beam. It's like he's my fucking child and just got the honor roll or something. He just leaves me in awe, the same way he did when he somehow got Amelia's to shut their doors to the public and let me frolic in their kitchen. It just floors me how someone can be that thoughtful.

And that incredibly hot.

I shake my head, realizing I'm late transitioning into downward dog. As I lift my core and push my rear up, I can't help thinking about how thrilling it would be to have Corbin behind me, watching. I can imagine his eyes craving me the way they do, making me feel completely stripped and defenseless. *What the hell is wrong with me? I can't even do yoga without thinking about all the dirty things I want to do to him.*

But there are still questions that lurk in the back of my mind and sneak up on me, reminding me to be cautious. Reminding me that every man has flaws, and Corbin is no exception. I frown, remembering the text on his phone and the late night phone calls. If I don't find out who Rachel is soon, it's going to eat me alive. I should just ask him, just come out and say, "Who the hell is Rachel?" But as much as I feel for him, I have no idea what he feels for me. Do I even have the right to ask him something like that yet?

Will I ever have that right?

I let out an exhausted sigh and get a few looks from the girls around me, including McKenzie. I whisper an apology and avoid McKenzie's eyes as they bore into me. I know she wants the dirt, and I know I can talk to her, but right now I just need to let my mind figure out some things on its own. I close my eyes, inhale deeply, and push everything out of my mind as much as I can so I can finish my class peacefully. The deeper I breathe, the more I let the soothing sounds of my instructor's voice and music wash over me. I let them envelop me in a tight cocoon, sheltering me from every pain.

As the tranquility sets in, I find myself daydreaming of the warmth of the sun on an exotic beach with the wind blowing through my hair. My long dress is whipping around my legs and the waves are crashing softly against the shore. As I look to my left, I see Corbin spread out on a light blue blanket. He motions for me to lay with him, and as I sink down next to him and his arms wrap around me, I smile. It's the safest, warmest, best feeling I've ever experienced.

Sweet paradise.

Work is dragging by at the pace of a handicapped snail. I swear I've looked at the clock at least thirty times and it's only changed by about ten minutes. I sigh and sink down in my chair, closing my eyes and rubbing my temples to try to alleviate the massive headache that's been plaguing me all afternoon. *Only a few more hours, Paisley. Keep it together.*

I glance at the card on my desk from all my coworkers thanking me for the treats I've brought in this week. There's several comments about how it's the best cookies/cupcakes they've ever had. They say this every time I bake, so I'm not sure if I should believe them anymore or if they're just trying to make me feel good. What if everyone actually hates my baking and just says things like this to be nice? As much as I want to throw myself a pity party, I can't really bring myself to believe that. I may not be the best in the world, but I know I have talent – mainly because I have such a passion for it.

I still can't believe I baked with Corbin. When I was happy, not sad. Or pissed. Or confused. I was genuinely happy and I baked. I haven't done that since college. Being in that kitchen brought back all the great things about baking. Not only has it been there for me through the hard times, but now it was slowly making its way into the great times.

I'm shaken from my daydream when I feel a sudden dip in my chair, making me feel like I'm about to tumble backwards.

"Shit!" I slap my hand over my mouth and turn in my chair to find Corbin smirking above me.

And by smirking, I mean he's doing that incredibly sexy smile just shy of his full blown smile. The one that makes me want to lift up my skirt right here in my office and not even say sorry about it. His blue eyes are blazing, almost as if he's thinking the same thing I am.

Maybe he is.

"Hey, potty mouth," he teases, his grin widening. I shake my head and open my mouth to call him a jerk, but he quickly leans down and pulls my mouth to his. He runs a hand through my hair as I slowly open my mouth and let his tongue in. He softly circles and I play back, a teasing game that makes me forget where I am for a moment. I reach out and grab his ass, pulling myself out of my chair and closer to his body.

"Easy, killer. I think we might want to save this for later," Corbin whispers, pulling back and nodding his head toward my office door. I turn and see Shannon practically breaking her neck to look in at us as she walks by. I laugh and walk over to close my door most of the way shut, flipping Shannon the bird discretely as I walk back toward Corbin. I hear her laugh behind me as I sit back down at my desk.

"To what do I owe this pleasure, Mr. Ray? Have you come to check up on the progress my creative team has made?"

"Yes," he answers, seating himself in the chair on the other side of my desk. He unbuttons his jacket and lets it fall open, reminding me of the first time I saw him in a business suit. I cross my legs and beg my ovaries to calm the fuck down as he continues. "But mostly, I came to see what my beautiful account manager was doing tonight."

I smile and feel my face grow hot. I can't believe this guy still makes me blush. "Well, she doesn't have any plans at the moment, so there's a possibility she could be persuaded to hang out with a handsome soldier."

Corbin returns my smile and his dimples appear as he flashes those beautiful teeth, "Good, I was afraid another friend would want to steal your time from me." His southern accent seems so out of place in this office. It's slow and sexy, and makes everything in the world sound simple and easy. It's a stark contrast to the muttered curse words and shuffling feet that fill the space around us.

"Nope, I'm all yours tonight. What do you have in mind?"

"Oh, something really naughty. Are you sure you want me to say it out loud here, at your place of employment?" His eyes are challenging me and that damn smirk is back, waiting for my response. I fidget in my seat and cross my legs the other way, making Corbin chuckle. He knows exactly what he's doing to me.

"I'm not afraid of you, Mr. Ray," I lie, knowing that I'm scared as hell of him in many aspects. I'm scared of the way I feel about him, I'm scared of him hurting me, and right now I'm scared I'm going to get fired for jumping a client in my office.

He laughs and shakes his head, "Oh, you really shouldn't have said that." He gives me another daring look and I gulp down the dry air in my throat. *Jesus, how am I supposed to resist him?*

"Relax, I'm actually thinking of a pretty low-key night, if you're up for it. I'm pretty exhausted from all the running around I've been doing."

I perk up at the word "relax." Exhaustion is still overpowering every other feeling in my body right now. I feel like I haven't slept in years and I'm running on nothing but adrenaline and caffeine. "That actually sounds perfect to me."

"Great, then it's a date," he says, rising out of the chair and buttoning his jacket again. I want to unbutton it along with every other button covering him with my teeth. "Just me, you, and a pair of sweatpants. I'll grab some wine and junk food on my way over."

I laugh as I get up to accompany him out. "Deal, but I hope you're okay with yoga pants. I lost the last pair of sweatpants I had a few months ago and haven't bought any since."

He stops abruptly and turns to face me, "I am more than okay with yoga pants." He grins devilishly and I imagine him ripping them off me. I blush and turn us back toward the front door, trying to push him out before I cause the biggest scene in the office since the Christmas Party last year when our intern got a little too tipsy and tried doing a strip tease on her desk.

"Alright, Mr. Ray, get out of here before I get myself fired and you have no account manager to work on your project," I lean up and give him a swift peck on the lips before he chuckles and exits the office. I'm watching his ass so closely as he leaves that I don't notice Shannon standing beside me.

"Yeah, I would totally tap that," she says, letting out a whistle and shaking her head. I smack her and turn on my heel to head back to my office, trying to contain my laughter.

"What?! You know I would!" she hollers after me and I flip her the bird again. I hear her laughter fade as I duck back inside my office and shut the door. I need a minute to cool the fuck down.

Even though I know we're just going to lay around my apartment, I know I have to look cute tonight. I showered as soon as I got home and blow dried my hair into soft, bouncy curls. I avoided using too much product and tried to make them look natural, like that's just the way my hair magically falls when I use a blow dryer. The truth is it turns into a crazy, frizzy mess unless I use a round brush and a dollop of smoothing cream.

I open the bottom drawer of my dresser and start sifting through my yoga pants, a collection that has grown significantly in the past few years since I became an avid yogi. I find the tightest ones I own that I purchased from Victoria's Secret not too long ago and pull them on. I fold down the hot pink top and turn to admire my ass in the mirror. *Thank sweet baby Jesus for whoever created yoga pants.*

I run my fingers through my hair a few times, loosening my curls and adding a little volume before grabbing a black racer back from my top drawer. I pull it on over my lacy black bra and turn sideways, making sure my curves are accentuated.

And they definitely are.

My phone buzzes and I race to my bed to retrieve it, hoping it's Corbin saying he will be a few minutes late. Who knew it took so much effort to look effortless?

- Hey, baby. Want to meet at our spot tonight? -

I smile at Tanner's text, I have seriously missed him. Even though last night was a little awkward, I'm convinced it's just me being an emotional girl and overanalyzing.

- Ugh, I would love to but I'm actually booked tonight.
Can I get a rain check? -
- Let me guess, Army boy? -
- :/ Why do you have to say it like that? -
- Just trying to look out for my princess. That's my job as the
Knight in Shining Armor. Didn't I tell you that? ;) -
- You're such an ass. GOODNIGHT, Tanner. -
- You love my ass. ;) -

I shake my head and toss my phone on the bed again. He's right, I do love his ass.

In a totally friends-only kind of way.

I think.

Fuck, can Corbin just get here already?

As if on cue, I hear Corbin knock at my door. I quickly run my Burts Bees chapstick over my lips and light the two candles in the living room as I scurry toward the door to let him in. I check one last time to make sure everything is cleaned up before pulling the handle.

And then I'm paralyzed.

Again.

Corbin looks up from the ground and shoots me his smoldering eyed smile. The right side of his mouth curls into a sexy half smile as his eyes devour me. The black t-shirt he has on is clinging to his muscles, making me jealous. It has a symbol in the chest area and beneath that a platoon name and "Hooah!"

Damn right, "hooah."

His gray sweat pants are hanging deliciously off his hips and I instantly want to run my finger tips along the hem line. I want to tease him and make goose bumps pop up all over him the way he makes me react to his touches.

This man is seriously delectable.

"I brought beer instead of wine, hope that's okay," he shrugs, holding up the bag in his left hand.

"You could bring me rat poison if you delivered it dressed like this," the words fly out of my mouth before I have the chance to stop them. I don't even have time to blush in embarrassment before Corbin is inside and kissing me against the door, the bags that were occupying his hands now dropped to the floor. He grabs my hips and pulls me into him, his mouth pressed hard against mine. A soft moan escapes my lips and he pulls back, both of us panting.

"You've really got to stop doing that."

"Doing what?" I ask, confused.

"Looking at me like you want me so bad you can't stand it."

I bite my lip, knowing that's exactly how I feel every time I'm around him. How am I supposed to stop doing that?

I grab one of the bags off the floor and head to the kitchen, Corbin following behind me with the rest. I grab the six pack of Shock Top and place it in the fridge, bending over to fill the last empty space I have on the bottom shelf. I hear Corbin inhale stiffly behind me.

"Everything okay back there, Mr. Ray?" I tease, lifting a brow as I glance back at him.

"Everything is absolutely great, Ms. Bronson. Did I mention that I *love* yoga pants?"

"Hm, I don't think you did," I say as I look back in the fridge. I pretend like I'm adjusting the Shock Top and sway my hips a little.

Corbin growls in response, "You're going to kill me, here."

I shrug as I close the door and start emptying the other bags, "I have no idea what you're talking about." Corbin laughs softly and shakes his head. I can already see where this night is going.

And I want to be there.

Like now.

After we make a platter of junk food with everything from Twinkies to Doritos and pop open the top on two bottles of beer we make our way into the living room. I fall into the couch and tuck my feet up underneath me, snacking on a handful of cashews as Corbin pulls three movies from the remaining bag.

"I didn't know what you like, so I got three different genres."

I wait for him to continue, but he just sort of stares at me. "Okay… what are they?"

"Well," he says, pulling the movies behind his back. "I could just tell you what they are, or I could tell you what you'll get based on your decision."

I scrunch my face up in half confusion, half suspicion. "Okay, I'll bite. Tell me what I'll get."

He smiles his full mega watt smile, the one where his teeth and adorable dimples make an appearance in all their glory. "I was hoping you'd choose my way."

Corbin moves next to me and pulls me into his lap, planting light kisses on my neck and collarbone as he speaks. "Option A is a little scary, but I promise to hold you the entire time and kiss you during the scary parts."

Okay, why do I need more options? Anything that involves kissing, I'm in.

"Option B is romantic, but I promise that if that's your choice, I will romance you in more ways tonight than the guy in this movie could even think of."

I smile, as cheesy as that was it was also incredibly adorable. How freaking sweet is this?

"And option C?" I ask, my curiosity piqued.

"Ah, option C. Option C is an old movie favorite of mine that I've seen a million times. If that's your choice, then you're stuck listening to me talk and I'll force you to talk to me, too."

My heart suddenly starts to beat so hard in my chest I'm afraid Corbin might be able to hear it. I bite my lip and fidget with the ring on my right hand before he gently grabs my chin and lifts it so I look him in those gorgeous, breathtaking blue eyes.

"Like I said, the option is yours. I'm not here to force you into anything." His brow is furrowed in concern as he searches my eyes, and I know that he wants me to pick option C. This man wants me to open up to him, he wants to open up to me.

And I'm acting like a scared little bitch.

And I'm so, *so* tired of it.

I clear my throat and try to sound unaffected, but I know he can see right through me. "Well, I hate scary movies and I don't want you to embarrass yourself trying to out-romanticize option B, so I guess option C will have to do." I smile, satisfied with my feigned humor attempt.

"Hey!" he says defensively. "I can be romantic! I mean, just look at this spread." He motions to our junk food tray and I stifle a laugh, shaking my head.

He pulls me closer and runs the back of his right hand down my cheek, staring into my freaking soul again with those eyes. "All jokes aside, I'm glad you picked C." He stares at me a few moments more before pulling my lips to his. His kiss is soft and sweet, but it still makes my stomach ache in anticipation. I can't help but want him.

"So, what is this old movie favorite?" I ask, pulling away from his toxic lips. I swear I could die by his kisses and it would be the sweetest death.

"Shawshank Redemption. Have you seen it?"

"Are you kidding me? That's one of my favorites, too. You can't beat Morgan Freeman."

"Or Stephen King. It's like a match you just can't mess with. Kind of like us," he adds, flashing his mega watt smile again before jumping up to put the DVD in. I kick myself inside because I'm acting like a little school girl, but I fucking *love* that he just said "us."

Like we're a thing.

Are we a thing?

Corbin sits down next to me again and pulls me close, his arm draped around me. I lean my head on his chest and trace my fingertip down the line between his abs. I feel him shiver and every inch of my body jumps to life. When my hand reaches the hem of his sweatpants, I slip my fingertip just beneath it and trace a line from his left hip to his right hip.

"Paisley, we're supposed to be talking," he breathes huskily, his hand now running through my hair as I bite my lip.

"I'll talk to you all night, tell you anything you want to know. But I won't be able to focus on a damn thing until you rip these yoga pants off me." I gaze into his eyes hungrily and lick my bottom lip before sucking it in between my teeth again. He groans and pulls my mouth to his, desperately pushing his tongue inside. I climb onto his lap and straddle him, weaving my hands in his hair as he nips and sucks down my neck.

"Do you know how fucking beautiful you are," he growls into my chest before kissing along the hem of my tank top. He bites me softly and I cry out, feeling my body ache in response. I pull my shirt over my head and throw it behind me and Corbin grabs my arms in his hands, pulling me back to let his eyes skate over my body.

"You're intoxicating."

My body practically explodes with his words. I want nothing more than to crush my lips to his, but he's still holding me in place and his eyes are consuming me. He slides his hands down to my wrists and pulls my arms behind my back before leaning in to kiss along my bra line. He moves up my neck, slips his tongue inside my mouth and tugs on my bottom lip with his teeth before tracing a line back down. I arch my back toward him, throwing my head back, and grind my pelvis against his hard on.

"I want to touch you," I moan.

Corbin smiles against my cleavage as he kisses, "I know you do. But I'm not done yet." He pulls back and lets go of my wrists. I immediately reach for him, but he pulls me back again. "I said, I'm not done yet." I pout in response, but Corbin just smiles more devilishly as he unclasps my bra and my breasts spring free.

"I get sixty seconds before you can touch me again, do you understand?" Corbin waits for me to nod before blazing a trail of fire with his fingers from my lower back up my abdomen and finally to my breasts. He cups them in his hands and I arch toward him again, my hands threatening to rebel against my will and reach out to touch him.

He takes both of my nipples between his thumbs and middle fingers and rubs them gently as his palms grip me. The shocking pleasure rips through my body and I gasp and moan and rub against him, my body squirming. My hands instinctively jerk toward his but he stops me again, "Mm, not yet. I still have thirty seconds."

I whine and bite my lip as he returns to torturing me with his touch. His hands move to my ass and he pulls me closer before tracing his tongue down my neck to my breasts. He sucks my nipple into his mouth and the heat current shoots straight between my legs. I feel my body clench and I throw my head back again, letting out a loud moan.

"Corbin, please. I want you," I pant, my body still squirming on top of his as he mercilessly circles my nipple with his tongue. He bites down gently and sucks hard, demolishing my control. I reach out for him and he lets me touch him this time, my hands starving for his body.

Suddenly, Corbin pulls me up to stand with him. I grip his triceps and kiss all over his shoulders before sliding my hands down into his pants. When my hands finally touch him he curses and lets his head fall back, his mouth slightly open. I run my hands up and down, feeling him grow even harder with every stroke.

"Fuck, Paisley." He tugs his pants down to the floor and lifts me back onto the couch, peeling my tight pants off as he does. His eyes light up when he realizes they were my last piece of clothing. I'm laying beneath him as he towers over me, completely naked.

Completely his.

I get brave and let my legs fall open, letting him see every inch of me. He bites his lip and pulls me back into his arms, my legs wrapped around him as he falls back onto the couch with me on top. He crushes his lips on mine and pulls my ass toward him, his hardness pressed against my stomach. I moan and try to lift up with my legs to slide him inside me, but he holds me down again, smiling against my kisses.

"Corbin," I whine, my body close to combustion if I don't have him inside me soon.

"Tell me you want me," he whispers against my skin, planting small kisses down my chest again. He sucks my nipple into his mouth and circles his tongue wildly.

"I want you," I groan, the sharp pangs of pleasure coursing through me.

"Say it again."

"I want you!" I scream. The entire neighborhood can probably hear me by now but I don't give a shit. I need him inside me. Now.

"Fuck," he groans, pulling my forehead to his. "Paisley, I've never wanted anyone or anything more than I want you." I don't even have time to react before he lifts me up and slides me down onto him, filling me with his desire.

I throw my head back, my body overwhelmed with the intensity of how he feels inside me. Corbin pulls my head forward in his hands and gazes into my eyes. As I move up and down, his eyes stay fixed on mine, and I know this is one of those moments. This is a moment in my life that I will never forget, one that will stain my memories forever.

Corbin moves his mouth to my chest again and the combination is too much. My legs tense around him and he pumps into me harder. My body can't control itself anymore and I lose it. I completely shatter around him, my body shaking as I scream out his name. He pulls my mouth back to his and as we both release, he kisses me. Slowly, softly, our moans and breaths mingling with each other in a beautiful symphony. As we both come down, I open my eyes and find Corbin's locked on mine again. Our breathing synchs as our chests rise and fall together, and we stay just like that – Corbin's hands weaved into my hair, my arms clasped around his neck, our foreheads pressed together and those gorgeous blue eyes stripping my soul bare.

For as long as I live, I will never forget the feeling of right now.

Chapter thirteen

Farsighted

I grab another handful of Doritos and lean back on the couch, laughing as Corbin recounts a time when he and Jack snuck out and threw a party down by the lake. His eyes have that shine in them again as he tells me all the crazy events of that night. It sounds like some crazy movie the way he explains it, with all the cliff hangers and getting away with things that seem impossible. I can't help but laugh with him as he remembers his best friend. It's contagious.

Morgan Freeman's voice fills the background as we talk, and I catch my favorite quotes every now and then. *"These walls are funny. First you hate 'em, then you get used to 'em. Enough time passes, you get so you depend on them. That's institutionalized,"* I hear him say. He's referring to the walls of the Shawshank prison, but I can't help but relate them to my very own walls. I think it's true about getting used to them, depending on them even. It's been easy to hide everything the past four years. Now that I've talked to McKenzie and Corbin is slowly peeling away my layers, I feel the threat of the unfamiliar territory on the other side of these walls crashing in on me.

I also can't stop thinking about the fact that I'm feeling some really intense things for a man who is leaving in a week. This is usually the part where I start planting the seeds to lead to a break up. I have my last few nights of fun, say goodbye, and move on without any hurt. But this is different. I don't want him to deploy. I don't want him to leave me at all.

My body is still weak as I listen to Corbin speak, sedated from his touches. It feels like I'm in a dream and my body is just floating along, taking a vacation until I wake up and put it through hell again.

"You two were crazy," I laugh, popping another chip into my mouth.

Corbin laughs and shakes his head, "That's only one story, I could go on all night about the mischief we caused."

I suck the chip remains off my fingers, "So tell me another one." When I look back up at Corbin, his eyes are dark and he's watching me suck my last finger.

"If you don't stop doing things like that, we're never going to get to talk."

I blush and shrug, grabbing a nearby napkin to wipe the rest off my hands.

"And no, I'm not telling you another story. Not until after you tell me something."

"I'm really not that interesting," I try to convince him, hoping I can stray just a little bit longer from talking about myself. It's not that I don't want Corbin to know more about me, I just know that if he finds out how messed up I am he might turn and run away.

I would.

Corbin grabs his beer from the table, taking a big swig. "I very seriously doubt that. I've only known you a few days and so far you've been the most interesting person I've ever met."

I tilt my head, confused. "What? Why do you say that? I'm so boring."

He laughs a little and shakes his head, playing with the label on his bottle. "You are far from boring, Paisley. I've never had anyone capture me the way you did that night we first met. I felt like you were already mine, like that guy touching all over you was threatening everything I held close in the world. And when you ran from me that night, I felt broken. I was exhilarated when I saw you the next day, and then shattered again when you left me that night. And I can't even explain what I felt when I ran into you while I was jogging."

Corbin's eyes are more serious than I've ever seen them and I kind of feel like shoving my head between the couch pillows. Seriously, what a bitch I sound like in this scenario.

"But ever since you stayed, since that day at the gym… I don't know how to explain it. When I'm not with you, you're all I think about. When I am with you, I can't think about anything else."

Except those damn phone calls. And Rachel.

Shut up, Paisley! He's being sweet!

"To say the least, you have been very interesting to me," he finishes, taking another sip from his beer. I can't help the goofy grin that spreads across my face.

"Well, I don't really know what to say. I'm not exactly used to talking about myself."

"That doesn't surprise me," he laughs again. "How about we try something simple. Tell me something that no one knows about you. A quirk maybe, or a fear."

I scrunch my nose up, trying to think of something – anything – that I can say. I could tell him that I sucked my thumb til I was eight, but I don't think that's exactly going to get me points here. I could talk about my love for Twitter and how I spend half my day on there, but again – lame. Why can't I think of a single interesting thing about me that I haven't told anyone about?

And then it hits me.

"Owls," I say, trying to swallow my last sip of beer and talk at the same time. "I like owls."

"You like owls?" He asks, raising a brow. "Like, the birds that can turn their heads all the way around and deliver letters to aspiring wizards?"

I chuckle at the Harry Potter reference. Could it be that Mr. Perfect has a nerdy side? "Yes, exactly like that. I used to draw them when I would take notes back in high school and all through college, too. And I have a couple stuffed ones in my room. I just love them."

"What do you love about them?"

"Well," I say, hopping up to grab another beer from the fridge. "Originally, when I was younger, I just liked the little owl from the Tootsie Pop commercials."

Corbin lets out a loud laugh, "The 'how many licks does it take' owl?"

"Yes," I reply defensively. "He was cute, okay? Anyway, after that I started doing a lot of research on owls, and I just really started to love them the more I learned. I mean, take this for example," I sit back down on the couch with my new beer and take a swig, tucking my legs beneath me. "Did you know that owls have special feathers that make them not make a lot of noise when they fly? They're like certified bird spies."

Corbin laughs again, almost spewing his beer all over me. I laugh, too, realizing how ridiculous I sound. "I know, it's crazy. But they're a really cool animal. Plus they're cute, can't leave that part out."

Corbin puts his beer down on the table and motions for me to come sit on his lap again. As I do, he pulls me in close and nuzzles into my neck. "You're cute."

I smile and plant a kiss on his forehead, pulling him closer to me. My heart aches thinking of not having him here with me, just like this, after next week.

Corbin pulls back and tucks my hair behind my ear, "You know, I actually know a little fact about your bird that I bet you didn't know."

"Pfft, yeah right! Hit me."

"They're farsighted," he says, his eyes deepening. "Yeah, they can see things in the distance very well, especially in the dark. But it's the things that are right in front of their eyes that they can't seem to see clearly." His eyes dart back and forth between mine, and I have a feeling we're not talking about owls anymore.

"Tell me who fucked you over, Paisley."

That same familiar panic washes over me and I feel the beer in my hand shaking a little. I set it down on the table and lift myself off Corbin's lap, pacing in front of him. "I know this shouldn't be that big of a deal, especially after all you've told me about Jack, but," I reach around in my scattered brain for the right words. "I just don't really know if I'm ready to go there yet."

Corbin looks defeated. The concern wrinkles up on his forehead and he looks down, peeling his label again. *Jesus, Paisley, just tell him! Talk to him! Do something!*

This is crazy. This man makes me feel more than I've felt my entire life and I can't even tell him why I ran away from him the first two times we were together? Well, technically the first time was because of the bet. Do I tell him about that? Do I tell him I'm a tag chaser? Well, not really a tag chaser, but that I date military men so I don't get attached?

Holy shit, this is not the conversation that needs to happen right now. I can't tell him that, he would never understand. I can't lose him, not like that.

But I have to tell him something.

I hear the movie playing behind me and my favorite quote leaves Tim Robbins' lips, *"I guess it comes down to a simple choice, really. Get busy living, or get busy dying."* Shit, even the movie is on his side. This is it, Paisley. Open up, give him something, anything.

"It was my dad," I sigh, plopping back down on the couch and pulling a pillow into my lap. I hug it like it's the only thing in the world saving me from myself. "My dad is the one who fucked me over."

Corbin studies me for a moment before taking another drink. He doesn't push, doesn't say "what happened?" He just sits there and waits for me to decide when to talk.

And it's exactly what I need.

He reaches out and grabs my hand in his, the pad of his thumb tracing up and down my wrist. I take another deep breath and try to decide what I could say without telling him everything. At least for now. I want to tell him everything, I want him to know all there is to know about me. I want to know all there is to know about him, just not right now. Not in this moment.

"Long story short, my dad was pretty much everything to me. I'm close to both of my parents, but I was Daddy's girl in every sense of the expression. I grew up thinking my parents had this fairy tale marriage, and from what my mom says, they did. Up until my senior year in college, anyway."

I reach for my beer, anything to keep my hands busy before I rip off every nail I still have, and take a swig before continuing. "My mom caught him cheating on her. And he didn't even apologize. I mean he did, but he didn't beg for forgiveness. He did the exact opposite. He *left* my mom, the woman who loved him for twenty-seven years, for the woman my mom found him in bed with."

I shake my head, still disgusted just thinking about it. It makes me want to call my dad right now and rip into him, but I refuse to give him the satisfaction. I haven't spoken a word to him since the day he sat me down and told me what happened. He's tried calling, tried coming by my apartment, my office. I don't care, I never want to talk to him again.

"I'm so sorry, Paisley," Corbin tugs on my hand a little and I know he wants me to come closer, but the space between us is about the only thing keeping me from freaking out. I bite my lip and will my eyes to suck the tears back in before they spill over and run down my face.

"The way I see it, my dad was the perfect man, and even he screwed up. He took my mom's heart, ripped it from her chest, tore it to tiny little pieces and fed it to some whore he was shacking up with," I take another drink, practically finishing half the beer in one swig. "I knew from that moment on that all the fairy tale bullshit I was fed by Disney and everyone else was nonexistent. I stopped looking for it, got more realistic, and I've been fine. Until now," I look up into Corbin's eyes. "Until you."

Corbin sets his beer down and grabs my face in his hands, brushing my hair from my face. His eyes look different, like a deep ocean blue instead of the usual icy, bright sky blue. "I can't promise I'm your fairy tale ending, Paisley. I'm by no means the perfect man. I'm fucked up in so many ways I couldn't even count them if I tried." My heart aches, I want Corbin to see himself the way I see him. He's so perfect, so beautiful. "But I can promise you that I will never, *ever*, hurt you the way your dad hurt your mom. I will do everything I can to be the man that you want, the man that the seven-year-old you used to dream about. I will bring you flowers, I'll take care of you when you're sick, I'll give you space when you need it and I'll never leave your side when you want someone there. I want to be better than I am because of *you*, Paisley."

He pulls me into a deep kiss, and I feel like my heart has literally melted inside me and is dripping out onto the floor. Like everything I thought I was just vanished, and now I'm this completely new person all because of this man with his lips pressed against mine.

I don't know how I'm going to explain to him what I've done the past four years, or why I ran that first night, or how I'm going to ever be enough of a woman to deserve him, but what I do know is that I don't want to be anywhere else in the world right now except right here, with him, just like this.

As much as I want Corbin to stay, I have to work in five hours and Corbin has another appointment for development on the gym. I'm in the kitchen throwing away the last of the bottles as he gathers up his things, wishing I could just call out tomorrow and run away with him.

"Paisley?" Corbin calls from the living room.

"Yeah?"

"What's this?"

I wipe my hands on the soft green towel hanging from my oven door before returning to the living room. Corbin is standing by the couch holding up Tanner's white NYU hat.

"Oh, that's Tanner's hat. He must have left it here last night."

"Who the hell is Tanner?" Corbin has the exact same look on his face as he did the night he saved me from Creepster. Even from the kitchen I can see his jaw clenching under his cheeks.

Shit.

"He's just a friend, one of my best friends actually. He's visiting from New York. That's who I was with last night." I try to make it sound nonchalant and casual, like it's no big deal, but Corbin doesn't budge.

"You didn't tell me that your 'friend' last night was a guy." Corbin's lips are sealed in a thin line and I can practically see the steam threatening to blow from his ears.

I walk slowly over to him, grab the hat, throw it on the ground, and wrap my arms around him. "I promise, you have nothing to worry about. Tanner is one of my best friends and has been for years, but that is *all* he is." I look up into Corbin's eyes but he won't look back down at me. His gaze is fixed on the wall across the room and he's still tense. "Corbin, please look at me."

He sighs, his chest releasing, and looks down at me. His blue eyes are shameless, showing me how much he cares about me and the possibility that I might have been with another guy. "I'm sorry, Paisley. I don't mean to act like some possessive boy, but I can't help it. I think I've made it pretty clear that I don't want anything, or anyone, taking you away from me."

I smile and lean up to kiss him, "Well then you better keep me *far* away from chocolate." He laughs into my lips and wraps his arms around me. I can't help but feel a little guilty, because technically I did almost kiss Tanner last night. But then again, that might have been me imagining it. I was a mess about my dad's birthday and Tanner's hot, but I seriously doubt he would ever kiss me. Either way, it didn't happen, so it's innocent, right?

"What are you doing this weekend?" He asks, pulling back from our kiss and brushing the hair from my face.

"I don't really have any plans, actually. I'm sure Kenz will want to go out somewhere, but we haven't talked about it yet."

"Do you think she could spare you for one weekend?"

I lift my brow, eying him suspiciously. "What exactly are you going to do with me for a whole weekend, Mr. Ray?"

He smiles devilishly and pulls me in for another kiss. This time, he forces his tongue inside my mouth and thrusts his groin into me. "That is for me to know, and for you to find out agonizingly slowly."

"Hmm," I moan into his lips, sucking his bottom one into my mouth gently. "I think she'll live for one weekend."

"Good," he breathes, kissing down my neck. "I'll need the whole weekend for what I have planned, from Friday when you get off work until Monday when you show back up. So don't make any plans, not even small ones."

"Yes sir," I half say, half moan as I pull him in to deepen our kiss. I don't care about the weekend right now. All I want is him in my bedroom. I slide my hands down his chest and push them down into his sweat pants, making him groan in response.

"Ms. Bronson, if I didn't know any better I'd say you're trying to get me to go for round two."

"If it was up to me, I'd keep you here forever and the round would never end."

He smiles before swiftly lifting me from the floor and carrying me back to my room, my body screaming for him the entire way.

Chapter fourteen
Ditched

"This is so not fair, tell Corbin he totally owes me for sharing you so much," McKenzie whines.

I laugh, "Okay, I'll tell him. I'll be at yoga tomorrow morning though, I promise."

"Yeah yeah, just give me back the best friend that promises me shots of tequila."

I laugh again and then see an email from Lydia pop up in my inbox. "Gotta go, the queen just emailed."

"Oh shit, better not keep her highness waiting. Text me later, skank."

"Well when you put it that way," I tease.

"BYE whore," McKenzie adds for emphasis before ending the call. I shake my head and laugh, relieved that my best friend is so understanding. We had plans to go to happy hour tonight but Corbin wanted to hang out. My time with him is so limited, I didn't have the heart to say no. Luckily, McKenzie wants me to be with someone so bad I'm pretty sure she'd let me light her on fire if it meant I was going on a date with Corbin.

Lydia has been emailing me all morning. She's having one of her frantic days where she decides to go through every open account we have and pick out the tiniest mistakes. And I do mean the tiniest ones. As in, we misspelled a word in our notes that the client will never even see.

I lean back in my chair and sigh, closing my eyes to drown out the computer screen for a minute. What happened to the days when I loved my job? I've always had a passion for creating things, for solving problems and keeping up with trends, but things have definitely changed. Lydia and her nonsense used to not bother me, but now it's all I notice. I used to love working with a new client, now I dread it.

"Ugh," I sit back up in my chair and begin typing out a response to Lydia. When I finish, I notice a text from Tanner.

- You're mine this weekend. -

I laugh, typing my response.

- Haha oh you think so? -
- I know so. At least give me tomorrow night. -
- I wish I could. Corbin has something planned for the weekend, he said it will take the entire time. Rain check for next week? -
- I leave on Sunday... -

Shit, how could I forget that Tanner was only in town for the week?

- Shit, I totally forgot. This kind of just got sprung on me last minute. -
- It's fine, I see how it is. Army boy gets my girl and I go home to New York broken hearted. :'(-

I laugh again, but I can't help the feeling in my stomach when I see that he called me "his" girl. What does that mean? That still means the same thing it meant before that almost-kiss the other night, right? As in, "his" best friend... not "his" *girl*. Right?

- Yeah yeah, back to all those girls more than willing to offer a shoulder to cry on. I'm sure it'll be such torture. ;) -

I'm a little surprised when my phone rings.
"Hello?"

"Okay one, I don't care about those other girls. Two, I'm not leaving without getting to say goodbye to you. So if I can't have you this weekend, I get you tonight. Deal?"

"Um," I fidget, trying to stall. I really want to see Corbin again tonight, but I know Tanner would never forgive me if I didn't hang out with him before he went back to New York. And honestly, I don't know the next time I'll see him. "Yeah," I finally say, "I can hang out tonight."

"Perfect. Let's go to Sticky's."

"Sticky's?!" I whine, sliding down in my chair again. "Why in the world would we go to Sticky's?"

"For old time's sake. And because I know it annoys the shit out of you." I hear Tanner laugh through the phone.

"You are seriously *such* an ass."

"And we've been through this. You love my ass."

I roll my eyes, "I think you love your ass enough for the two of us."

"Damn right, it's a nice ass. Be ready at eight."

"Make that nine, I have to pack."

"Pack? For what?"

"I'm not sure, exactly. Corbin gave me a packing list for this weekend. He said half of it is stuff I'll actually need and the other half is made up to throw me off."

"Oh, such a clever little Army boy," Tanner scoffs.

"ANYWAYS, I have to go. Lydia has been on my ass all morning. I'll see you tonight." I hang up the phone and immediately type out a text to Corbin.

- I have to bail tonight, I'm so sorry. Tanner leaves
this weekend so it's my last chance to see him. –
- I don't like sharing with Tanner. –

I have a feeling Tanner feels the same way.

- You have nothing to worry about, I promise. Just get some
rest for our big weekend together. I'm really excited. :) –
- Ugh, I hate this, but okay. Don't stay out too late.
I need you awake for tomorrow. ;) -
- Yes sir! -
- Oh, I like when you call me sir. –

I blush and bite my lip, tossing my phone in my top drawer so I can focus on work. My head is spinning with the fact that my plans just switched three times in a matter of ten minutes. Last week I spent almost every night alone in my apartment eating ice cream. This week I'm running out of time in the day.

"Paisley," I jump a little in my chair as Lydia pops her head in my office. "Finish whatever you're working on and come to my office. I need your help with a new client."

Oh joy, another client. Too bad none of these clients come with pay raises.

"I'll be right over."

Lydia nods and eyes me suspiciously before stomping toward her office, her brown kitten heels clicking against the floor the entire way. For once, I'm actually excited to go to Sticky's. I'd go just about anywhere if it'd get me away from the ice queen.

"I can't believe I let you talk me into coming here," I scream over the crowd as we inch our way to the bar. Tanner laughs and grabs my hand, pulling me through the sea of drunk college students.

"Don't act like you don't love it," he says when we reach the bar. He's right, I really do love this place, but I feel way too old to be here. Even though I'm only a few years removed from this scene, I much prefer the laid back feeling of going downtown. Maybe it's because I don't have to illegally sneak drinks anymore, or maybe it's because

I actually like to enjoy my drinks instead of feeling like I'm drinking a shot the entire time, but whatever it is – it's not the same at Sticky's anymore.

Except that I'm here with Tanner, which somehow makes it feel familiar all at the same time.

Tanner flags down the bartender, who's all too eager to take his order. She's a very petite brunette with blonde highlights and big brown eyes. When Tanner flashes his smile, she practically jumps across the bar and into his arms. And even though I'm not allowed to be, I'm a little protective.

"What can I get you, sexy?" She bats her lashes and leans over the bar, showing her cleavage even more than the push up bra/skimpy tank top combo she has going on. I roll my eyes, this girl is shameless.

"Let me get two Jack and cokes, and bring two shots of Jack Honey with that, too." Her face falls a little as he signals to me as the other person the drinks are for. I slide my arm around his and lean my head against his shoulder, smiling at her. When she walks away, I release his arm and laugh a little.

"Someone's jealous," Tanner says, calling me out. He lifts his brow and smiles, and I completely see why the little brunette was so easily pulled in. It's a good thing Tanner isn't a killer, he'd be able to get a victim in a creepy van no problem at all.

Damnit Paisley, focus.

"I'm not jealous," I say defensively as the bartender brings us our drinks. "I just enjoy seeing the joy drained from the eyes of young college girls." He shakes his head at me and laughs as he hands me my shot.

"Cheers," I go to take my shot but Tanner stops me.

"Wait, we need a real toast. After all, I probably won't see you again for at least a year." My face falls at that and I feel his words wrench my gut. I don't want him to leave.

"To us, to all the crazy shit we've gotten into over the years and to always having each other to get through the rough stuff," he goes to cheers, but I pull back this time.

"And to looking damn good even though we're old as shit compared to all the fucks in this bar," I clink our glasses together and down my shot before Tanner has the chance to add anything else. He shakes his head and throws his back, handing me my drink and grabbing my free hand to lead us back through the crowd.

"Where are we going?" I whine, sucking down my drink so I can actually handle the fact that I'm back at Sticky's. It's crazy how the place that I used to go practically every night of the week in college can feel so alien now. We pass a couple making out sloppily and another table of girls trying to squeeze in for a selfie. I chuckle, that definitely would have been me and McKenzie.

"We're going to dance, obviously." Tanner turns back to grin devilishly at me. Shit, I really don't want to dance. The last time I danced was when that creep was all up on me. I smile a little, thinking of Corbin, but then remember where Tanner is leading me.

"I'm going to kick your ass," I say, draining the rest of my drink and slamming it down on a table as he tugs me through the last bit of the crowd and onto the dance floor. He immediately pulls me into him and wraps his arms around me, grabbing my hips and making me sway with him. He slides his leg between mine and I feel guilty as shit because I kind of like it.

Okay, I really like it.

The song on is a fast, sexy one. The lyrics are talking about having sex in a club and I feel like that's exactly what we are doing, even though our clothes are still on and we're barely touching. Tanner pulls me in closer and his eyes are intensely fixed on mine. *Shit.*

"Tanner, I need another drink." I'm trying to stall, to get out of this situation before I do something stupid. Tanner pulls back and eyes me suspiciously.

"You're not getting out that easily," he says, grabbing a nearby frat boy by the shoulder. "Hey, I'm an alumni and judging by the way you can still stand, I assume you're a pledge." The boy looks at him like he's bat shit crazy, but Tanner continues. "I need you to do me a favor. Here's twenty bucks, go get two jack and cokes from the bar and you can keep the change." At that, the boy's eyes light up and he's headed to the bar before I have the chance to argue.

"There, problem solved. Now turn around," he growls, grabbing my hips and whipping me around to face the other way. I feel his hips press into my ass and we start swaying again. He moves the hair off the right side of my neck and I can feel his mouth hovering inches from my skin. We used to dance like this all the time, but this time feels different. It doesn't feel like we're doing the friendly, drunk, let's just dance because we're shitfaced kind of dancing. This is definitely different, closer.

Hotter.

The frat boy returns with our drinks and Tanner shoos him away again, handing me my fresh glass. I chug half of it in one gulp, desperately trying to ease the nervousness coursing through me.

"Damn, thirsty?" Tanner laughs, pulling my drink away.

"A little," I shrug. He sets our glasses down on a nearby table and pulls me into him again, causing my breath to grow shallow.

Calm down, Paisley. I wish the almost-kiss would have never happened, I feel like a fucking mess. Nothing strange is happening but yet here I am, overanalyzing everything and acting like a weirdo. Okay, no big deal. It's just me and Tanner out at Sticky's like old times. No reason to freak out.

I take a deep breath and relax a little, reaching for my drink again. I finish the rest and Tanner downs his, giving me an excuse to drag him to the bar. We manage to find two seats at the very corner and we squeeze into them. I'm so thankful to not be dancing I could hug whoever left these chairs vacant.

"Want to get out of here?" Tanner asks before I have the chance to order another drink.

"Absolutely," I say all too quickly. He laughs and I notice again how pretty his eyes are. I'm not sure how I never noticed before.

"Okay, we can go, but on one condition."

"Ugh, I hate your conditions," I groan, signaling to the bartender for a refill. Luckily, this one is a male so I actually get service.

"After we leave, I get one more dance. I get to choose the song and you can't bail until it's all the way over."

I squirm in my chair. It's not that I hate dancing with him, but I do kind of dread it now that my body is betraying my brain and getting hot anytime Tanner touches me.

"Okay, fine. Just get me out of here before I do a keg stand or something." I drink half of my new drink and hand it to Tanner, who downs the rest. When we make it outside to the parking lot my ears are still ringing from the noise.

"So now where to?"

"Where do you think?" he smirks, opening his door and sliding inside.

I'm stumbling a little bit as we walk down the path to our spot. I've got the bottle of Jack we stopped to get on the way in one hand and the other one is holding on tightly to Tanner's. Even though I feel like I haven't had much to drink, my brain feels fuzzy and I've got this goofy grin plastered on my face that I can't erase.

"I can't stay out too late, I promised Corbin I would get some rest for tomorrow," I giggle, hiccupping.

"Chill, I'll get you home before you turn into a pumpkin – I promise."

I punch his arm playfully before removing the top off the bottle of Jack to take a swig. "Easy killer," Tanner says, grabbing the bottle. "I want you to still be conscious for our dance."

I groan and throw a little fit as he lays out the blanket he grabbed from the car. He places the bottle down and pulls out his phone as I kick out of my wedges and fall back onto the blanket, staring up at the stars.

"What are you doing?" he asks, giving me his sideways "I'm amused" smile.

"Come here, come lay down beside me."

He sighs, but does what I say. "Why do we have to grow up, Tanner? Why can't things be as simple as they were when we were in college?"

"Because things are never simple. Looking back, it feels like things were simpler back then, but we had problems then, too. We just know now that they weren't really that big of a deal. But at the time, it felt like they were."

"Like not having anything to wear to a party?" I ask, leaning up on my elbow to look at him.

He laughs, "Exactly. Or in my case, not having a girl to bring home at the end of the night."

"Ass!" I laugh, punching him again.

"You know," he says, leaning up with me. "You've really got to stop talking about my ass so much. People might get the wrong impression." I laugh a little, but the intensity in Tanner's eyes cuts it short. We stay there for a moment before he jumps up, reaching his hand down for mine.

"Okay, no more stalling. Time to dance, and no groaning about it, either."

I bite my tongue and let him pull me up, my body threatening to betray me again. He plays with his phone for a minute before setting it down on the blanket. A few seconds later, a slow rhythm starts playing.

Tanner bows dramatically as he reaches out his hand for mine. I laugh and try my best to do a dramatic curtsey, but I'm a little buzzed so I focus more on not falling. I place my hand in his and he pulls me in close, wrapping his arm around my waist as I place mine around his shoulder. He presses his cheek against mine and starts swaying slowly, humming a little with the song.

My will to fight is broken, these words I left unspoken are burning a hole in my heart.

"Who is this?" I ask, my cheek still pressed against Tanner's.

"Kyle Tyler. He's an indie artist from NYU. He played this song live at a coffee shop about a year ago and ever since then, whenever I hear it, I think of you." He pulls me in a little closer and I start really listening to the lyrics.

I need you like a flower needs a cave, but I can't help it - you're the only thing I crave.

Tanner pulls back and stares into my eyes. I swallow hard, begging my eyes to look away but they're not listening. We stop swaying and Tanner runs his hand across my cheek and back through my hair, pulling me into him. Slowly, carefully, he pulls my lips to his.

And we kiss. Not like a best friend kiss. Not like the drunk kisses we would occasionally have back in college. No, this is a full on, lines crossed, friend boundary gone kiss.

I can't help it, I pull him into me, deepening the kiss. He inhales stiffly and slides his tongue between my lips, massaging mine. His mouth tastes minty and sweet like the honey whiskey we've been drinking. I weave my hands in his hair and he wraps his arms around me, pulling me against him. I can feel his excitement pressed against my stomach and I kiss him harder. I've wondered what this would feel like with him for so long, wondered what it would feel like to have him really kiss me. But now that it's happening, I can only think about one thing.

Corbin.

I pull back, covering my lips with my hand and looking down at my feet. "I'm sorry Tanner, I can't." I glance back up at him and immediately regret it. His chest is moving frantically up and down with his breaths and his eyes are boring into mine, questioning me.

"Paisley, I – "

"Please Tanner, just take me home." I turn and grab my wedges off the ground as I head back toward his car. He doesn't move for a moment, but eventually gathers up the blanket and bottle and follows behind me. As we slide inside his car, I seriously contemplate bashing my head into the window so I can be unconscious for the ride home.

"I'm sorry, Paisley. I didn't mean to upset you," Tanner says, but he sounds more upset than I could ever be. I want to tell him he didn't upset me, that I actually loved feeling his lips on mine, but I can't find the words to explain that even though that's true, I don't want him the way I want Corbin. So I just say nothing and look out the window, letting the silence eat both of us alive the whole way back to my place.

When he parks outside my apartment, I get out of the car before he has the chance to say anything else. I almost run inside to avoid saying goodbye, but the fact that I probably won't see him for a long time threatens to drown me. I turn back toward his car and lean inside his window.

"I'm sorry, Tanner. You didn't upset me. The fact is, I loved what happened tonight." Tanner's eyes light up. He reaches for my hand and I let him hold it, and for a moment it feels like he holds my entire heart in that hand of his.

"Then why did you run?"

My heart aches. I wish I would have just walked inside, but that's the old Paisley. I'm done with running, I want to start facing the shit that scares me.

"Because that's not us, Tanner. You're my best friend, and I never want to lose that, but that's where it stops with us."

He drops my hand and grips the steering wheel, "This is about Army boy, isn't it?"

I don't know what to say, so I just nod. Tanner sighs and shakes his head, starting the car. "It's okay, I get it. You better get inside and get some sleep for your big weekend."

"Tanner please, I don't want you to leave with us like this."

"Like what?" he asks, his beautiful eyes locking onto mine. I bite my lip, tears welling up in my eyes. Tanner turns away from me, "Goodnight, Paisley." I stand back as he squeals off, leaving me alone in the parking lot. As I cross my arms and slowly walk to my apartment, the tears slide down my cheeks. Why do I have the feeling I just lost my best friend?

Because I did.

Chapter fifteen

The Playlist

"I told you to get some rest," Corbin laughs, brushing the hair from my face to reveal the zombie eyes I've had all day. Even though Tanner dropped me off at two, I couldn't fall asleep to save my life. I kept thinking of our dance, our kiss, and the miserable look in his eyes when he drove away. Sleep wasn't going to happen and I knew it.

"I know, I'm sorry. I just need some coffee and I'll be good to go, I promise." I try to sound convincing, but I don't think Corbin is fooled. He just smiles his sideways smile and moves his hand from resting on top of the gear shift to resting on my thigh. My skin immediately buzzes to life and I shiver, making him smile a little broader.

"Don't worry about it. Actually, this works out better. It's going to be a long car ride. You should sleep."

"I don't want to miss the whole trip," I whine. "And where are you taking me? Can you tell me now?"

Corbin shakes his head, lacing his fingers with mine and bringing my hand to his lips for a soft kiss. "Not yet. Seriously, get some sleep. I won't let you sleep the whole time but you look exhausted and we still have a long night ahead."

I smile and nod, knowing he's probably right and I should take advantage of the time to sleep. I always used to sleep in the car when I was little, which is probably a huge reason why I want to fall asleep anytime I drive for more than two hours. I grab my phone and check the time. Four fifteen and still no word from Tanner. I tried texting him this morning and again after lunch, but no response. I type out a quick text to him before setting an alarm on my phone for seven so I don't sleep too long.

- Corbin picked me up from work early and we're heading out now. I still don't know where we're going, but I'll let you know as soon as I do. -

I hit send, but immediately realize how stupid it is to be texting him about Corbin. I want to be open and honest with him, but part of me knows it's probably killing him to read that text.

- Tanner, please answer me. I really am sorry for last night. I don't want to lose you. You mean more to me than anyone else in the world and I don't know what I'll do if you leave to go back to New York with us like this. -

I wait a few more minutes for a response, but when nothing comes in I sigh and toss my phone in the cup holder. I wait for a red light to lean over and give Corbin a slow kiss, taking my time and running my fingers through his hair.

"How am I supposed to focus on driving with you doing that?" He mumbles into my lips. I smile and shrug, falling back into my seat.

"That's nothing. You don't want to try to drive with what I really want to do to you."

Corbin's eyes get wide and I wink before leaning my seat back and closing my eyes, willing the fatigue from last night to sweep over me.

Relax, Paisley. Forget about Tanner and focus on your weekend with Corbin. I don't want to fight with Tanner, and I definitely don't want to lose him, but there's nothing I want more than to be with Corbin right now. Riding shot gun in his truck heading God knows where, I feel happier – safer – than I have in years. At that, I find Corbin's hand and kiss it one last time before my exhaustion takes hold. Before I can wipe the stupid smile from my face, I'm out.

I hear Corbin's voice in my dream, but I can't make out what he's saying. Slowly, I come to and realize he's on the phone. He's speaking softly, probably to try not to wake me. I leave my eyes closed and listen, my curiosity piqued.

"I bet you do… Yeah… No, I would love that… Of course." I strain my ears to hear over the music. That stupid feeling in my gut tugs at my heart. Is this Rachel?

"Okay, well I have to go. I'm actually with a friend right now and we're about to go out. I'll call you later. Okay. You too, bye."

My heart feels like it's about to beat out of my chest. It's thumping hard against my rib cage and I'm half convinced there's no way Corbin can't hear it, too. *What the fuck was that?* Why did he just lie and say he was going "out" with a "friend?"

Then it hits me.

He probably knows I'm not sleeping. Or even if he doesn't know for sure, he doesn't want to chance it. Maybe he's just trying to keep it a surprise wherever he's taking me.

Jesus, Paisley. You always assume the worst.

I roll over onto my side and tuck my legs up, feeling ashamed even though Corbin has no idea the freak out I just had internally. I focus on returning my breathing and heart rate to normal, reminding myself that I'm about to have an amazing weekend with a guy who was sweet enough to plan a surprise and keep it that way. Before Corbin, the sweetest thing a guy had ever done for me was bring me flowers and make me dinner. At this point, Corbin has already secured a spot in the date hall of fame.

My breathing finally slows, my heart rate steadies, and soon I'm drifting off – back into a blissful sleep.

"Paisley," Corbin gently shakes me, his hand on the inside of my left thigh. My body immediately reacts, waking me with a delicious electric shock. "Wake up, beautiful."

My eyes flutter open and I realize by the darkness in the sky that I drastically overslept my alarm. "Oh my God, what time is it?!"

Corbin smiles, "Relax, it's 11:30. But the night is just beginning, so it's a good thing you slept."

"11:30?! I set an alarm for 7:00!" I try to lean my seat up, but Corbin stops me.

"It's fine, Paisley. Really, I swear. You didn't miss anything but the drive."

"We've been driving for that long?"

He nods, leaning over to gently place his lips against mine. I breathe him in, his earthy scent surrounding me. His kiss is practically restraining me, keeping me fixed in my seat with my hands by my side, unable to move even to touch him.

"I'm going to need you to put this on," he says, pulling out a sleeping mask. It's satin and bright red. It reminds me of my mom's, which makes me laugh a little.

"What happened to the blindfold?" I tease, referring to our baking date.

"Oh don't worry, I've got plans for it later." Corbin's eyes blaze in the darkness of the car and I swallow hard, my thoughts completely blurred. He smirks, "Put on the mask."

"Okay... what are you up to, Mr. Ray?" I scrutinize him before lifting the mask and securely fastening it around my head. It's completely black with the mask covering my eyes, but I hear Corbin get out of the truck and then open my door shortly after. He grabs my hand and guides me up before grabbing something from the backseat and closing the door.

"Do you trust me?" He asks, that same simple question he asked last time he had me blindfolded. Last time, I had temporarily freaked out, overanalyzing if I trusted him. This time, I don't even hesitate.

"Of course."

Even though I can't see him, I swear I can feel him smile. "Come on, it's a tricky path but I promise I won't let you fall."

He tugs on my hand and we slowly walk, our hands swaying gently at times and him carefully guiding me at others. After a few minutes, he stops me.

"Take your shoes off."

I slide my sandals off and bend down to feel for them, grabbing them both in my left hand. We walk a little further and now my mind is racing as I analyze the feel of the surface beneath my feet. First concrete, then rough, scratchy wood, and finally – sand. The sand is chilly and feels powdery and light. I hear small waves caressing the shore and I know we must be at a beach. The question is, what beach are we at that it took him so long to drive me here?

We stop again, and this time Corbin takes the sandals and drops them before taking both my hands in his. "I knew that this would be our only chance to spend a weekend together for a very long time, and I knew that for that reason – it had to be special." Corbin gently runs his thumbs along the back of my hands, sending his current through me. "There's a place I've always wanted to go, ever since I was young. Jack and I used to talk about coming here and all the things we would do. It's been on my bucket list ever since, and after he passed, I vowed that I would only come when I found someone special enough to share it with. I didn't know if that would be a friend, a coworker, or hell, even a dog, but I knew I wanted them to be as special to me as Jack was."

I bite my lip as he continues, tears threatening to soak the mask wrapped around my eyes. "One thing is for sure, I never expected it to be a girl. I never expected to go from being the way I was, perfectly lonely, to wanting someone – no, needing someone – more than anything else in my life. But then I met you, and every rule I had, every truth I thought I knew, was completely shattered. All I know now is there is no one else I would rather share this with, and I can't wait to spend an entire weekend with you."

Corbin releases my hands and slowly lifts the mask off my eyes. I blink a few times, trying to clear my vision and take in the scene.

We're the only two people on a stretch of beach. I look to my right and see a small boardwalk, which explains the wood I felt under my feet. The water is a deep blue and the moon is brilliantly bright, casting a beautiful glow on the sand that's reflected in Corbin's crystal eyes.

"Do you know where we are?"

I shake my head, trying to narrow down the beaches that would take such a long drive. "Are we in North Carolina?"

He laughs and shakes his head, "Far from it. We're in Key West."

I smile what I'm sure is the biggest smile I've had in years and throw my arms around him, "Key West?! I've always wanted to come here!"

"You mean you've never been?" Corbin asks, pulling back but still holding me firmly in his arms.

I shake my head, "No, but I've wanted to come forever, like since I was a little girl. I can't believe you brought me here. I can't believe we're in Key West!"

Corbin smiles his full wattage smile, his gorgeous teeth blazing in the moonlight. He swoops me up in his arms and kisses me hard, weaving his fingers in my hair and pulling me into him. I slide my tongue between his lips and deepen our kiss, dragging my nails along his lower back.

"Mmm," he groans, breaking our contact. "Okay, before you distract me with your temptress kisses, there's one other thing I have to show you." He pulls his phone from his pocket and begins thumbing through it. After a moment, he holds it up near my chest, "May I?"

I tilt my head, confused. "May you what?"

Slowly, *devastatingly* slowly, Corbin slides the phone between my breasts and nestles it in my cleavage. Every time his finger grazes the bare skin above the hem of my tank top my entire body lights on fire.

"Sorry," he shrugs. "I'm going to need my hands." I bite my lip, my mind racing to all the places I would love him to put his hands.

"I originally made this playlist for you to hear on our way down, but someone didn't listen to me when I told her to get some sleep last night, so that plan changed." He smiles a cocky smile and I stick my tongue out in rebuttal. "But, it's actually better this way, because now I can make you dance with me."

My mind flashes back to last night with Tanner. How strange to think less than twenty-four hours ago I was dancing by our lake with him. Now, I'm by the ocean about to dance with Corbin. I shake Tanner from my head and focus on Corbin.

"I made this playlist when I got home from your place the other night. I couldn't get your adorable face out of my mind," he laughs softly, running the pad of this thumb across my cheek. "So I started listening to music. I know you never know the songs I play for you, but I hope that when you hear these songs, you'll think of me. Because I know that they're forever seared in my brain with your name written all over them."

He runs his thumb across my temple and slides his hand back through my hair. Then, he blazes a trail with his forefinger along my jaw bone, down my neck, across my collar bone, and he slowly pulls it down between my breasts, sending little bumps exploding all over my body. When he reaches the phone, he taps the play button and immediately the soft waves are accompanied by the crooning of a slow country song. Corbin pulls my hands up behind his neck and gently trails his fingers down my arms, my sides, and eventually rests them on my hips, pulling me in close.

As we sway to each new song that comes on, I completely lose all sense of time. Corbin's eyes capture me, keeping me transfixed on the uncontrollable sensations flowing through my body with each touch he gives me. When he leans in for a soft kiss, the hair on every inch of my body stands on end. When he gently grips my hips, the heat explodes between my legs. I'm so entranced I don't even realize when the music stops playing.

"So, what do you think of our playlist?" He asks, planting small kisses on my lips.

"I think you'll have to send me a copy because I didn't hear a word they said." Corbin pulls back, confused. "Corbin, I can't focus on anything when you're touching me, except maybe on how much I want you to touch me again."

"Oh," he says, his head falling a bit. Oh shit, did I upset him? I'm about to open my mouth to try to plead insanity when he continues, "Well then, I guess we'll just have to get you to our room so I can show you what I was saving the blindfold for." He runs his tongue along his bottom lip and I instantly need new panties.

Lord help me.

Chapter sixteen
Roses are Red

We check into a third story suite in a quaint condo-style hotel that sits on the water near the top of the key. When we walk in, there is a kitchen to our left and a dining/living area that spreads out in front of us. Just beyond the couch is a large sliding glass door that reveals a porch equipped with a table and chairs. To the right across from the kitchen are stairs that I assume lead up to our bedroom. The entire suite is painted white with a light turquoise band around the top. Beach pictures are hung on every wall, along with specks of shells and jars of sand that are intermingled here and there.

"This is so pretty," I breathe, the reality that I'm in Key West with an insanely attractive man washing over me.

Corbin grabs our bags, "I'm going to take these upstairs. Just relax, I'll be right back." He kisses me softly before turning and heading up the stairs. I try to make my feet move, but I'm not successful until he's all the way up and around the corner. I'm convinced I could watch that man's ass walk up a flight of stairs for my entire life.

I wander around the room, checking out the kitchen first. The fridge is fully stocked with fresh fruit, vegetables, meat, drinks, and condiments. I find myself wondering if it comes that way or if Corbin arranged it. I grab a handful of red grapes and pop one in my mouth as I venture into the living area. There is a large couch and a love seat, both a pale, sky blue. A small glass coffee table rests in front of them and there's a large flat screen TV mounted on the wall with shelves lining beneath it. I toss another grape in my mouth before sliding the glass door open and stepping out onto the balcony.

There's a soft breeze blowing in off the water, whisking through the trees that surround the balcony and blowing my hair off my neck. I inhale deep, taking in the salty smell of this small piece of paradise. Closing my eyes, my mind flashes back to the dream I had about me and Corbin on our private exotic beach. Maybe dreams really do come true.

"You're so beautiful," Corbin says softly, sliding up behind me and wrapping his arms around my waist. He rests his chin on my shoulder as we both stare out at the moonlight reflecting off the water. I turn to face him, holding up my last grape.

"The fridge is stocked, I helped myself to some grapes. Want one?"

Corbin nods and opens his mouth, challenging me with his eyes. I instantly feel his intoxicating current roar through me as I place the grape between his lips. He pulls it in with his tongue and gently nips at my fingers. I suddenly feel weak, my body leaning toward him, yearning for him to touch me.

"Turn around," Corbin whispers, pulling the blindfold from his left pocket.

I start to tremble slightly as I turn back to face the water. Corbin slowly fastens the blindfold around my eyes, "Is that too tight?"

I shake my head, words completely lost to me at this point. Suddenly, he lifts me up and tosses me over his shoulder. I laugh, feel around for his ass, and smack it playfully. "I can walk, you know."

"Maybe, but you better save your energy for what's coming." Corbin doesn't return my laugh and his voice is husky, dark. I can imagine the hungry look in his eyes that always comes before he devours me. I shiver.

I feel him walk me through the door and up the stairs before he gently lays me down on what feels like the softest bed ever. The goose down comforter is icy against my hot skin and sends chills racing all the way down to my toes.

"Get undressed," he commands. He's no longer touching me and I have no idea where he is in the room. I suddenly feel very naked and all my clothes are still in tact. I slowly strip off my shorts and lift my tank top over my head before falling back onto the bed.

"All the way undressed." Corbin's voice is tantalizing. I want to rip off the blindfold and throw him down on the bed, but the other half of me is aching to know what's coming next. I lean up and unclasp my bra, freeing my breasts. Slowly, I run my hands down my ribcage, stomach, and hook my thumbs in the lace of my panties, sliding them off and flinging them to the side. I hear Corbin growl from somewhere in the room, "Fuck, Paisley. I could stare at you all night."

"Come put your hands on me," I plead, arching my back.

"Ah, not so fast," he says, but I feel him join me on the bed. I reach my hand out and frown, feeling his jeans.

"No fair, these need to come off."

"In due time, Ms. Bronson. Now," he grabs my wrists and pulls both of my hands above my head. "Keep your hands here, no matter what. If you move them, my clothes stay on. Deal?"

I nod, the breath hitched in my throat. Suddenly, I feel a soft, velvet like fabric touching my cheek.

"Can you tell what I'm touching you with?"

I try to identify the fabric as he plays with it on my cheeks, my lips. "It feels like a flower."

"It's a rose. I picked this one very specifically because it reminds me of you." He runs the petals across my lips and then trails a line down my neck, across my chest, and draws a heart on my stomach. "Because it's soft, and beautiful, just like you."

I feel the softness disappear and suddenly the rose scratches me between my thighs, "but it's also painful sometimes, much like you." The scratches don't hurt, but they bring my skin to life. The wetness pools between my legs and my left hand jerks forward instinctively to touch him.

"Ah, ah, ah! What was our agreement, Ms. Bronson?" Corbin

teases, placing my wrist back above my head as he goes back to sliding the petals up and down my stomach.

"This is torture," I moan, arching toward him. I know he's smiling right now, loving every minute of this. The rose glides up my side and circles around my left nipple, sending tiny bolts of electricity through me each time it touches.

I don't think I'll ever look at another bouquet of flowers the same way again.

Finally, Corbin pulls the rose down my body, toward the place I'm aching for him to touch. He stops just above and runs the rose across from my left hip bone to my right one, making me squirm for him to take it just a little lower. Just when I think I can't take anymore, the rose is gone and instantly replaced by Corbin's tongue, blazing a fire between my legs.

I try to bite my lip and control my breathing, but tiny moans keep escaping my lips with every lash of his tongue. He slowly slides a finger inside and I arch toward him, swiveling my hips.

"You make the sexiest sounds," he breathes, planting hot kisses on my inner thighs as his fingers work. My body tenses and I know I'm about to fall apart at his touch, but then he stops. I rip the blindfold off, panting.

"Why did you stop?" My legs are still trembling, but when my eyes adjust to the darkness I see Corbin's naked body caressed in the moonlight streaming in from the window. He's standing above me, the hardness of his body towering over me like a Greek god as his dark stare sears through the air between us, lighting my insides on fire.

And it is by far the sexiest, most enticing thing I've ever seen.

I lean up to grab his neck and pull him down on top of me, crushing my lips to his. Our hands run feverishly over each other, as if we've never felt another human being before. And I haven't, not like this anyway. I've never wanted anyone the way I want Corbin. I swear it's like he's the most addicting drug known to man and I'm his biggest fiend. I run my fingertips down the dip in his back, feel his hard on pressed between my legs, right against where I'm aching for him to push inside. I bite his lower lip and he growls in response, flipping me over to rest on top of him.

I lean up and look down at him as his eyes skate over my body. "You are so fucking gorgeous," he growls again, leaning up to suck my left breast into his mouth. I throw my head back, rubbing against him. I want him inside me so bad, but I want to give him the same torturous pleasure he gave me. I find the rose and drag it down his torso, tracing each ab along the way. Tiny goose bumps explode all over him as I get lower. When I'm just above, I do the same tease he did with me and drag the rose from hip to hip. He smiles his full watt smile, his teeth blazing in the soft light of the room.

"Are you giving me a taste of my own medicine, Ms. Bronson?"

"You could say that," I tease, biting my lower lip. I fling the rose to the side and slide my body down his so that my head is resting just above his hips. I look up the length of his body, admiring every inch. *Good Lord, this man is blessed.*

Corbin's eyes are wide and I give him a devilish grin before pulling him in my mouth. He instantly groans, his body tensing. "Oh my God, Paisley."

I keep my eyes locked on his as I pull him in and out of my mouth, rolling my tongue along his length. Corbin moans and tosses his head back, his eyes closing. I know he's ready, but I don't want it to end yet. I slide my tongue up his abs, bite softly at his chest, and climb back on top, sliding down on him as he crushes his mouth on mine.

He's pushing into me harder, faster. I can't control it any longer. I throw my head back and cry out as the electricity tears through me like never before. Corbin tenses and I feel him release, both of our bodies shaking and moving together in a steady rhythm as we come apart at the seams. I fall back onto the bed and my hair covers half of my face as I try to catch my breath.

"That. Was."

"Yeah." Corbin finishes for me, pulling me onto his chest. "It was." My body is still aching, pulsing from his touches as he glides his fingertips softly up and down my arm. He kisses my forehead and brushes the hair from my face, "You're incredible."

"Ditto," I laugh, leaning up to face him. He smiles, melting my heart with those damn dimples, before pulling me in for another long, slow kiss.

"Welcome to Key West," he smiles into my lips, speaking between kisses.

"I never want to leave."

Chapter seventeen
The Perfect Day

I'm laying on my side, my head propped on one hand as I watch Corbin dress in the soft sunlight streaming through the room. I'm still sedated from him waking me up the same way we fell asleep last night. I don't think I could ever get tired of this man's touch.

"I'm going to go make us breakfast," he smiles, sitting down on the edge of the bed. I lean up and kiss him slowly, willing him not to leave. He shakes his head and laughs softly against my kisses, "Don't tempt me to stay in bed with you all day."

"I think that sounds like the perfect day," I giggle, planting small kisses down his shoulder.

"As much as I agree with you, we have plans. So I'm going to go make breakfast," he stands up and grabs my phone from the bedside table. "And you're going to call your mom, get dressed, and join me downstairs in thirty minutes."

"Why do I need to call my mom?" I ask, confused.

"Because she's called twice already this morning. And because she's your mom, silly."

"Ugh, she probably just wants to know if I've called my dad yet. I swear she's never going to give it up."

Corbin's eyes soften and he sits back down on the bed, putting his hands on either side of my face. "Don't think about that, about him. Not today. Today's about us." I smile softly and nod as he pulls me in and plants a kiss on my forehead before standing up and heading downstairs.

I check my missed calls and sure enough, two from Mom. I don't expect anything, but I check for texts from Tanner just in case.

Nothing.

There is one from McKenzie, though.

- Okay, I'm dying here. Where did Mr. Perfect take you?!
Call me ASAP, slut. -

I laugh, only McKenzie. I dial her number and fall back on the bed, pulling the cool, feathery covers up and around me.

"Oh my God I was seriously about to lose my shit. I can't believe you didn't call me last night!" McKenzie screams into the phone.

"Well good morning to you, too. And I didn't exactly have time last night."

McKenzie gasps, "You little whore! Tell me where you are!"

I laugh, "We're in Key West."

"KEY WEST?!"

I lean up in excitement, pulling the covers with me. "Yes! Kenz, he was so freaking sweet about it. He took me to the beach first, that's when he told me where we were. Then we came back to our suite and it's GORGEOUS. It's seriously the sweetest thing any guy has ever done for me."

"Um, I think it's the sweetest thing any guy has ever done ever, period. I'm so happy for you!"

"Thanks, girl. I wish you and Derek were here, too."

"Oh please, you don't wish we were there and you know it," she teases.

"Okay fine, but I miss you. I have to go, he's making us breakfast."

"HE'S MAKING YOU BREAKFAST?! Ugh, I'm just going to go kill myself now."

"BYE, Kenz," I laugh. I hit end and immediately dial Mom.

"Hi, sweetie," Mom's voice rings over the line. She's always had the most comforting voice.

"Hey, Mom. Sorry I haven't called, I've been really busy."

"Oh it's okay, I was just getting worried about you. How was the rest of your night with Tanner?"

"Fine. Hey Mom?"

"Yes, sweetie?"

I hesitate, reaching for the right words. "When you and Dad met, when did you know you loved him? I mean, how long did it take you to realize you wanted to be with him?"

"Oh, I absolutely hated your father at first," Mom laughs. "He was such an arrogant asshole!"

I gasp, "Mom! I don't think I've ever heard you curse!"

"Well, he was!" she laughs again. "But he was a persistent asshole. He kept popping up, no matter how hard I tried to avoid him. Eventually I just stopped fighting it and started enjoying his company. It didn't take me long after that before I knew that I loved him. Why are you asking me this? Is this about Tanner?"

I sigh, "Not exactly."

"Is there someone else? Is this another one of your military men?"

"Yes, but it's complicated. I didn't know he was in the Army when I met him, and for a little over a week now we've been getting close. He cares about me, Mom. And he gets me to tell him things that it took me forever to tell other people. I don't know what it is, but he makes me want to knock down all the walls I've put up and let him inside. And it scares the shit out of me."

"Oh honey, don't be scared of falling. Falling for someone is the fun part. Yes, you can get your heart broken, but don't focus on that right now. You're young, smart, beautiful – and you deserve to just have a little fun."

"But that's the thing," I pull my legs up and tuck them under me, trying to speak softly into the receiver. "I don't think this is just a little fun anymore. At first I did, but it's different with this guy. He's supposed to leave at the end of the week for deployment, and for the first time I'm actually sad about it. I'm dreading it, actually. I don't want him to leave. I think I really like this guy."

"Well, let yourself like him, then." My mom laughs a little before continuing, "I know you're scared to have something end the way it did with me and your father, but I wouldn't change anything about the love we had. We may not have lasted, but before your dad broke my heart, he filled it with happiness and joy that it had never experienced before. Sometimes you have to walk out on a limb, knowing you could fall thirty feet to the hard ground, just to see if that apple on the edge is worth the risk like you think it is."

"And what if it's not?"

"Then you get up, dust yourself off, and keep walking til you find the next tree."

I smile, loving my mom for knowing exactly what to say when I need to hear it. "Thanks, Mom. I love you."

"I love you too, honey. Now go be young and have fun and stop worrying so much. You're going to have gray hair at thirty if you keep this up."

"Yes ma'am," I laugh, ending the call and falling back onto the bed to look up at the ceiling. Maybe Mom is right. Maybe there really is something worth risking the hurt for. Maybe, just maybe, it's not about playing safe.

A knot forms in my stomach as reality crashes in on me. I care about Corbin, and if I care about him, I have to tell him about the bet. I sigh, covering my face with a pillow. Corbin's earthy scent fills my senses as I breathe in. Even the pillow can't shake this man.

Tonight is the night I tell him. Tonight, I jump over the last wall separating us and take the full leap. It might hurt like hell, but I know more than I've known anything else in my life that he is worth that risk.

I stretch out on the front of the boat, letting the setting sun soak into my pores. There's a gentle breeze rolling in off the water as we cruise slowly. The boat has about twenty onboard, but Corbin and I are the only ones snuggled up on the front. His back is pressed against a pole and I'm leaning with my back against his chest, both of us looking out at the water and sipping the frozen drinks prepared by the boat crew.

Everything is pretty perfect in this moment.

"What was your favorite part today?" Corbin asks, kissing the side of my neck. He pulls me in a little closer and the pad of his thumb traces secret words on the skin just above my bikini line.

"I don't know if I can choose," I reply, taking another sip of my piña colada. After he made me a full breakfast buffet complete with omelets, fresh fruit, and hand squeezed orange juice, he surprised me with an all day water adventure. We've been on the boat all day and have done everything from scuba diving to parasailing. "I think this is my favorite part. This moment right now."

I turn to face him, the setting sun cascading over his smoothly tanned skin. His eyes are illuminated by the soft orange glow and I don't think I've ever seen him look more beautiful than he does right now. He smiles a sideways smile before running his finger gently down the side of my face.

"I'm so happy I went to that stupid bar that night." His eyes dance between mine before he pulls me in for a soft, deliciously slow kiss. He takes his time pressing his lips to mine, nipping at my bottom lip and running his fingers through my hair. My heart beats fast in my chest. How does he still have such an effect on me? Will I ever be able to breathe when he touches me?

He pulls me back against him and nuzzles his nose into my hair. "The day's not over yet, you know."

"There's more?"

"Of course, there's more. First, we're going to watch this sunset. Then, when we get back to shore, you're going to change into a dress and we're going to do something better than sex." Corbin bites my neck softly and tiny electric bolts shoot down my body to below my bathing suit bottom.

"I don't think there's anything better than sex with you," I breathe, pleading with my heart to not beat right out of my chest.

We sit there silently sipping our drinks, sharing a kiss here and a touch there. His arm never leaves my waist and his finger tips are still lazily drawing on my skin. It feels like I've known this man my entire life, like he was made for me, for this moment. It's as if every shitty thing in my life is completely gone and the only thing left for the rest of my time on earth is moments like this with him.

My gut twists at the thought of telling him about the bet, about my past. I know that I have to tell him, but everything in me feels it's not the right time. What other choice do I have? If I keep waiting, it'll only hurt more when I tell him. At least right now, I feel like he would understand. I think he sees how I feel about him and that things are different. Hell, we might even laugh about it. With him leaving in a week, I know I can't risk the chance of telling him last minute. Besides, I want him to know the truth. I want him to see how different I am with him, how much he's opened me up.

I just don't want to lose him in the process.

As the sun starts to dip below the water line, the sky breaks out into a watercolor portrait of pinks and oranges. "It's so beautiful," I say, breathing in the colors.

"Yeah, it is." I turn to look at Corbin, but he's not looking at the sunset. His eyes are locked on mine and I'm one hundred percent positive I've never been looked at the way he's looking at me right now. "I always thought I would see this place with Jack. I thought we would get rowdy on Duval Street, go fishing on a boat, get into all kinds of trouble." I see the ghosts come back into his eyes, making me want to pull him in and shield him from the memories. "But being here with you, watching this sunset, it feels like there's nothing and no one that could make this more perfect. I want to watch a million sunsets with you. I want to watch so many that I can close my eyes and see the way the sun looks in your hair. I am so incredibly happy right now, and I haven't been happy in years."

My eyes are welling with tears as I pull him in and kiss him, the last of the sun sinking away to leave us alone together in our perfect moment.

"I can't believe you bought me a dress," I tell Corbin. I'm sitting in his passenger seat as he drives, his hand resting on my thigh just below the hem of the sequined black dress he surprised me with just a short hour ago. It's such a simple gesture, his hand resting there, but my body aches for him to slide his hand up higher and relieve me of all the tension that's been building all day.

"I can't believe how amazing you look in it," he lifts one brow as he looks over at me, giving me that sexy half smile. "I'm going to have to really kick someone's ass tonight, I can feel it."

I laugh and swat his arm, "Don't get us thrown out of Key West, Mr. Ray."

"No promises," he says, still smiling. I take in his classic look – his amazing smile, those fiery eyes, and the all black outfit he's put together, complete with a black blazer that hangs open just the right way. He's driving me absolutely wild and all he's doing is driving. It's like he's a Calvin Klein model, which makes me really want to get him to pose for those underwear shots.

We pull into a parking spot on the side of a small road and all I see are little shops that have closed their doors for the day. "Are you taking me shopping? Because that's not better than sex with you," I tease. "I mean it's close, but still not better."

Corbin laughs, "No, not shopping. You're not exactly the patient type, are you?" He jumps out of the truck and opens my door for me, helping me slide out. As soon as my heels hit the pavement, he wraps me in his arms and pulls me into him, his eyes searching mine. "God, you are so beautiful." He lifts my chin and pulls my mouth to his. As people walk by us I hear the girls swoon, "How sweet!" "He's hot." "I want to be kissed like that."

I pull back and smile, "We better get going wherever you're supposed to be taking me before I push you back in the truck and make you take me home, instead."

Corbin's eyes smolder and his grin widens into his full watt smile, "Tempting, Ms. Bronson. Very tempting."

He kisses me again softly before grabbing a long black box from his pocket. "I got something for you." When he opens the box, a tiny gasp escapes my mouth. Inside is a beautiful white gold necklace with an owl pendant glittering with small gemstones.

"Corbin, it's beautiful!"

He smiles, "I just thought it might be a good reminder that I want to know everything about you, even the things you think are nerdy." He pulls the chain from the box and fastens it around my neck before pulling me in for another kiss. I try to deepen the kiss, wanting to strip myself bare for him right there, but he pulls back. "Come on, we can't waste that dress."

He grabs my hand and we walk a few blocks, his thumb gently rubbing the inside of my hand, before he suddenly stops, "We're here."

I look around. We're standing at an intersection, a very quiet one for Key West. There are a few small shops that are closed, and it seems like the street a few blocks down is the busy one. A man covered in lights and riding a bike just as decked out as he is rides past us, music blasting from his boom box. The few people that were on the street start to follow him as he rides past.

"I'm confused, what are we doing exactly?"

Corbin motions across the street to a small building, and I notice the sign on the door.

Better Than Sex

A Dessert Restaurant

I turn and smile at Corbin, "Wow, it really is better than sex."

"So they say," he returns my smile, but his eyes are challenging. "But I'll let you be the judge of that."

I swallow hard as he grabs my hand again and we walk across the street. When we slide inside the small restaurant, a friendly gentleman welcomes us.

"Good evening, and welcome to Better Than Sex. Do you have a reservation?"

"Yes, two for Corbin Ray," Corbin pulls me in closer, as if he wants everyone in the small establishment to know I'm his.

And I fucking love it.

"Ah yes, we'll seat you in just a moment, Mr. Ray." He hands us each a light up menu, which is absolutely necessary seeing as how the entire place is dark with just a few golden lights radiating among the many shades of red that cascade the room. "Please feel free to browse our menu while we get your table ready."

Corbin takes the menus, but when we sit in the corner of the small seating area, we barely even look at them. He plays with the hem of my dress absent mindedly as he stares into my eyes, the flickering candle in the corner illuminating his desire. I turn my head to break his spell for a minute so I don't explode right here when I see a strange object near where the host is standing.

"Corbin, is that a penis?" I point to a long, brown, penis shaped statue sitting next to a small vase of flowers on the table.

Corbin laughs softly, "I do believe it is, Ms. Bronson."

As I look around, I notice all the photos hung are sexy shots of men and women together. Some are just of naked women, some of kissing, some of playful silhouettes under the sheets. "This is kind of turning me on," I laugh, turning back to Corbin.

"Just wait til you taste the chocolate," the host interrupts, winking at me. "We're ready for you now."

Corbin and I laugh as I turn as crimson as the walls. The host guides us a to a small corner table in the back of the restaurant. I notice as we walk that there can't be more than fifteen tables total in the entire place. As Corbin and I take our seats across from each other, the host places our menus back in front of us. "I'm sure you'll need a little more time to look this over," he winks again. "Your server will be right with you."

When he walks away, Corbin tries and fails to stifle his laughter, "Busted."

I kick him playfully under the table, "You're such a jerk! That was so embarrassing."

He smiles, his eyes dancing in the candlelight. "I thought it was adorable." He grabs my hand from across the table and pulls it to his lips, softly kissing my skin. "And personally, I'm glad you're getting turned on."

I bite my lip, looking back at my menu. *How the hell am I supposed to make it through dessert like this?*

Corbin orders us our drinks first, two "Caramel Over Me's," which turns out to be a glass of white moscato dipped in delicious caramel that slowly drips into the wine and down the side of the glass. As we drink, a small drop beads down onto Corbin's finger. I take his hand in mine and slowly lick it off, trying my best to be sexy but not sure if I'm failing miserably or not.

His eyes take on a new hunger, "You're trying to kill me, aren't you? First the dress, then biting your lip, and now this."

"Hm, guess you'll have to punish me later," I tease, wiping a small drop of caramel from the corner of my mouth.

"Just remember you said it." Corbin smiles devilishly and takes another sip of his wine. His gaze lights my skin on fire and I'm pretty sure my panties have already melted, or disintegrated into a burst of flames.

We each order a dessert, which turns out to be too much because they're both huge. We share, nibbling off each of the plates and taking sips between bites. There are sexual playing cards on the table, so we take turns reading off questions and answering them, which only gets us even more amped up. By the time I take my last sip from my second glass of wine, I'm so ready to go back to the suite I can barely stand it.

"So, are you taking me back to the room now?" I smile, biting my lip again.

Corbin laughs softly, looking down as he signs the receipt. "Not just yet, and you better stop biting your lip or I'm going to make you hate yourself for it later." He closes the receipt book and looks back up at me, his eyes blazing. I want so badly to jump across the table and have him right here, right now, but he stands and grabs my hand again. "Let's go."

We drive to Duval Street and find parking nearby before joining the rowdy crowd that's spilled all over. Crowds singing with a band fill the streets, mixed with the sounds of street performers, mic announcers, glasses clinking and laughter. The street is so alive with energy, it's intoxicating. As much as I want to get Corbin back home, I can't help but want to join in on the fun.

After we grab drinks at Fat Tuesday's, a small daiquiri bar, we venture inside Key West's Coyote Ugly. I somehow get suckered into dancing on the bar, which actually turns out being a good thing when they pull Corbin to join me and "make me" take a body shot off him. We venture inside each bar, seeing what they all have to offer, before finally ending at Irish Kevin's. There's a live performer making jokes about everyone in the bar and hitting on women as they walk by, but he also plays all my favorite 80s songs and Corbin and I sing along at the top of our lungs, laughing and drinking in between.

After he performs *Livin' on a Prayer* by Bon Jovi, the performer starts telling a story about him and his brother and a fight they got into over that song at a bar once in college. As he speaks, I watch Corbin laugh, his beautiful smile lighting up the whole bar. I want to tell him right now, I want him to know everything about me and I want him to know about my past, even though I'm not proud of it. I want him to see that he's changed me, that there's something about him that makes me not want to run. I want him to see that for once, I want to stay. I never want to leave.

"What are you thinking about over there, Ms. Bronson?" He smiles at me, brushing the hair from the front of my face and tucking it softly behind my ear.

"I was just thinking that this really has been the perfect day." It sounds cheesy, but it's true. I can't think of any other way I would want to spend a day than doing everything I did today with him.

"Well, it's not over yet," he says smoothly, pulling me in for a kiss. The crowd is thick around us, but he kisses me like we're in a room alone. He pushes his tongue inside my mouth, dancing with mine as he runs his hands through my hair. I pull his hips into me and feel him hard against my stomach, making me instantly ache for him.

"Want to get out of here?" he breathes, pulling back from our kiss. I can barely nod before he's pulling me out the door and we're headed for the truck.

Chapter eighteen
Jumping Into Bed

Corbin carries me through the door, my legs wrapped around him and my hands weaved into his hair. His lips are still crushed to mine as he maneuvers up the stairs, stopping halfway up to throw me against the railing. He moves his lips down my neck and across my collarbone, licking the dips in my skin that drive me wild. A soft moan escapes my lips and Corbin growls in response, picking me up again and running up the last few stairs.

He tosses me to the bed and comes crashing down on top of me, holding his glorious body just inches from mine as he stares down at me. His eyes are piercing through the night air, glowing in the moonlight that streams into the room. He doesn't even take the time to rip my dress off. In one swift movement, he pulls off his pants, shoves them to the floor, and enters me, tugging on my hair a little as he pushes in.

I arch my back toward him and throw my head back in ecstasy, completely engulfed in his desire. "Fuck," he groans, pulling my hair a little more. We move together, our bodies in perfect rhythm. I'm about to come apart at his touch when he slows, kissing me softer.

"Don't stop," I moan, willing him to move quicker with my hands on his ass.

He smiles into my neck, still planting soft kisses. "Mmm, remember what you said?"

I moan again, my body aching so bad I think I might catch a cramp. "I don't remember anything right now, just please don't stop."

"Ah," he says seductively, looking up at me with his icy eyes as he trails kisses down the cleavage line on my dress. "But you said I would have to punish you, remember?"

He pulls me up from the bed, lifting my dress above my head, and stares at my naked body. I didn't wear a bra under the dress, and my panties were non-existent from the beginning of the night, so I stand completely bare in front of him, my chest rising and falling with the anxious breaths vibrating through me. Corbin is bare except for his dress shirt, which is unbuttoned and hanging open enough to show his tight abs that flex beneath it.

"You really are fucking gorgeous, Paisley," Corbin breathes, cupping my cheek in his hand. He lets it drop slowly down my body, my skin twitching beneath his palm with every gliding movement. When he reaches my hips, he swiftly dips his hand between my legs and pushes one finger inside, making my head fall back in pleasure.

"Corbin," I pant, reaching out for him. He pulls my wrists behind my back with his free hands and begins nibbling and kissing down my neck as his fingers work. My body is on fire, crying out for Corbin to let me feel him again. Every pulsing movement sends tiny jolts of electricity soaring through me, ripping me seam from seam. I shake and tremble beneath his hand, completely his.

He fucking owns me.

I want so bad to release, but every time I come close, he slows down or pulls his fingers out completely, making my body scream.

"Do you want me?" he asks, breathing into my ear.

"Yes," I barely whisper, my voice shaking.

"I said," Corbin breathes again, this time pulling my nipple between his fingers and pinching gently, sending a jet line of electricity straight down my body. "Do you want me?"

"Yes!" I cry out, freeing my wrists from his grip. "I want you, Corbin. I need you."

With that, Corbin pulls my bottom lip into his mouth and sweeps me back onto the bed. He pushes inside, releasing my tension. My body aches and I tighten until I explode into a blazing fire, completely coming apart with him inside me. The pleasure rocks through my body, making me shake and tremble.

I have never, and I mean ever, orgasmed like this.

I have never felt like this.

It's like until this point, I've never felt pleasure. I've never felt what it's like to come apart at the touch of a man. Not the way he makes me come apart.

Corbin pushes in one last time, moaning out loud as he releases. I feel him pulsing inside me, our foreheads pushed together as our breathing synchs. Once again, I look up into his smoldering eyes and feel him look into me, *through* me, into my very core. I want so badly to say something, to capture the feeling inside me and find the words that match so I can tell him what he's doing to me, but I'm speechless. My body is completely wrecked, in the best, most delicious way possible.

Corbin moves beside me and pulls my back into his chest, folding his legs into a pretzel with mine. We lay there, our breathing coming down together, his arms wrapped around me and our bodies fixed together like two puzzle pieces that complete the final picture. He kisses the back of my neck, and without any words being spoken, we have the deepest conversation. His body speaks to mine in ways I'm not meant to understand. For the first time in years, I feel complete.

I feel safe.

As Corbin's breathing steadies out and I feel him drift off to sleep, my mind wanders back to the inevitable conversation I have to bring up. I should have told him tonight, but I couldn't – I couldn't ruin this amazing day. But tomorrow, no more excuses. Corbin makes me feel so alive, he makes me want to fall and never think twice about what might be at the bottom, and I can't let him truly see that unless I let him see the real me, past and all.

I close my eyes tight, willing my brain to be quiet. For now, I don't want to worry about anything. I don't want to think about anything. I just want to be the lucky girl wrapped up in Corbin's arms. I want to be happy, I want to let myself fall for him, and I want to let him take me deeper into what is by far the most intense connection I've ever had with anyone in my life.

So that's what I'm going to do.

Corbin's soft kisses on my forehead wake me, "Good morning."

I smile and slowly open my eyes, "Good morning to you, too."

Corbin gently runs the pad of his thumb across my cheek as his eyes study me. The morning sun is lazily drifting in through the window, occasionally disappearing behind the clouds and casting shadows along the bed. "I'm going to take a shower. Do you want to join or sleep a little longer?"

As tempting as it sounds to shower with him, my body is still sedated from the night before and sleeping a little longer sounds like paradise. I snuggle into the covers and peck his cheek with a small kiss, "Five more minutes."

He laughs softly, brushing the hair from my face and kissing me slowly. I probably should be horrified that he's kissing me before I've brushed my teeth, but his kisses are toxic and I don't have time to think about preparing for them.

"I'll wake you up when I get out and we can go grab breakfast. I've got one more thing planned before we head back to Orlando." He kisses my forehead one last time before disappearing inside the bathroom. I smile to myself and close my eyes, willing my body to drift back into the blissful sleep it was just in, when I hear Corbin's phone ring. It rings four times before the room is silent again and I start to drift, but then it rings again.

"Ughhh," I sigh, reaching for his phone to turn it on silent. My heart jumps in my throat when I see the name illuminated on the screen.

Rachel.

My pulse is thumping loudly in my ears, my mouth suddenly dry. My hands shake and I go to answer, but stop myself. *What are you doing,*

Paisley? You can't just answer his phone. The ringing stops again and I let out the breath that I've been holding. I turn the phone on silent and toss it back onto the bed, but as I go to lay back down, her name illuminates the screen again.

Before I have the chance to talk myself out of it, my hand shoots for the phone and I answer it, "Hello?"

There's a pause on the other end, but I can hear breathing.

"Hello?" I ask again.

"Where is Corbin?" Her voice is airy, light. It almost sounds like she's a fairy, or a Miss America contestant. Except she sounds really pissed off.

"He's in the shower, would you like me to leave a message for him?" I try to sound calm even though my stomach is tight and I've lost the ability to swallow.

"The shower? Who the hell is this?!" The fairy's voice rings in my ear, making me pull the phone away from my ear.

"This is Paisley, Corbin's..." I pause, not really knowing what to say. What am I to him, really? "Friend."

I hear a scoff on the other end, as if she's utterly amused by my interpretation of the situation. "Well, *Paisley,* this is Rachel, Corbin's GIRLfriend. And I highly suggest you get as far away from him as you can before I get there because you do NOT want to see what will happen if you're still there."

The word slams into me and knocks me to the ground. I fall onto my knees and cover my mouth, my breath caught in my chest and tears stinging at the corners of my eyes. His girlfriend? He has a girlfriend?

"I, I'm so..." I try to speak, try to formulate some sort of sentence to apologize to this woman I don't even know, to this woman I currently hate and envy and despise all at once.

"What? Did you really think he was interested in you? Did you think you were going to move back home with him or write him letters while he was deployed? You're just another tag chaser, and he's got one in just about every city."

I shake my head, the tears now pooling and threatening to spill over. "Corbin isn't like that, he wouldn't do that."

"No?" she laughs, a sarcastic, bitter laugh laced with venom. "Go ahead, ask him. And just a tip? Maybe you should actually get to know someone before jumping into bed with them." The line goes dead, and the phone falls slowly from my hand onto the floor.

A girlfriend? How can this be possible? Corbin cares for me, he does things for me that no other guy has ever done. How can he...

But then it hits me.

My dad did these same things for my mom, he loved her, he cared for her, he made her feel like she was his one and only.

And then he left her.

I wipe the tears from my face, cursing under my breath. How the hell could I be so stupid? How could I let him in when I KNEW this kind of shit would happen? I find my phone and find Tanner's number as fast as I can. I don't even know what I'm going to say, but I know he's the only person in the world I want to talk to.

"Hello?" Tanner answers and I start crying again, not even able to say one word.

"Shit, Paisley, what happened? Where are you?"

"Key West," I manage to spurt out between sobs.

"I'm booking you a flight now. Get to the airport and I'll text you when I have more information."

I nod before realizing he can't see me, "Okay. Thank you, Tanner."

There's a pause on the other end before Tanner answers, "You never have to thank me. I love you, Paisley. Just get to the airport."

We hang up and I wipe the tears from my face again, but it's no use. I throw on the closest pair of shorts I can find and pull a tank top over my head before fastening my hair in a ponytail. I'm tossing my clothes into my bag, tears still burning scars into my cheeks, when I feel Corbin's hand softly grab my arm. Even when I want to hate him, the electricity from his touch surges through me.

I rip my arm away, "Don't touch me." The words come out as more of a whisper, choked behind my tears.

"Paisley, please. Don't run away from me, talk to me," he tries to grab me again, but this time I whip around to face him.

"Don't fucking touch me!" I scream. My chest is heaving, the breaths running rampant in my chest. His eyes are searching mine, they look hurt, destroyed. I immediately want to run to him and throw my arms around him, to cry into his shoulder and beg him to be with me, to stay with me, but then I remember what Rachel said.

Maybe you should actually get to know someone before jumping into bed with them.

"Paisley, I don't understand," Corbin speaks softly, like he's defeated. I see the same look in his eyes that was there that day in the gym, when he asked me not to run.

"Well let me make it really simple for you, Corbin. Your girlfriend called, you should probably call her back." I spit the words out like they're poison on my tongue, trying to light him on fire with my eyes. I want him to feel the pain coursing through me right now.

"My what? Paisley, let me explain." Corbin moves in my direction, his arms reaching out to hold me.

"I called Tanner, I'm leaving." I turn back to my bag and continue shoving clothes inside, not really caring at this point if I leave anything behind.

"You called Tanner?" he asks, his voice cold. I continue packing, ignoring his gaze fixed on me. "Well, I guess you've got it all figured out then, don't you?" Corbin throws on his basketball shorts and a t-shirt and storms down the stairs. I hear him mumbling and cursing under his breath before the door opens and slams behind him.

I fall onto the bed, pull my knees to my chest, and cry. I cry because I want him to come back and hold me. I cry because I want to kick myself for being so stupid. I cry because in a way, maybe Rachel was a little right about me, maybe this is Karma's way of kicking my ass. But mostly, I cry because I feel betrayed. I've never felt for anyone the way I feel for Corbin, and all I am to him is his Orlando play toy.

My phone buzzes with a text from Tanner.

- The earliest flight doesn't leave until 2.
If I drive down there I can be there around 3. What do you want to do? -

I check the time and cringe when I see it's only eight thirty in the morning. I definitely don't feel like waiting in an airport all day, but what other choice do I have?

- I'll just wait for the flight. Thank you so much, Tanner.
I don't even know what to say. –
- Stop thanking me. Just get home so I can hold you. –

I round up the last of my things and throw them in my bag before calling a cab to take me to the airport. We're only about a mile away, and I think about walking, but just like any girl I definitely didn't pack light for this trip.

My heart races as I stand outside waiting for the cab. I want Corbin to round a corner, pull up in his truck, anything. But he never does. Instead, a dusty yellow cab pulls in and as I sink down in the backseat, I feel the last bit of my heart break. When the driver asks me where I'm going, I start crying again.

Should I tell him the truth? That I'm heading absolutely nowhere? That I'm emotionally stunted and when I finally do let my walls down I get thrown to the ground?

"Airport," I manage to say softly. He nods, a sympathetic look in his rough eyes looking back at me through the rearview mirror. As we pull away, I realize I forgot my owl necklace on the dresser.

Chapter nineteen
Traitorous Heart

The cab drops me off at the airport and I check in my bag. I still have hours to kill, so instead of going through security I walk back out the doors and down the road about a half a mile to the beach where Corbin took me the first night we got here. It's slightly overcast and there's a strong breeze rolling in off the water. I find a small palm tree near a boardwalk and sit down in the sand.

How did my entire world just get turned upside down with one phone call?

I absentmindedly run my fingers through the sand, drawing a heart and then erasing it. Drawing a smiley face and then wiping the mouth away and making it sad. I wish my life were as easy to erase as the sand beneath my fingers, wish I could just wipe away the bad parts and redo them. After about half an hour of letting my numbness consume me, I pick up my phone and dial McKenzie.

"Hey slutface, you on your way back from Fantasy Island yet?" McKenzie laughs on the other end, but when I don't say anything back her tone immediately changes. "Oh shit, Paisley, what happened?"

"Karma just slapped me in the face with a frying pan," I reply, trying to find humor in my tragedy. I spill all the details to McKenzie, about our perfect day, about our night together and how I was going to tell him about the bet, and then about the phone call. Reliving it makes me want to throw up.

"So what did he say when you told him he needs to call his girlfriend?"

"He said 'Let me explain.'"

McKenzie pauses on the other end for a moment, "So, did you let him?"

"Of course not," I huff, getting up from my spot in the sand and pacing around the small palm tree. "What is there to explain? Apparently, he has a girlfriend and a million other little girls he keeps waiting on him in other cities and I was just another piece in that game. It's seriously like I got exactly what I deserved, exactly what I dished out to the guys I've dated in the past."

"Bullshit, Paisley."

McKenzie's bluntness catches me off guard. Whose side is she on?

"It's bullshit and you know it. You didn't let him explain because you were afraid that maybe he had an explanation. Maybe he was going to break up with his girlfriend when he got back anyway, or maybe she's a crazy ex. You have no idea, and you didn't give him a chance to talk."

I slump back down in the sand, covering my face with my free hand. *Shit, she's right.*

"It gets worse," I groan.

"Oh jeeze, what now?"

"I got pissed and told him I called Tanner and that I was leaving."

"Paisley! You know he isn't comfortable with your friendship with Tanner, why would you say that?" McKenzie is scolding me like an eight year old caught looking at a porno mag.

"That's exactly why I said it, Kenz! I wanted him to hurt, I wanted to piss him off."

"Well, did it work?"

I sigh, "Unfortunately, yes. He stormed out and I haven't seen him since." The sickness in my stomach spreads to the rest of my body and I literally think I might be sick on the beach. "But what if it's true, Kenz? What if he does have a girlfriend and I was just nothing to him?"

"If it is true, then he's an asshole and you get up and move on and learn from him. But just ask yourself, do you really think with the way he treated you, with the things he said to you, that he doesn't care about you? Do you really think he just does these things for every girl he meets?"

Everything in my gut wants to say no, to say that there's no way he could look at every girl the way he looks at me. "I don't know, Kenz. I think if he's good enough at what he does, if he's anything like my dad, then yeah, probably."

"Well," she sighs. "Then you're not as smart as I thought you were."

We both sit silently for a moment, and I know she's probably right, but the bigger part of me is hard at work building back the walls I broke down, scowling at me the entire time. "I'm flying in, I'll be home later this afternoon."

"Come see me when you're done with Tanner, okay? And seriously, I don't think it would be such a bad idea to call him."

"Okay, I'll talk to you soon." I hang up and stare out at the ocean. More people are gathering on the beach now and I study all of them, letting the hours pass by. There's a small family of three kids and a mom, but I don't see the dad anywhere. I wonder to myself if he's just at work, or if maybe he's an asshole like mine.

A couple down the beach catches my attention. They're walking hand in hand with their feet barely grazing the water. Suddenly, the man swoops the woman into his arms and goes barreling into the ocean. The woman is squealing and laughing the whole time until she gets dunked under water. When she comes back up, she leaps into his arms and they kiss what has to be one of the most soulful kisses I've ever witnessed not being acted out on a movie screen. The way they look at each other, the way they touch, it's so comfortable, yet so electric.

It's exactly how I felt with Corbin.

And probably how I'll never feel again.

The flight lasts barely an hour and we descend into Orlando just as quickly as we left Key West. The tiny plane carried myself along with about twelve other passengers, so I had no one in the seat beside me. I looked out the window the entire time, trying to focus on not being sick, and watching the sun reflect off the top of the clouds.

Mostly, I thought about Corbin.

Maybe I should call him. Maybe he really does have an explanation, and maybe I am just letting my insecurities and fears stop me from hearing it. In a way, I guess I've been preparing for us to fail since the moment I met him. It only makes sense that the first time something shitty happens I automatically jump to the worst conclusions and run away. I told him I was done running, even told myself that, but did I ever really believe it?

I step off the tram and walk towards baggage claim, Disney displays guiding the way. Funny how I always used to love Disney as a kid, used to truly believe in the magic and the fairy tale endings. In reality, Disney is just setting us up for heartbreak. There are no princes, no true love kisses, instead it's just lies and secrets and eternal longing.

When I reach the escalator that leads to baggage claim A, I immediately see Tanner. At first, he seems pissed off. His fists are balled up and his jaw is clenching as he watches me descend. I tilt my head to the side, questioning him, and he softens, giving me a half smile and a shrug. I try my best to smile back and shrug, too, as if we're both in agreement that shit happens and life sucks.

"Hey," I say quietly when I reach the bottom. "You look so mad, are you okay? Are you still mad at me?"

Tanner shakes his head and pulls me into his arms, wrapping me in a tight hug. He plants a small kiss on my forehead, "I don't even know what the shithead did and I want to kill him."

I laugh softly, tears stinging the corners of my eyes again. I don't think anyone will ever be able to know exactly what I want to hear the way that Tanner does. He grabs my hand and leads me to the conveyer belt where we pick up my bag.

"Where do you want to go?" Tanner's eyes are searching mine, and I know he probably wants to go to our spot, but right now all I want to do is soak in a hot bath and cry.

"I just want to go home."

Tanner puts his arm around my shoulder and leads me out to his car without another word. As he drives, he holds my hand in his and rubs my fingers softly. I lean my head against the window as the outside world blurs past me. I feel like I'm in a movie, or a really tragic dream. Flashes of my weekend with Corbin strike me hard without warning, like a line drive straight into my stomach.

"Tanner?"

"Hm?"

I pause, not sure how to phrase what I want to ask him. "Do you think I let my fear hold me back? I mean, do you think maybe I run away from the problems in my life?"

Tanner plays with his grip on the steering wheel, biting the inside of his lip. "I think you do what any smart person would do. You protect yourself. It's a lot more than most people can say and honestly, I think the broken hearted fools envy you."

I nod and look back out the window, running his words through my head. I may protect myself and not get as hurt as those broken hearted fools, but when all is said and done, at least they've had moments worth living for. At least they have loved someone. At least they've *felt* something.

I think I'm the one who envies them.

"Feel better?" Tanner asks, pulling me in for another hug. I'm wrapped in my soft, light yellow bath robe, my hair still wet and falling around my face.

"Kind of," I lie, because it's better than sounding like a whiney little girl. Tanner pulls back and plants a soft kiss on my forehead before pressing his to mine.

"You're an awful liar," he takes my hand and pulls me down on the couch with him. "Tell me what happened."

It's even more painful reliving everything with Tanner. Partly because it's like reopening a wound, and partly because every time I mention how perfect my weekend with Corbin was, Tanner's lips purse together and I know he hates hearing it. Now that the line is blurred between us, I don't know what is okay to say and what's not. It's like he's the same best friend I've always had, yet at the same time he's someone I don't know at all. It's both familiar and terrifying.

"Jesus, I can't believe the asshole has a girlfriend," Tanner shakes his head. "And I can't believe he didn't tell you, especially after you told him about your dad."

"That's the thing," I lean up and turn to look at Tanner. "I'm not exactly sure he does. He tried to explain himself, but I kind of told him to fuck off."

Tanner scoffs, "Well, what is there really to explain? It's not like some girl is just going to lie to you for her own health. He's a skeeze and he got caught in his own game. Of course he wants to explain himself, he still has a few days left to play with you."

Tanner's words slam into me, forcing me back against the couch. "Do you really think that?"

Tanner's eyes soften and he brushes the still drying hair from my face. "What I really think is that he has got to be bat shit crazy to let you go, and he doesn't deserve you." His thumb slides down the side of my face and he cups my face in his hands. I lean into him, closing my eyes and feeling his comforting touch. When I open my eyes again, Tanner's stare has changed. His eyes are hungry, determined, yet he looks afraid.

"I want to kiss you," he breathes, his voice barely above a whisper. My heart immediately starts drumming in my chest. "I want to kiss away all the pain in your heart, all the doubt in your mind that tells you you're not the most beautiful girl in the world. Please," he pleads, "let me kiss you."

I can't speak, the words completely stolen from my mouth. I nod softly, my eyes blurring with tears. Tanner pulls my face to him and presses his lips to mine.

The kiss starts out soft, just like it did the night before I left, but suddenly I feel a need consume me. I deepen our kiss and weave my fingers in his hair, tugging softly. Tanner moves on top of me, pushing me down onto the couch. His hands run the length of my body, feeling every curve under my robe. I let out a soft moan as he moves his lips to my neck, biting and sucking softly.

He leans up on one arm and slowly unties my robe, letting it fall open. It's the first time Tanner has ever seen me naked, yet it feels so natural, like he already knows every inch of my body. He cups my left breast in his hand and leans down to kiss the swell above his palm. I let my mouth drop open into a soft "o" and tiny breaths escape between my moans.

I reach my hand down and swiftly unbutton his pants before rubbing him through his boxers. "Oh God," he breathes against my chest. I feel him harden beneath my hands and every inch of my body is begging me to pull him inside me. My body is screaming for him, screaming for me to take in everything his glorious body has to offer.

But my heart is traitorous, it beats only for Corbin.

"Tanner wait," I press my hand against his chest. He lifts himself above me, his chest still moving rapidly with his breaths. His eyes search mine and I know he sees it, he sees my heart. He pushes back and sits at the other end of the couch as I pull myself up and wrap my robe tightly around me.

"I'm sorry," I whisper, as if it's enough, as if those two words that some man invented to right wrongs has ever really worked when feelings like this are involved.

He runs his hands through his hair, shaking his head. "I don't understand, Paisley. Why?"

My eyes blur again and I just shake my head, because honestly I don't have the words to answer him. Before Corbin came into my life, I think I could have been with Tanner the way he wants. But now, it's like I've gotten a tattoo on my heart that no surgery can change. It's done, it's irreversible.

Tanner stands, pacing around me. "Don't you see how perfect we are for each other? You can't sit there and deny that you don't feel completely at home when you're with me, that you haven't felt something more for me, that kissing me just now didn't make you feel *anything*."

"It did, Tanner. I do feel for you," I speak softly through my tears.

"Then why won't you be with me?!" Tanner stops pacing and stands in front of me, his hands outstretched. "This is it, right here. This is what you want. You want a man who will treat you right and love you and never do you wrong, well that man is me. It would be so easy with me, Paisley."

"You think I don't know that?" I wipe the tears from my cheeks, standing to look him in the eyes. "You think I don't know that everything would be easy with you? There's no danger in getting hurt, there's no risk. We're comfortable together and I know I can tell you anything. I can completely be myself with you."

Tanner moves toward me and I know he wants to pull me into him, to hold me like he always does, but I stop him. "No, let me finish." I breathe in a deep breath and try to steady my voice, "I know all that. But I have spent the last four years of my life choosing easy. I've chosen easy with every guy I've so-called 'dated' since my dad shattered my heart and expectations of men into tiny, fragile pieces. I know easy, I know how easy feels. I may have never gotten hurt, but I never felt anything either. I was numb, like a piece of nothing just floating by and watching my life instead of living it."

My voice grows stronger as I speak, the realization burning through me. "But Corbin is different. He makes me want to take the risk. He makes me feel like not only can I be myself, but I can be the better version of myself. I know there's a chance he could leave me, that he could walk out of my life with that woman on the phone or any other girl in the world and never look at me again. Never even think of me again. That my heart could end up completely stripped and tortured," I shudder, knowing that very well could be what happens, or what has already happened if I don't save it. "But I also know that I have never felt more alive in my entire existence than I have with him in the past two weeks. And I know that if I let him go without fighting to keep him, I will become a shell of a woman who will never truly love anyone else again."

Tanner falls onto the couch, his eyes staring out into nothingness. I know what I'm saying isn't what he wants to hear, but it has to be said. I sit down next to him, "Corbin is not my easy, Tanner, but he is still the one my heart wants."

He shakes his head, "I just don't understand, Paisley. He's confusing, he makes you happy one minute but you're pissed the next. You're vulnerable. I've seen you cry more in the past week than in the past seven years I've known you. Work is hell and you've got so much shit you need to straighten out there, it just doesn't make sense to have him in your life screwing with your emotions even more than they're already screwed with." Tanner turns toward me, his eyes begging me to hear his reason. "He's the last thing you need right now."

I smile softly, knowing he's right but also so terribly wrong. "Sometimes the last thing you need is the only thing you want, Tanner. I can't help what my heart feels."

His eyes gloss over and I reach out for his hand, but he leaps from the couch. "I told him the truth about you, Paisley. About us." His back is turned to me and one hand is kneading his forehead.

"What are you talking about, Tanner?" I stand, walking toward him. My heart is pounding in my throat and the overwhelming urge to be sick is coursing through me once again. "What do you mean, Tanner?" I demand, my voice louder.

"He was at the airport," he says, whipping around to face me again. "He tried to find you in Key West but I guess you weren't in the airport when he went. So he got in his truck and raced against your flight to get here before it landed. He showed up right before you did, and I knew it was him when I saw him. Everything about him screamed that he was a man who'd royally fucked up."

My heart melts, "He came for me?"

Tanner's face hardens, "Yeah, after he fucked you over he tried to save himself. When I saw him, everything inside me wanted to punch him square in the nose, but I didn't want to get kicked out of the airport. So I hurt him the same way he hurt you."

Everything is slow, morphed. The words that come from my mouth don't even sound real, "Tanner, what did you tell him?"

"The truth! I told him the truth, Paisley. I told him that he was nothing to you but another tag to put on your chain. I told him that you loved me, and that we had kissed the night before you left. I told him about the bet and about the other guys who filled the same slot he does before he came along. I told him that when he leaves, I will be the one still here with you. He doesn't make sense for you and he knows it, and now he knows that he wasn't the only one who had a secret. Now he knows that you don't need him either, and he can hurt the way he hurt you."

My hand flies up to my mouth as I stare at Tanner in shock, "How could you?" My words are just above a whisper, but then the rage courses through me. "How could you?!"

I run back to my room and throw on the first pair of shorts and shirt I find, throwing my hair into a messy bun. My tears are completely dried out, my face hard as stone.

"Where are you going?" Tanner is standing in my doorway, his hands tucked into his pockets.

"I have to see him, I have to explain," I push past him and grab my keys off the table. As soon as my hand finds the door knob, I feel Tanner gently grab my arm.

"Please, Paisley. I love you, and I know you love me, too. You don't need this guy, all he's done since he met you is tear you up inside. Don't fight me, I know you feel for me."

"I do feel for you, Tanner. You're my best friend in the entire world, but you just hurt me more than you could ever know." I pull the door open and Tanner drops his hand from my arm.

"Paisley, I'm begging you. Don't walk out that door."

I stand with the door open, the breeze drying the last few wet stains on my face left from my tears. I know right now that I could just close this door and go back to the couch with Tanner. I know he would hold me and love me and that maybe in a few years, we would get married and everyone would marvel at how our friendship bloomed into a true love.

But I know in my heart that I would never, could never, truly love him. My heart belongs to someone else, someone who deserves an apology from me. I take a deep breath and step forward, "I love you, Tanner, but I have to go." With that, I close the door behind me and run toward my car, my heart breaking more with every step.

Chapter twenty
Pumpkin

My heart is racing when I reach Corbin's hotel room. I have no idea what I'm going to say, no idea how I'm going to save what we have. Before I have the chance to change my mind and run, I knock on the door.

"Please answer, please answer," I mumble under my breath.

The door clicks and swings open, but it's not Corbin inside. Instead, I'm greeted by a young, beautiful blonde woman. Her skin is tan and smooth, her legs stretching out under the tiny shorts she's wearing. Her hair is short and layered, her eyes a gorgeous chocolate brown.

"Oh, I'm sorry. I think I have the wrong room," I say hopelessly. Corbin has checked out. He's gone, and I can't do anything about it. I turn to walk away, but the young woman stops me.

"You don't have the wrong room, but you are messing with the wrong guy, or the wrong girl, I should say."

I turn around slowly, "Rachel?"

She nods, eyeing me slowly as she crosses her arms and leans against the door frame. "You've got a lot of nerve showing up here."

I bite my lip, knowing she's right. He has a girlfriend, I'm a piece of shit, and I really have no right to be here. "I know, I'm sorry. Please, I have to see him. Just let me talk to him."

She laughs, shaking her head. "Are you insane? Why in the world would I let you talk to him?"

I know I'm crossing the line, that I don't belong here and she's the one in his life, but I came this far and I'm not backing down now.

"Corbin!" I yell, trying to get him to come to the door. "Corbin please, let me explain."

Rachel laughs again, "Scream all you want, honey. He's not here. And if you know what's good for you, you'll leave now before I tear every strand of that sloppy bun out of your head." Her lips purse together and I know she's not bluffing, and I can't say I blame her. If Corbin were mine and some girl was threatening that, I'd kill her.

But he's not mine.

"I just want you to know that I'm sorry. I never knew he had a girlfriend, if I had I would have never have done the things I did with him." I know it's stupid trying to explain myself, but this woman deserves an apology from someone, and I don't know if Corbin has given her one. "And I know you think I'm just a tag chaser, and had you met me two weeks ago you would have been right. But I've never felt for anyone the way I feel for Corbin."

Rachel's eyes soften, and I can't tell if she is really listening to me or if it's just a façade she's putting up to make me leave. Either way, I have to keep speaking.

"I just had to tell you, I had to make sure you knew where I stand. And I respect you, but I want you to know I'm not giving up. Until he tells me to fuck off and leave his life, I'm going to fight for him."

I don't give her a chance to reply. I turn on my heels and race for the stairs, foregoing the elevator. I sprint to my car and frantically dial his number, knowing it's probably no use. I call him over and over with no answer as I speed to the gym. When I get there, I slam on my brakes and skid into a parking space before running to the door. His truck is nowhere in sight, but I bang my fist on the door anyway.

"Corbin! Corbin, please," I knock over and over, my fist rapping on the glass. The tears I thought were gone start pricking my eyes again. Suddenly, my phone rings.

"Corbin?"

"What do you want, Paisley?" His voice is cold, hard. It's almost as severe as the night we met, the way he talked to the creep who put his hands on me. I feel like an alien, like a disgusting specimen that he can't stand to be associated with.

"Corbin, please, let me explain."

"Explain what, Paisley?! That you're a tag chaser and all I ever was to you was a distraction from all the shit you're running from?"

"It's not like that, I swear."

Corbin cuts me off, "I opened my heart to you, I never hid anything. I thought you were giving in to me, that maybe I was cracking the code and you would be the girl to break me down, too. That we would find ourselves together."

The pain inside me resurfaces and I remember that I'm not the only one in the wrong, "Oh yeah? Would that happen before or after you told me about your girlfriend, or would you have even mentioned her at all? Don't pretend like you're innocent in all this."

"She's not my girlfriend, she never has been and never will be. And if you would have stayed with me in Key West instead of running to Tanner, you would know that." His words slam into me, knocking the wind from my chest. I turn my back to the gym door and slide down the glass, sitting on the warm cement.

"I don't understand," I whisper.

"Rachel is Jack's little sister. Ever since he died, I've been there for her, and she's always been protective of me. She's had a crush on me for years and she thought when she turned eighteen that we would be together. When that didn't happen, she still stuck by my side. She's even helping me get things together with the gym, which is why she flew in today. She's seen me try to find love before and fail miserably, and yes, she wasn't lying about the other girls. I'm not going to sit here and pretend like I'm an angel and I haven't had my fair share of one night stands, Paisley. But you were different, or so I thought," he laughs, sarcasm laced in his words. "Turns out you're worse than all of them put together."

"Corbin, I swear, if you just give me a second to explain –"

"Oh, like you let me explain in Key West? No, not this time. I'm not running after you this time, Paisley. You got what you wanted. You wanted a guy to entertain you for a few days and then walk out of your life, right? Well congratulations, this is me walking."

"Please, Corbin. Just wait a second," I plead, the panic rising in my throat.

"I'm done waiting, Paisley." The line goes dead and I throw my phone across the parking lot, sobs violently racking my body. I hug my knees and try to breathe, but I can't. It's like everything in my world is crashing down around me and there's nothing I can do to stop it, nothing I can do to even salvage a tiny piece of what's left of me.

I'm ruined.

After what feels like hours of painful, rib-crushing sobs, the numbness washes over me again. I stand and wipe my face. I know what I have to do, where I have to go. I know this is it, the breaking point that was inevitable. There's only one person who can save me from myself now.

It's the first time I've seen my dad's new house, though I guess since he's been here for three years now, it's not technically new anymore. It's a small house, much smaller than the one we used to live in as a family. It's white with stones peppering the driveway and flowers growing in a small garden that lines the front. It seems like every light is on and the sun just barely set ten minutes ago. I inhale a deep breath and knock on the door, my stomach in an even tighter knot than before.

I hear shuffling inside and my dad's voice suddenly fills my ears as he tells his dog, Gizmo, to get away from the door. Gizmo used to be our dog, but Mom made Dad take him when he left, he was always closer to dad, anyway. The door cracks open and Dad looks out at me, confused. Then realization spreads across his face.

"Oh my God. Pumpkin, is that you?" He's always called me pumpkin, ever since I can remember. I used to love that nickname, but it feels so out of place right now.

"Hi, Dad." I whisper, because it's all I can manage. His eyes take in my appearance – my messy hair, tear stained face, shaking hands.

"What happened, baby?"

"Can I come in?" I ask, ignoring his question.

He steps aside quickly and opens the screen door, "Of course, please. Here, come sit in the kitchen. I'll make us some coffee."

I take a seat at the small glass table. Gizmo excitedly jumps into my lap and licks my face, making me smile even when it felt impossible. His tail is wagging uncontrollably and I think he might explode.

"He's missed you," Dad chuckles, pulling two coffee cups from the cabinet. I finally look at him, actually study him. Even though it's only been three years, he's aged what seems like ten. His hair is graying some and the wrinkles in his face have deepened, but he's still just as handsome as he always has been. His tall and confident demeanor has always made him appear so unbreakable to me, and his smile reminds me of Corbin's – full of life.

Dad joins me at the table and sets a full cup of coffee in front of me. "With milk and sugar, just like you used to like it," he smiles. I try to smile back, but fail miserably. I pull the cup toward me and cup my hands around it. Even though it's at least ninety degrees outside even with the sun gone, I'm shivering and tiny goose bumps are parading up and down my arms.

"Did your mom make you come?" he asks, sipping from his cup. I shake my head, still trying to figure out the words I need to say. He sits patiently, sipping slowly from his cup and petting Gizmo, who has since crawled into his lap and is now softly snoring.

"I'm a fucking mess," I finally say, because I figure I might as well start with honesty. "And it's your fault." I lift my eyes to meet his, my hand still cupped around my mug. I can't even think about eating or drinking anything, but I'm thankful for the warmth.

He exhales, a sadness flooding over his eyes. "I never meant to hurt you, Paisley. You were my world, you still are."

"Then why did you do it? Why did you betray mom, betray me?" I choke on my words as the tears threaten to pour from my eyes. It still feels like I have no more tears to shed, so instead of actually crying, my throat strains against it and my lips quiver.

Dad is still petting Gizmo, his eyes staring out into nothing. "I don't have an answer that you're going to like, but I can tell you the truth." He looks back up at me, "I loved her, your mom. I did. I will never love another woman the way I loved her."

I laugh sarcastically, but hold off on the remarks racing through my head. I came here to make him explain, and that's not going to happen if I don't let him.

"I know you don't believe me," he says, his voice shaking a bit. "I don't blame you, but I did. What we had was comfortable, like she was my oldest friend in the world. I felt safe with her and she with me, and we fell into this easy kind of love."

"But there was something missing, Paisley. Your mom knew it, we both did. When I met Jani," I flinch at her name, the woman who tore my whole world apart. "There was a passion there, an electricity that was undeniable. I didn't go looking for her. I didn't know that I wanted anything else in my life, I thought I was fine. But when she came into my life, everything changed."

He pauses, waiting for me to respond. I still don't have anything to say, it's like the only thing I can offer right now is my silence. I feel like I've opened every wound that consumes my body and now I'm just bleeding out at the table with no way to stop it.

"I never wanted to hurt you, and honestly I tried to get away from Jani. I told her I couldn't hurt you or your mom, that you two were my life. I made her leave me alone, but then every second of every day I ached for her, Paisley. It was killing me inside, and that's when I started acting poorly towards your mother. It killed me."

I shake my head, not wanting to accept his honesty, but at the same time completely understanding it. It's just like me and Tanner, it's that battle between what's comfortable and easy versus what makes you feel alive.

"Why did you come here, Paisley?" He asks, reaching his hand across the table slowly. He waits to see if I'll pull away, and when I don't, he wraps his hand around mine. It's the first time I've touched my dad in three years, and it immediately sends tears sliding down my face. I want to scream at him, to slap him across the face and tell him I hate him, but I don't.

The truth is, I love him. I miss him.

And right now, I need him.

"I fucked up, Dad. I ruined my friendship with Tanner, and I finally found someone who makes me want to trust and believe in something again, but I lost him." Dad wipes away the tears now streaming down my cheeks with the pad of his thumb, offering a soft smile.

"Baby, there's nothing you could do that would ever ruin what you have with Tanner, and if you met someone who had such an effect on you, I can't see them not being affected by you in the same way."

I break down and tell him everything, not just about Tanner and Corbin, but about the past three years of my life. About how I've hidden behind this mask and built up my walls, how I've hurt those around me, and now, how I've hurt myself in return. It takes hours to tell him everything, but he sits there unwavering, still holding my hand in his as he listens.

"I don't know what to do, Dad," I finish, sniffling. I feel absolutely deflated and defeated.

Dad sits back in his chair, his hand finally leaving mine. He crosses his arms across his chest and thinks quietly to himself for a few minutes. "Well," he finally says, "I have to admit it hurts like hell hearing that I put you through so much, Paisley. I'm so sorry for that, for everything, even though I know that doesn't change anything."

I sigh, "It's not just you, dad. I used you because it was easy to blame my own insecurities on you after you left."

"Maybe," he says. "But either way, I had a role in this, and for that, I'm sorry. But right now, the most important thing you have to ask yourself is what do you want, what do you *truly* want?"

"I want Corbin," I half whisper, half cry. "I've never wanted anything or anyone so much in my entire life."

"Then go get him back," Dad says, as if it's so simple. As if I haven't already tried. "And I don't mean by calling him on the phone or writing him a text message, I mean go get him back. Make him look you in your eyes and tell you he doesn't want you, that what you did is unforgivable and he doesn't feel anything for you. If he can do that, then yes, maybe you will have to walk away. But my money is betting he won't be able to do that, because if he could, he's an idiot. And my baby girl doesn't fall for idiots." He smiles, grabbing my hand again.

I inhale deep, weighing the option. I know what's between us is real, and maybe if he let me see him, if he let me explain, we could work through this. God knows I want to, and I want to believe that he does, too.

"What about Tanner?" I ask, my heart breaking again just like it has every time I've spoken his name since I left him standing in my apartment.

"Tanner will still be there, just like he always has been. Yes, things are going to be different, and you're going to have to draw a line that neither of you have had to have before now, but he loves you and he's not going to leave your life, not like this."

I'm not so sure, but then again I do believe Dad's right about one thing – Tanner does love me. The question is, does he love me enough to be my friend without being anything more?

"When do you see Corbin again?"

"We have a meeting tomorrow to review the first draft of creative for his logo, but I don't know if he'll even show."

"He will," Dad reassures me. "And if he doesn't, then you go to him after work. One last time, you take the risk and leave your heart on the table. Show him that you feel the same way he does, that he's found a place in you that didn't even exist until he came into your life. Make sure that if he leaves again, if he walks out for good, that you did everything you could to stop him."

"Did Mom try to stop you?" I ask, knowing I'm probably not ready for the answer.

"She did, but not as much as she could have. She knew in her heart that Jani made me happy, and just like Tanner, your mom loved me enough to know that was really what she wanted for me more than anything. She wanted me to be happy."

I bite my lip, picturing my broken hearted mother crying in her room. I wonder if Tanner is crying over me. "Does Jani still make you happy?"

He smiles, and it's the same smile that radiates through me anytime I talk about Corbin. "Yes, yes she does, pumpkin. She has completely changed me, almost like I wasn't living until I met her."

I smile back. It's a weak smile, one that I have to force a little, but at least it's a smile. "I'd like to meet her, I think."

"I would love that," his smile widens and he stands, reaching his hand out for mine. "Now come give your old man a hug, I feel like a piece of me has been missing these past few years."

I let him pull me into him. He kisses my forehead softly, "I love you, kiddo. I hope you know that. I always have and I always will." I wrap my arms around him tightly, holding the one man who completely broke me and who may have just helped me start putting the pieces back together again.

"I love you too, Dad."

He pulls back, "Do you want to stay here tonight? I'm sure you have to work in just a few hours."

I shake my head, "No, that's okay. I need to shower and make myself presentable. I'm trying to win back my guy tomorrow, remember?" I smile, nudging him with my elbow.

"Go get him, pumpkin."

"Thanks, Dad." I hug him one last time and make plans to get lunch soon. It's as if the giant hole that's existed in my heart is slowly closing, or at least filling itself with something to make it a little more complete. When I get back to my place, I find a note from Tanner on my pillow.

I love you. I'm sorry. Please call me.

I move the note to my desk and collapse into bed, the weight of my exhaustion finally hitting me. I barely set my alarm before I fall asleep, dreams and nightmares of Corbin battling in my head.

Chapter
twenty-one
Don't Let Go

Even though I fell asleep quickly, I tossed and turned throughout the night. At about four in the morning I finally gave up and got up to shower and get dressed. I took extra time on my hair, curling it to perfection, and picked out the cutest business appropriate dress I own. It's a bright yellow, form fitting dress and I paired it with a black blazer and tall black heels, along with a chunky black and silver necklace. I still can't fathom eating anything, so I forego breakfast and head into the office early.

It's just shy of six when I walk in and though we don't officially open until eight, it doesn't surprise me to see Lydia's light on in her office. I try to sneak by, but again her cat like instincts detect me.

"Paisley, is that you?"

Fucking A, this woman is insane.

"Good morning, Lydia. I was just coming in to catch up, I have some important client meetings today." One in particular, but she doesn't need to know that.

"Well you'll have a little more time now, I just received a call from one of your clients, Mr. Ray. It seems his trip has been cut short and he's leaving town this morning. He asked me to put a hold on his project until he returns."

I race to her door, almost tripping on my heels. "What? Why is he leaving, when did he call? Did he ask for me?"

Lydia is unmoved by my urgency. She's still sitting at her desk, lazily sifting through some paperwork. "Now why on earth would he tell me why he was leaving, Paisley? It was a short conversation and the only thing you need to know is to put his project on hold and bill him for the time spent so far."

"Shit," I curse under my breath, letting my head fall back against her door. "Lydia, I have to go. I'll get Shannon to reschedule my meetings for today."

I turn to leave, but Lydia stands, "Excuse me? You'll do no such thing. You're meeting with two very important clients today, including one that we're currently trying to hook for a half a million dollar account."

"Lydia, I'm sorry, I'm sure one of the other account managers can handle it."

Lydia cuts me off, moving in front of her desk. "Paisley, are you *involved* with Mr. Ray? Because if you are, you do understand that is grounds for termination."

She crosses her arms and taps her heel at me, pursing her lips together in dissatisfaction. It's like it's the final push, the last thread of string that was holding me together. Before I can stop myself, I storm over and push my finger in her face.

"You know what, Lydia? I'm tired of your shit." Lydia gasps, clutching her imaginary pearls in horror. "If it's so easy to fire me, then do it. Better yet, I fucking quit." I turn on my heels and storm out of her office.

"Don't be crude," she laughs, her voice shrill with panic as she chases after me. "Of course I wouldn't fire you, I was merely asking, that's all. I think you're right, I think you do need the day off. I'll just have Shannon –"

"No, not this time, Lydia. I'm over you walking all over me and acting like I'm the dirt beneath your feet. I'm talented, I'm valuable, and I'm worth a hell of a lot more than what you pay me. Consider this my two minute notice," I flip my middle finger up, smile smugly, and slam the door behind me.

Part of me wants to jump in the air, the adrenaline coursing through me is absolutely toxic. But right now, the only thing I can think of is getting to Corbin. I have to find him before he leaves, I have to explain. *God, please don't let him be gone already.*

I bang on his hotel room door, praying under my breath, "Please be here, please don't be gone." The door swings open and my chest deflates when I see Rachel.

"He's not here," she says, crossing her arms.

"Rachel, please, tell me where he is. Is he at the gym? Did he leave already?"

"They called him back for early deployment, they're leaving earlier than expected. He's supposed to fly out at eight. I'm packing up the last of his things and driving his truck back home for him. He left over an hour ago for the airport."

I don't even let her finish before I'm racing back down the hall.

"Paisley!" she yells after me. I stop and turn, panting. "I just wanted to say I'm sorry, for lying to you. And I hope you catch him, he deserves to be happy." Her eyes are soft, sad. I think of my mom, of Tanner, and I wonder how many hearts are broken in order for two hearts to be happy. I smile and nod, hoping she'll see that I understand, and then push through the exit door and barrel down the stairs.

When I reach my car, I floor it and speed the whole way to the airport. I pull into the drop off lane and park my car.

"Excuse me, miss! You can't park here!" A security guard yells after me. "Miss!"

"Tow it!" I scream back, racing through the crowd and ducking inside. I run to the first monitor I can find and scan the departing flights. There's one to Tulsa at nine thirty, but none for eight.

"Damn it," I mutter, scanning the list again. I see a flight into Oklahoma City for eight fifteen, that must be the one. The screen indicates an on-time flight departing in just twenty-five minutes. I race to the ticket counter, dodging families in Disney gear and grumpy business men the entire way.

"I need one for Oklahoma City at eight fifteen," I tell the attendant, my breathing erratic and strained. She takes her sweet time, asking me if I have bags and if I will require any travel insurance. Finally she hands me my ticket and I take off running for security. My heart sinks when I see the lines backed up into the lobby.

"Shit," I let out a frustrated sigh. "Shit, shit, shit!"

"Miss?" I turn and see an elderly man in a security outfit staring at me, his brow raised in amusement.

"Oh God, I'm sorry. I didn't mean to be so loud."

He chuckles, "It's quite alright. You look like you're in a hurry, can I help you?"

Hope courses through me again, "Yes, please. I need to get to gate A27. There's a man about to board that plane and if he leaves before I talk to him, I... I'll..." I don't even know what to say, what would happen to me if he left before I got there?

"I understand, miss. Please, follow me this way." The man moves hurriedly through the crowd, me on his heels. He shows his badge as he passes and moves me to the express lane, ahead of everyone else in line.

"This young lady is a VIP passenger and needs to be assisted without hassle and as quickly as possible," I hear him tell the officer behind the podium. He leans in and whispers something else I can't hear, and the young man smiles at me.

"Of course, right this way miss."

I turn to thank the elderly man, but he just winks, "Go, you can thank me later."

I nod and smile, taking my shoes off and placing them in the bucket. Less than a minute later I'm through security and sliding onto the tram just before the doors close. I check my watch, eight ten. Can this tram move any slower?

Finally we reach the terminal. I take off through the doors and race down the lane, counting the terminals as I pass. A23, A25...

A27.

My heart is catching up to me, beating so mind numbingly loud in my head I think I might faint. I scan the seats for Corbin, but he's nowhere to be found. The screen is blank above the terminal and I don't see a plane taxied out front.

Shit, I'm too late.

I run to the desk where a young brunette is typing on a computer. "Ma'am, did the plane for Oklahoma City already leave?"

The brunette looks up at me and smiles sweetly, "I'm sorry sweetie, I just got to this gate. They switched some things around, but it looks like there's not another flight out of this gate until ten fifteen, so I'm afraid the flight you're referring to has already departed."

The balloon of hope inside me deflates, sucking the air from my chest.

"Would you like me to see if there's a later flight we can get you on?" She asks, reaching out to take my ticket. I shake my head numbly and walk to a nearby chair, sinking down and covering my face in my hands.

I'm too late.

I lost him.

The weight of everything is crashing down on me and I'm almost positive I'm actually going to be sick this time. Suddenly, a small finger taps me on my shoulder. I look up through my fingers to see a little girl staring back at me. Her eyes are the biggest green eyes I've ever seen, her soft blonde hair pulled up into two curly pigtails, and she's smiling at me sweetly.

"Hi sweetheart, are you lost?" I look around for a sign of her parents, but they're just across the lane at A28 watching us intently. They're both smiling, and I'm instantly confused. The little girl extends her hand out to me. It's balled up in a tight little fist like she's holding something.

"Here," she says. "For you."

I open my palm and gasp when she drops a small fragile chain with an owl pendant into my hand.

My necklace.

"Where did you –" I look back up to ask the little girl, but she's gone now. Instead, standing where she was, is Corbin.

Tears immediately spring to my eyes, blurring my vision slightly. Corbin falls onto this knees in front of me and takes my hands in his.

"I thought you left," I say softly.

"They just delayed the flight, bad storms in Oklahoma City."

I nod, unsure of where to go from here. "Corbin, I'm so sorry. I should have told you about my past, I swear I planned on it. I was so scared, I'm always so scared."

Corbin smiles and shakes his head, "I'm sorry, too. I should have listened to you, and I should have told you about Rachel before I did. You were open with me about Tanner, and I should have done the same."

I feel guilt pour over me, "I wasn't exactly honest about Tanner, either."

"I know," he says, pulling my hands up to his mouth and planting a small kiss on my fingers. "He told me."

I cringe, knowing that what Tanner said and what actually happened are two completely different stories.

"Please don't believe what he said, he was angry. I never said he was my boyfriend or that you meant nothing to me, I swear."

He laughs softly again, "No, I mean he told me the real truth, about everything. He called me this morning right after I left for the airport. I tried calling you, but you didn't answer."

I scrunch my face up, "I kind of threw my phone across the gym parking lot last night."

Corbin smiles, "Poor phone." We sit silently for a moment, his eyes searching mine while my brain tries desperately to find the right words to say.

"Corbin, I know I'm not perfect. I'm afraid of getting hurt, I run away from my problems, and frankly I'm just a huge pain in the ass. I'm not going to lie to you and say that my past isn't ugly, because it is. I'm not proud of the things I've done, but I also don't regret them, because somehow all the shit I've been through has led me to you," I squeeze his hand, hoping my words are enough, that he hears me.

"You really are a pain in the ass," he laughs. I swat him playfully, laughing too as a single tear rolls down my cheek. He wipes it away and tucks my hair behind my ear, "But you're my pain in the ass. Yeah, we're not perfect, neither of us, but I can't deny the electricity between us. There's something there that we aren't meant to understand. Jack's sister is important to me, just like Tanner is to you, and I know we're both going to have to really trust each other if we want to move forward and make this work. I've hurt you, you've hurt me, but yet here we are," he motions to the space between us. "I'm willing to break myself down a little further and open up to you, to give you all of me, but I have to know that you're willing to do the same. No more running, no more hiding secrets, just me and you and everything we have to offer."

I smile, tears still streaming down my face. "Corbin, I don't know if I'll ever be able to break down all the walls I have. I can't promise you that I'll never run again, or that I'll never shut down. But what I can promise is that I've felt more alive in the past two weeks than I ever will again if you walk out of my life. I can't lose you, and if I try to run again please, chase my ass down and tie me to a chair or something," we both laugh. "And don't let me go. Don't ever let me go."

Without another word, Corbin swoops me up in his arms and pulls me into him, pressing his lips against mine. The electricity is more intense than I've ever felt, and I know without a doubt in my mind that this is right where I belong.

We pull back and I realize the crowd around us is clapping and cheering. Corbin laughs and I blush, hiding my face in his chest. He pulls the owl necklace from my hand and fastens it around my neck. "Come on," he says, whispering in my ear. "My flight doesn't leave for five hours, and I've got a pretty good idea of how to pass the time."

I bite my lip, his delicious current racing through my body and suddenly I ache for his touch. He puts his arm around my shoulder and we fall into a rhythm as we walk, kissing occasionally, and Corbin tells me more about his exes, opening his heart to me again. As he talks about the girls of his past, for once I don't feel threatened or annoyed. In fact, they each remind me a little of myself. It's funny, what started as a bet with my crazy best friend ended up bringing me what I wanted all along. I've spent all this time running, hiding, being a tag chaser. I have no idea how to handle a deployment, no idea how I'm going to live without him for almost a year, but I do know that there's no one in the world more worth waiting for than Corbin. Yes, I have been a tag chaser.

But now, I'm officially a tag catcher.

THE END

Epilogue

It's been exactly seven months, four days, and six hours since I last saw Corbin. He's been in the states for about a week now, but today he's finally flying in to Orlando.

Today, I finally get to feel him in my arms again.

Today, he finally comes home for good.

The past months have been absolutely brutal. The service is so bad overseas I was lucky if I got a ten minute Skype session or a message on Facebook. Luckily, Tanner has visited from New York three times and helped me on the rough nights when I felt alone. He's been more supportive than I could imagine, and I think I love him more than I did before. Even though things are still a bit tense between us, I think we're slowly falling back into our friends-only rhythm.

McKenzie has been a huge help, too. When she's not "not dating" Derek, anyway. I swear, they're going to just show up at my doorstep eloped one day. I've been learning to open up to her more, and we've grown closer than ever. She even went with me the first time I had lunch with my dad not too long after Corbin left. I needed her more than anything that day, and I'll never be able to fully repay her.

Even with their help, I still wasn't ever fully prepared for what deployment would bring. Mostly, it was letters and packages and the bottom line is that nothing will ever suffice as a proper substitute for that man's touch.

Fuck, do I need his touch.

Okay, calm down Paisley, keep it in your pants.

My heart is racing as I stand at the foot of the escalators, waiting for them to deliver my soldier. While he's been away, I've been hard at work on his gym project. He pulled his account from the agency and let me take over, and I took it on myself to do a little more, getting a jump start on building the field behind the gym and looking into what kind of equipment would be best. I've also been insanely busy with working on my own project, opening a bakery just a mile and a half down the street from Corbin's gym.

I can't wait to show him everything, but more importantly, I can't wait to get my hands on him. I'm biting my nails almost to the bone when finally, I see him. My heart starts doing flips and my stomach is turning, I don't think I've ever been this excited in my life. His skin is even darker than the last time I saw him and his facial hair is grown out just enough to give him the sexy rugged look that I love so much. His white t-shirt is hugging his newly defined arm muscles, teasing me and making me wish I was the shirt, instead. He flashes his full watt smile and I can't stand it anymore, I race up the down escalator, murmuring apologies as I scoot past disgruntled travelers. Corbin laughs when I finally reach him and pulls me into his arms. The people around us clap and laugh, and I have déjà vu to the last time we were in this airport.

"Oh my God, I've missed you," I breathe between kisses. His lips are like a delicious drug and I'm an addicted fiend.

"I've missed you, too. More than you know." He pulls back and stares into my eyes, those same icy blue eyes that completely own me devouring every inch of my skin.

When we reach the bottom of the stairs, we grab his bag and head for my car. "So, why are we stopping at the gym first? I think if you give me the chance I could make a strong argument for making your apartment our first stop," he grins devilishly and thumbs the skin beneath my tank top.

"Behave, Mr. Ray. I promise, it will be worth it."

We pull into the gym and I make Corbin close his eyes. I lead him through the doors and stand him in the perfect spot, making sure he can see the field being built behind the fountain.

"Okay, open your eyes."

When he does, a huge smile spreads across his face. I see him take in the fresh paint, the office I had put in, the new furniture, and the updated walls. Then, his eyes catch sight of the field, and he turns to me, wonder in his eyes.

"You really are the best girlfriend in the world, aren't you?"

I blush, "Second best, I'm pretty sure no one will ever be a better girlfriend than Emma Stone."

He laughs and pulls me into him, pressing his lips to mine. "I beg to differ, Emma Stone could never look as sexy as you do right now in that dress."

The heat builds in my stomach as his hands glide over my skin, taking their time as they roam every inch.

"I want to make love to you, Paisley. Right here, right where we did the first time."

I nod, breathless, my body wanting him so bad it's painful. I try to deepen our kiss, but he pulls back. I push my lip out in a pout, "No fair, I don't want to be teased right now."

He laughs softly, "No teasing, I promise. I just have to tell you something first."

I bite my lip, "What is it?" Suddenly, nerves crash over me. Is it something bad? What could he have to tell me?

"Paisley, these past months away from you have been hell for me. I've never missed anything or anyone so much in my life. There were days I wasn't sure I would make it, I thought my body would give out on me and make itself sick with wanting you so badly. The only thing that kept me going was the chance that I might be able to see your pixelated face on a Skype call for a few minutes or hear your voice on the other end of the phone."

I smile, "Trust me, I feel the same."

Corbin brushes the hair from my face, running his palm against my cheek. "I love you, Paisley."

And there they are, the three words I've been wanting to hear for months. The three words I thought I would never hear from Corbin, that I would never fully be able to understand. The three words I thought I'd never say myself.

"I love you, too." I barely get the words out before his mouth crushes down on top of mine and he picks me up, carrying me across the room. We're frantic, our bodies needing to touch, to feel. He pushes me against the glass, the same glass he took me against the last time we were here, and our bodies react to the familiar feelings.

As we make love, I'm overwhelmed with the realization that this man has completely changed my life for the better. Because of him, everything that I hated about myself is gone and replaced by everything I always wanted to be but never thought I could. With those three words, he kicked down the last block that was left standing from the walls that once stood so tall around my heart. It's official.

I am completely, irreversibly, undeniably his.

And this time, my feet are planted firmly on the ground.

Keep reading for an excerpt from *Song Chaser,* Tanner's story.

Acknowledgements

Wow, where to even start? This journey of writing and publishing my first novel has been both exciting and extremely trying, and I have so many people to thank for supporting me along the way.

My first thanks goes to my wonderful husband, Ryan. Thank you for always understanding when I needed to run to my laptop to write something down before I forgot it. Thank you for reminding me of my strengths when I just felt like giving up. And most of all, thank you for being the romantic, loving, amazing husband you are and giving me so much writing ammo to work with in my books.

A huge thank you goes out to every single member of my family, especially my mom. All of you have been tremendous pillars of support throughout this journey and I couldn't thank you enough for always asking how the book was going and requesting signed copies. And Mom, I will never be able to truly thank you for everything you have done for me throughout my entire life, but thank you again for always being my rock.

Thank you to my friends who had to listen to me talk about this book and the characters for hours on end throughout this past year. A special thank you goes out to Sasha and Sean for inspiring many characteristics of some major characters in this book. You know which ones and I'm sure when you read them, you laughed just like I did. Also a huge thank you to Stacy and Little Penguin for always asking how the book was going. It always made me smile to know that you cared. I love you all so much and appreciate you being there for me and supporting my dream.

There were so many people who helped make this book happen.

Betsy, thank you for editing my horrendous grammar mistakes and making this book the best it could be before going to print. Also, I could never really thank you enough for listening to me talk about this dang thing every single day. I appreciate everything you did for Tag Chaser more than you know.

Austyn, thank you for being the bad ass photographer you've always been and helping me turn the crazy thoughts in my head into a beautiful cover. I also can't forget to thank my beautiful model, Katie. You're gorgeous and you made this cover flawless. It's perfect, and I can't thank you both enough.

To my beta readers – Kellee, T, Novo, and Big – thank you for reading Tag Chaser along the way and giving me your feedback, both good and bad. You are truly what made this book what it is. Without your (sometimes harsh) critique, Tag Chaser would have been mediocre at best. Thank you for seeing the potential in my characters and helping me bring that out. I have to give a special thank you to Kellee, because without you I really don't know what I would have done. You were not only a fabulous beta reader, but you were also an unmatchable support system in my times of stress and worry. Thank you for encouraging me and for just being awesome.

A HUGE thank you goes to Jillian Dodd for being kind enough to take time out of her insanely busy life to answer the questions I had about self publishing for the first time. You are honestly one of the nicest people I have ever interacted with and a truly talented author. I look up to you and appreciate your advice more than you know.

Of course, I can't forget one of the most important thank you's that goes to YOU – my readers. Some of you have followed my journey from the beginning, some are just joining now, but the bottom line is without you, Tag Chaser would just be a document on my computer collecting virtual dust. Thank you for reading my blog, keeping up with my page, and most of all, for buying this book and telling your friends about it. I have always said I write for my readers, not for anything or anyone else, and that will never change.

Lastly, and most importantly, thank you to God for blessing me with a writer's heart. It's an emotional life to live, but I wouldn't change it for anything and I'm so thankful for every blessing He has given me.

About the Author

Kandi Steiner is a Creative Writing and Advertising/Public Relations graduate from the University of Central Florida living in Tampa with her husband, Ryan Steiner. Kandi works full time as a social media specialist, but also works part time as a Zumba fitness instructor and blackjack dealer.

When Kandi isn't working or writing, you can find her reading books of all kinds, talking with her extremely vocal cat, and spending time with her friends and family. She enjoys beach days, movie marathons, live music, craft beer and sweet wine – not necessarily in that order.

Connect with Kandi:
www.KandiSteiner.com
Facebook (http://www.facebook.com/KandiSteiner)
Twitter (http://www.twitter.com/KandiSteiner)

If you loved this book, please take a minute to review it on the site where you purchased it. Your time and thoughts are greatly appreciated and valued.

More from Kandi Steiner

For more than a year, Tanner West has tried to shake his feelings for his long time best friend, Paisley Bronson. She was the perfect girl to fit the lyrics in all his favorite songs – the girl he had always wanted. When she fell in love with another man before Tanner had the chance to tell her how he felt, he was left with no resolve to find love again. Burying himself in school and easy girls has become his new lifestyle, but when Kellee Brooks shows up at his favorite bar, he begins to think there may be another verse to his song, after all.

Kellee Brooks moved to New York City for one thing: escape. Growing up in a small town where her entire life was planned out for her, she's desperate to break free and find herself without following the same path as her mom. Kellee thought working at the local dive bar would mean more money for school, but when she meets the smoldering, scarred honey eyes of Tanner West, she finds there's much more hiding in the smoky building than just a few tips.

With Paisley still haunting Tanner and Kellee vowing to save anyone the trouble of loving her, will the pain and fear keep them apart – or will they find a way to rewrite their song together?

Break free with this heartbreaking story of letting go and letting love in.

And now, an excerpt from *Song Chaser*…

Song
chaser

*"Maybe the key to finding the perfect song
is simply rewriting the lyrics."*

kandi steiner

Prologue

The Drive

Tanner

There were no words I could say to make her stay. I knew it as soon as they started flying out of my mouth. I could practically see her heart beating for him, yet there I stood, spilling out every ounce of blood I had left in my pathetically beating heart right onto her floor to try to get her to lay back down on that couch with me and let me hold her until all her pain was gone.

I think in my head, I already knew she was out of my grasp. I knew it the moment I showed up on her doorstep that Sunday and took her to our spot and watched her emerald green eyes squeeze tight into a smile because of another guy. I was too late, I'd waited too long to tell her how I felt, but I did it anyway.

And I hurt her.

On the ride home, I played that scene in my head over and over again, like a fucking torture scene in a horror movie. Flashbacks surrounded me as I drove, my eyes blurrily focused on the road that laid out in front of me – the road that would never lead to her. She had said to me, "Sometimes the last thing you need is the only thing you want, Tanner. I can't help what my heart feels." Driving back to New York, I actually laughed at that. How ironic that the woman I couldn't help but love was preaching to me about how we can't help what our hearts want?

But that wasn't what plagued me most, that wasn't the nail that dug itself deep into my skin and poisoned my blood. No, the words she said to me just before walking out her front door would be the ones that would never leave, the ones that would be a constant reminder of one of the biggest mistakes I had ever made.

"You're my best friend in the entire world, but you just hurt me more than you could ever know."

So I drove, in tortured silence, not allowing myself the pleasure of turning on the radio. I just sat and thought about the one girl I had always written my perfect song for, the one girl who had made me think of her with every lyric I ever sang, the only girl in the world to ever make me feel nervous because I knew deep in my gut that she was completely out of my league. I thought I had found my perfect song, my own personal soundtrack that I would keep and have forever as mine.

Instead, I had chased her away.

Chapter one
Breathe

Tanner

I really fucking hate the stench of cigarette smoke. I do, I hate the way it clouds up the space I sit in and the way it stays in my clothes long after I leave. So I guess it doesn't really make sense that I'm sitting in this shitty hole in the wall bar where the smoke is thicker than the women who work here, but here I sit, because NYU insists we take these damn social retreats while in the Pediatrics Residency Program.

But if I'm being honest, I kind of want to be here. Probably because it's the only place in this whole fucking city where I can feel her.

In the past two years that I've lived in New York, Paisley Bronson has only visited one time, and it wasn't even me that she was visiting. She was here for some work conference and she only had time to meet me for a drink the night before she went back home. This is where I brought her, to The Box. Out of all the classy bars and out of this world night clubs that exist in New York City, I brought her to the one bar that is most like the little ones back home in Orlando. And the crazy thing is – she appreciated that. She's not a city girl, she never has been, and she finds value in the little things like having a bartender who knows your name and your order or having a karaoke night where no one who can actually sing ever shows up.

So I come back here, every Sunday, just to feel her. Sometimes it's with the other residents in the program, but most times it's by myself. To sit here and think about how it might have been different if I'd taken her to dinner instead and told her back then that I was so in love with her that I could barely breathe when she wasn't with me. But instead,

I took her here, and we drank the same Jack Daniels and Coke that we always drank and I held my tongue and tried not to brush that single strand of hair from her face and tuck it behind her ear. And kiss her.

God, I wanted to kiss her.

I drain the rest of my drink and signal to Sal, the bartender on my end of the bar, for another refill. He sees me every Sunday and knows exactly what to pour, and God love him he hasn't cut me off yet, even though I've given him plenty of nights where he should have. The group of girls singing right now makes me want to shove my head into a fucking dryer and slam the door shut over and over again. They're laughing and slurring their way through a Britney Spears song and no doubt think they're the hottest pieces of ass this bar has ever seen. They probably came as a joke, as a one-check-on-the-bucket-list sort of dare, but apparently I'm the only one who sees it for what it is because the rest of the men in the bar are hooting and elbowing each other like it's the best damn show they've seen, including some of the guys in the program with me.

Benny stands and applauds as the girls leave the stage before turning to me. "Cheer up, T Dubs! You look like you're at a funeral."

Does the death of my fucking heart count?

I smile, "Sorry man, long week."

Long year would be more accurate. When I left Orlando, I thought I'd never see Paisley again, that she'd never want to look at my face again after what I did to her. But she called me, just a few months later, and somehow we worked through it. Corbin, the guy she fell in love with, deployed right after he and Paisley made up and it's been hard on her. I've been there for her through the whole thing, even flying to Orlando a few times to be there when I knew she just needed to be held. But it was different than it used to be because she knew how I really felt. Every time I held her, I felt her stiffen. She didn't feel the same around me, and that just made me feel shittier around her.

Benny shakes his head and slams his fist down on the bar, "Sal! Can I get another whiskey for my friend here? Put it on my tab. And if you've got any happy pills back there, slide those in, too." He nudges me in the ribs and I laugh, pushing him off me. Sal was already working on my drink, but at least it won't be on my tab now.

"Alright, alright, I get it. I'll put on my fucking happy face."

"Attaboy," he laughs. "And don't think you're getting out of singing tonight. You haven't sang in over a year and we're breaking that streak tonight."

I nod to Sal as he sets down my fresh glass, "Keep dreaming, Benny."

"Aw, Tanner, please! I miss that dreamy voice of yours," Charlie says, her voice low and seductive. She traces her finger along my bicep and I shake her off. She's beautiful, in an easy target kind of way, but I'm not in the mood to put up with her shit.

"Well you'll have to keep on missing it. I'll drink all the whiskey you feed me, but I'm not singing." I haven't sang since I left Orlando that day, after calling Corbin and telling him the truth about Paisley – the real truth. I told him that she was crazy about him, that we were just friends, and that he'd be insane to let her go.

And as much as I knew it would make her happy, it still fucking killed me.

What I had told him before the truth was that Paisley had kissed me – that she loved me and not him and he was just another set of tags to hang on her chain.

Yeah, I know it was shitty, but I was desperate to keep her.

I didn't know what else to do.

But, after I saw how hurt Paisley was when I told her that's what I had said and after she walked out on me – I knew I had to make things right. I called him the morning he was supposed to get on a plane to go back to his base and laid out the truth. I even told him I was a fucking idiot who was trying to save the woman I loved for myself even if it wasn't what she wanted. Corbin, surprisingly, understood – but in the end he got Paisley back.

And I got a broken heart.

"Why won't you sing?" I hear a smooth, almost angelic voice coo behind me. I turn in my barstool and literally choke on my drink. Sal has moved down to the other end of the bar and standing in his place is a fucking angel. No shit, this girl is glowing. Her long, sandy blonde hair is falling all around her and her soft eyes are like two illuminated wells pulling me in deep. I can't see what color they are, which kind of intrigues me, but what I notice most is her freckles.

Damn, I have never seen freckles that sexy before.

"Are you okay?" she asks, tucking her hair half behind her ear. Probably because I choked on my drink and still haven't found one word to say.

I set my whiskey on the bar and turn to completely face her, "I'd be better if I knew your name." I turn my game on and break out the half smile, the one that usually lands a girl in my bed within a few hours.

"I'll tell you my name if you sing," her brow arches as she grabs the white towel hanging off her shoulder and begins drying a glass. She's dressed modestly in a pair of jeans and a bright yellow tank top, but her skin looks freshly tanned and a sliver of skin just above her hip bones makes me want to trace it with my fingers and send goose bumps down her body.

"How about you tell me your name, and if you're lucky, I'll sing to you later when you're in my bed?" I know it's a cocky line. Hell, for once I feel a little stupid saying it, but in all honesty I'm a guy, and this girl looks like the perfect distraction from Paisley. Still, I can tell this girl is different, and I somehow feel embarrassed that the words tumbled out of my mouth.

As I expected, she rolls her eyes and swings the towel back over her shoulder before leaning across the bar. "Trust me, honey. If you got me in bed, you wouldn't be able to speak, let alone sing."

The corners of my mouth turn up as she pushes back from the bar. Her eyes are challenging mine, and damn if I don't like a challenge. I'm just about to shoot back with a clever quip when she tosses her towel on the bar and runs her fingers through her hair, "How do I look?"

I shake my head, "Do you even have to ask?"

She laughs, "Not really, but I wanted to see if your jaw would hit the floor again or if that was just a one-time thing." She winks at me, lifts the end of the bar up and walks up to the stage, her ass swinging the entire way.

Yeah, she definitely knows I'm watching.

She stands to the side with the DJ, pointing on his laptop screen and asking him questions. Benny and Terrence are doing a very drunken version of *Ice Ice Baby* and I can't help but let my mind wander back to Paisley. She was never into music as much as I am, but she would always try to keep up with my tastes and listen to whatever I threw at her. That's why it shocked the shit out of me the night I took her to one of my fraternity parties and she started busting out every line in this song when it came on. I laughed so hard I almost fell over. I can still remember it, like it could be happening right here, right now. She had her hands in the air and her wavy auburn curls were swaying all around her. She kept getting in my face like she was a gangster and when the chorus came on, she would rub her arms like she was cold as she mouthed the lyrics at me.

Everyone in that party thought she was such a nerd, but all I saw was perfection.

She never knew it, but almost every song I ever played for her was about her, or made me think of her. I was convinced that she was my perfect song, the perfect lyrics to any melody I would ever hear. Every time I heard a new underground band play, or heard a classic song on the radio, or even when I got adventurous and jotted down some lyrics of my own – she was always there, dancing in my head to every word. When we talked about everything after our fight, I told her that she was the girl in all my songs.

She probably thought I was insane.

Benny and Terrence stumble off the stage as the song ends, laughing all the way back to our place at the bar. The other residents cheer and laugh and the rest of the bar seems annoyed. I thump them both on the back and order shots for all of us, desperately trying to drown my thoughts of Paisley. As we slam them down and the liquid burns through my throat, I hear the DJ announce the next singer.

"Alright, we got a special treat tonight. This little lady is all the way from upstate New York and just graced us with her presence three nights ago. She serves a mean whiskey sour, but that's nothing compared to what her voice can do. Give it up for Kellee Brooks!" A few people clap, the men hoot and the rest of the bar continues drinking, but when she steps under the shoddy spotlight, a blanket of silence falls over the entire place and it's like no one can breathe until she says something.

She nervously grabs the mic and her eyes scan the audience until she finds mine. The cockiness she just threw at me from behind the bar is completely gone, and it's almost like she's nervous now. "Hi y'all," she says sweetly, the spotlight playing on her blonde hair. "Thank you for coming out tonight, I hope you won't be too hard on me. This is one of my favorites by Faith Hill, and I hope y'all enjoy it. It's called *Breathe*." She closes her eyes, and that's the last thing any of us can do – breathe. It's like we're all holding in our last breath because we're afraid we'll never breathe the same after we hear her sing.

The music starts playing, and for the next few minutes it's all I can do to sit there and not walk straight up to that stage, pull her down, and kiss her lips like they've never been kissed before. I hate karaoke, I hate when people try to sing when they can't. But in this girl's case, I could fucking listen to her for the rest of my life. I almost pull out my phone to record her, but I know it won't capture anything real about this moment. Plus I'd probably look like a psychopath stalker. So instead, I sit just there and soak it all in.

"Dude, I would so tap that," Shane says beside me, nudging me. I want to kick him off his barstool but instead I punch his arm, "Don't fucking talk about her that way."

"Chill dude," he says, rubbing his arm where I just hit. "Do you even fucking know her?"

I don't answer, I just turn back to the stage as she finishes the song, her eyes still locked on mine. I'm not really sure why I reacted that way. Hell, any other girl and I probably would have bumped his fist in agreement. Maybe my heart has been broken for so long I'm starting to grow a vagina or something.

Or maybe I just really want to be the only one to "tap that".

When she ends the last note, the whole bar bursts into applause and the cutest fucking blush I've ever seen spreads across her face. If it's even possible, she looks sexier than before and my cock twitches as I imagine searching the rest of her body for hidden freckles. She smiles, "Thank y'all so much." Before she steps off stage, she looks back out to me, her brow rising again, and I know it's a challenge.

It's my move, and I'll be damned if I'm not going to make it.

Purchase Song Chaser at your favorite book retailer.

CPSIA information can be obtained
at www.ICGtesting.com
Printed in the USA
LVOW04s2241111216
516840LV00024B/1908/P

9 781492 822608